Novels by Vince Flynn

The Last Man
Kill Shot
American Assassin
Pursuit of Honour
Extreme Measures
Protect and Defend
Act of Treason
Consent to Kill
Memorial Day
Executive Power
Separation of Power
The Third Option
Transfer of Power
Term Limits

And by Kyle Mills

Oath of Loyalty
Enemy at the Gates
Total Power
Lethal Agent
Red War
Enemy of the State
Order to Kill
The Survivor

CODE RED

VINCE FLYNN

**SIMON &
SCHUSTER**

London · New York · Sydney · Toronto · New Delhi

First published in the United States by Emily Bestler Books / Atria Books,
an imprint of Simon & Schuster, Inc., 2023

First published in Great Britain by Simon & Schuster UK Ltd, 2023

13 5 7 9 10 8 6 4 2

Simon & Schuster UK Ltd
1st Floor
222 Gray's Inn Road
London WC1X 8HB

Simon & Schuster Australia, Sydney
Simon & Schuster India, New Delhi

www.simonandschuster.co.uk
www.simonandschuster.com.au
www.simonandschuster.co.in

A CIP catalogue record for this book
is available from the British Library

Hardback ISBN: 978-1-3985-0084-6
Trade Paperback ISBN: 978-1-3985-0085-3
eBook ISBN: 978-1-3985-0086-0
Audio ISBN: 978-1-3985-2299-2

Printed and Bound in the UK using 100% Renewable
Electricity at CPI Group (UK) Ltd

MIX
Paper | Supporting
responsible forestry
FSC
www.fsc.org   FSC® C171272

ACKNOWLEDGMENTS

As I bring the Mitch Rapp era of my career to a close, I find myself thinking back on all the people who made it possible. My agent, Simon Lipskar, for first pondering the possibility. Sloan Harris and Emily Bestler for their confidence, support, and unwavering professionalism. David Brown and his team for their inexhaustible energy and creativity. Lara Jones for keeping all the moving parts working in harmony. Ryan Steck for his unparalleled knowledge of the Rappverse and for giving me the benefit of the doubt. Rod Gregg for patiently explaining the complexity of firearms and keeping me out of the sights of the aficionados. Elaine Mills for all her critiques and encouragement. And, finally, my wife, Kim. The woman who puts up with me, talks me down, and gives it all purpose.

Most of all, though, I want to thank Vince's fans. I was overwhelmed by your enthusiasm for this project, the speed with which you welcomed me into the fold, and your passion for the character and the world he inhabits. Taking over for one of the leading lights in the genre was terrifying, and it was the people out there rooting for me that kept me going.

My undying gratitude to you all. It's been an amazing decade, and there's a lot more to come.

CODE RED

PROLOGUE

THE mist that had blurred the sunset was becoming more oppressive as the night wore on. Visibility was still passable thanks to the powerful lights of Salerno's commercial dock, but Absaar Mousa wondered if that would last.

Only if Allah willed it.

He wiped the condensation from his binoculars and once again glanced behind him. The first few trees glowed green, but beyond that the darkness was impenetrable. The steep slope had been difficult to descend even in daylight and now the journey would be too treacherous for even the drug addicts and graffiti artists who normally haunted this section of ancient wall. Still, it would be unwise to rely too heavily on that assumption.

He put the binoculars back to his eyes and swept them slowly across his field of view. The verdant mountains and artistically lit castle ruin. The modern city and dark sea beyond. Finally, he focused on what had brought him there: the city's port.

Mousa had become something of an expert on intricate operations over the past year, but the scale and complexity of this one still astounded him. He examined a docked transport ship as a series of cranes plucked brightly colored containers from its deck. From this distance, the impression was that of a swarm of highly specialized insects carrying away the toys of some unseen child.

This, as much as anything, encapsulated Western society. The constant flow of goods that fed their materialistic frenzy. The meaningless possessions that they used to fill the place that Allah—and only Allah—had the right to occupy.

He backed a few paces into the trees, searching for relief from the intensifying rain. After finding a bit of protection, he focused on a garish yellow container stacked on a dock to the east. The smugglers he'd contracted had taken great care to make sure that it was in no way remarkable, and they had done their job flawlessly. Even knowing what he did, it seemed so insignificant. So unworthy of the effort that had been expended to get it there.

Ostensibly, it was full of parts used in the repair of farm equipment. Less known was the fact that hidden inside them were fifteen metric tons of captagon, a narcotic rarely seen in Europe, but extraordinarily popular in the Middle East. He himself had taken it while fighting for the Islamic State in Syria and had later become involved in its manufacture and distribution. The small white pills stamped with two crescents had served a surprisingly pivotal role in the fight to spread God's law. They provided billions in hard currency to finance jihad and suppressed fear and fatigue in the men carrying it out.

The drug in that container, though, was nothing like the substance he'd handled during his days as a warrior. It was a unique formulation powerful enough to change the tide of the war against the West. To tip the scale back in the direction of God's army.

Under the direction of unseen benefactors, Mousa had spent

the last twenty months developing a European distribution network made up exclusively of Believers. It hadn't been difficult to find disaffected immigrants unable to integrate into the societies they found themselves surrounded by. Young men thirsting for someone to blame for their misery. A cause to give their lives meaning. Purpose. All things that Mousa had become an expert at providing. He'd learned from the imams of his youth to speak with unwavering certainty about discrimination and corruption. Imperialism and heresy. To describe in the most lurid and visceral detail the eventual seduction of these men's daughters and wives by the easy pleasures of the West. And if those lofty ideas failed, Mousa simply offered the money that his shadowy masters seemed to have in unlimited supply.

The army that Mousa had built was now complete. European government officials had been bribed, clandestine distribution centers had been set up, weapons had been secured, and devoted personnel had been put in place.

Finally, after so many failures, the war had begun anew. But on a very different battlefield. It was time to admit that the followers of Islam would never be a match for the West's military. His movement would never be victorious trying to penetrate the armor of its enemy directly. No, they had to be hit where they were weak. In the soft flank that had been ignored by his brothers as they became more interested in glory and vengeance than victory.

The phone in his pocket began to vibrate, but he didn't bother to read the text. He knew what it would say. His man had reached the port's entry.

Mousa adjusted his gaze to the trucks passing through the initial security checkpoint, seeking out a bright blue one hauling a white container. He felt his stomach clench as it pulled up to the guardhouse and the driver—a particularly faithful young man named Ja'far Saeed—handed his identification through the window. Not that the act was visible with the intervening glare and rain, but Mousa had become so familiar with the dock's rhythms that it was hard to differentiate between what he actually saw and what was playing out in his mind's eye.

Mousa let out a relieved breath when the truck cleared security and started toward the area where it would be relieved of its empty container. Satisfied it was safe, he redirected his attention to a crane moving along a stack of containers that included one originating in the Syrian port of Tartus. The one that he'd spent almost two years of his life preparing for.

Everything progressed as he'd come to expect during the endless hours spent surveilling the port. Over that time, its repetitive efficiency had become strangely soothing. Today, that meditative spell had been broken by a trickle of adrenaline.

With its chassis unloaded, the truck set out toward the crane that had closed its grip around the container in question. Mousa watched as it was lowered to the ground and retrieved by a loader. His man stopped in the designated area and the lumbering machine placed the metal crate on his chassis.

The rest should have been little more than formality. A brief mechanical inspection followed by a check of his driver's paper-work. Instead, two service cars parked nearby suddenly accelerated and blocked the truck front and back. Hidden spotlights sprang to life, casting a piercing glare over a series of port workers, who were revealed to be armed with everything from handguns to assault rifles.

Mousa barely managed to keep from vomiting. It wasn't just the last two years. In reality, he had labored his entire life for this moment. The madrassas of his youth. Deadly battles fought across the Middle East. His infiltration into Europe and recruitment into the organiza-tion he now directed.

The leak that led to this disaster hadn't come from his team. Of this he was certain. He'd attended to every detail. He'd chosen only the most fanatical and obedient men. He'd compartmentalized information in a way that provided no one person with enough to create a failure on this scale.

The only plausible explanation was that he'd been betrayed. One of the unseen men he worked for had been compromised by the European authorities. It had to be.

Mousa's initial shock transformed into a mix of rage and despair as he used his cell phone to send a brief text. While the army of the godless had undoubtedly won this battle, their victory would come with a price. The Italians were about to learn that they were no longer dealing with the old women who made up their mafia.

A new kind of drug demanded a new kind of criminal.

Ja'far Saeed squinted through the windshield, examining the vehicle blocking his path and the armed men who grew in number with every passing second. The spotlights, initially blinding, were made even more disorienting with the swirling light bars of police vehicles.

A trap.

He looked in his side mirror and saw men moving cautiously toward his door, staying close to the container he had been charged with hauling to safety. A ping sounded on the phone mounted to his dashboard and he read the message as someone began shouting Arabic instructions into a megaphone.

Roll down the window!

Put your hands through it so they can be seen!

He hadn't come here to be martyred. His job had been to get the container to its destination outside of Bergamo. He knew nothing more than that. Not why. Not what it contained. Not who would be waiting for him. He didn't need to know those things. Feeling God's presence and being of service to Him was enough.

But now the mission had failed, and his orders had changed. There was only one thing left to do. One final act that would carry him to Allah's embrace.

Saeed put the truck in gear and rammed the vehicle in front of him. It rocked on its wheels and began skidding sideways, hopping awkwardly until its tires were torn from the rims. The pitch of shouted orders rose, but no one fired their weapons. They wanted him alive. They wanted to torture him. To force him to give up his brothers and turn his back on God.

Sparks began to fly from the back of the vehicle stuck to his grille, and then, suddenly, he was free of it. He moved through the gears, increasing his speed as the people on the dock tried to escape. He clipped one and managed to hit another head-on, pulling him beneath the truck's wheels and causing the suspension to jerk satisfyingly.

The gunfire finally started when he wrenched the wheel left and accelerated toward a fleeing man dressed as a dockworker. Holes appeared in his windshield, but he paid no attention. Something impacted the window next to him, embedding glass in the side of his face and blinding him in one eye. Despite this, there was no pain. Only hate and elation.

Saeed twisted the wheel again as his quarry cut right, but this time the trailer lost traction and the weight of the container began pulling it over. He threw his door open and leapt out, enthralled by what he knew would happen next. He'd been given authorization for one last act of vengeance against his people's oppressors, and now he'd use it.

His feet hit first, but the momentum was too much to overcome, and he found himself rolling uncontrollably across the dock. His position on the ground was enough to save his life when the bomb at the back of the truck's cab detonated, but not enough to keep his clothes from igniting. Again, there was no pain. Only the yellow firelight visible in his still-intact eye.

Saeed fought his way to his feet and saw the vague outline of a human a few meters ahead. The bullets impacting him were barely noticeable as he charged forward and dove at the figure, holding on with what strength he had left as the flames enveloped them.

By that point, he could no longer see but, praise be to Allah, he was still capable of hearing his victim's screams.

CHAPTER 1

MITCH Rapp raised a fist before crouching next to a jumble of boulders. The men behind him would do the same, melting into the darkness and scanning for threats.

Sometimes, though, those threats were hard to see.

To the north, the Hindu Kush mountain range was outlined against the stars. A few of its taller peaks were still holding on to snow that shone dully in the celestial light. They dominated everything in this region, providing mortal dangers to the local inhabitants as well as the means for their survival. Even the shallow canyon Rapp found himself in was the result of ancient glaciers that had made their way across the valley floor.

Water was scarce, but the fact that the ditch to his left was lined with low grass and scrub hinted at its presence just beneath the surface. Not enough to sustain anything that most people would recognize as civilization, but sufficient for a few hearty souls to eke out an isolated existence. And for all their faults, no one could say that the Afghans weren't hearty souls.

A broad agricultural plot ahead suggested that they were closing in on their target and that's what had prompted the stop. Confirming what he'd seen on the reconnaissance photos, it appeared to have gone fallow some time ago. A few stone barriers and terraces were all that was left of what was once probably not much former glory. Most likely a family poppy operation with a few goats thrown in. Afghanistan the way it had been before and now was again.

The war was finally over, and it had ended pretty much how Rapp had always expected. To some extent, America was a ceaseless victim of its own success. Over the course of a couple hundred years, it had gone from a British colonial backwater to the most powerful country of the modern era. It had developed the ultimate secret sauce and was happy to pass out the recipe to anyone interested. Who wouldn't want that? When the US military rolled across your border, it wasn't to subjugate your country, it was to deliver you from oppression, provide education and health care, and build infrastructure. To create a pothole-free path to peace, freedom, and prosperity.

With all those rainbows and unicorns, what could possibly go wrong?

Same answer as always. Everything.

The Americans had never managed to assemble an Afghan government that wasn't a combination of the Three Stooges and Dr. Evil. That had created an environment in which the US military had to take over the administration of the country's affairs, while Afghan officials focused on stealing everything that wasn't nailed down. Ironically, what had kept Afghanistan on a reasonably even keel during the occupation wasn't their confidence in their own government, but rather their confidence in the American one. Much like the Romans of the distant past, the US could be more or less counted on to live up to their agreements, pay people on time, and generally get shit done.

When that abruptly ended, the locals had a choice to make, and they'd chosen the Taliban. It was something Rapp had warned Washington about more times than he could count. While the Taliban were brutal and repressive, they were also predictable. And in this part of the world, predictability was about the best facsimile of stability anyone could hope for.

Back in the US, the mess of a war was inevitably followed by the mess of a pullout and then a mess of finger-pointing. Generals at politicians, politicians at the intelligence community, officers at generals, enlisted men at officers. The truth was that it was a failure at every level. One that the exhausted American people now preferred to pretend never happened.

All of which had combined to bring him to this place at this moment.

There were still a little over twenty Americans trapped in-country under various circumstances. Unfortunately, that wasn't a story anyone wanted to tell. It didn't fit into the former president's image of godlike master of the universe, and the media didn't see any profit in giving airtime to a subject that made Americans reach for the remote. Fortunately, with a new occupant in the Oval Office and Irene Kennedy back in control of the CIA, the clandestine services were finally able to start tackling the issue.

Or at least that was the theory.

After two minutes of motionlessness, Rapp hadn't heard anything that couldn't be attributed to the air filtering through the mountains. He motioned for his men to follow and continued along the degraded trail.

They'd already managed to get eight hostages out the easy way—with money. Taliban rule had plunged much of the country into poverty so abject that even the tough-as-nails Afghans were having a hard time hanging on. Famine was on the horizon and reports of people being forced to sell their children just to survive were becoming increasingly common.

It was a level of desperation that made even the most hardened jihadist forget about revenge in favor of finding the means to feed their families. With one exception, every kidnapper they'd contacted had been happy to just take the cash. And now Rapp had returned to Afghanistan to deal with that exception.

Based on the Agency's network of informants, the two American nationals in question were being held in a village not far from there. Negotiations carried out by a local intermediary had gone nowhere, and after an offer of a million US dollars hadn't even rated a response, Kennedy decided it was time to extract the hostages by a more direct method.

The question was, why didn't this group want the money? Why were they looking to start a fight they were destined to lose? Based on the best intel available, they weren't even Taliban. Just an extended family group consisting of maybe forty individuals living in the middle of nowhere. They had no dog in this race. Hell, there *was* no race anymore.

In the end, Rapp suspected it had less to do with the Afghans than it did the former US president and his CIA chief. Anthony Cook had only managed to stay in the White House for a short time, but he still cast a long shadow—particularly at the Agency. His authoritarian views had found a surprising number of sympathetic ears in the organization, as had his plan to turn it into an apparatus with no purpose other than to consolidate his power. Kennedy was still trying to sort out who could be trusted and who needed to be shown the door, but it was a difficult and sometimes painful task. People they'd known and worked with for years had been seduced by Cook's vision and were still working to undermine her.

With that hurricane blowing in Langley, it wasn't particularly far-fetched to think that a faction still loyal to the former administration was trying to lure Rapp into an ambush. He'd been Kennedy's operational right hand for decades and losing him would be a significant blow to her. Maybe even a fatal one given the current political environment.

A village perched on an east-facing hillside emerged from the darkness and Rapp signaled his column to stop again. He dropped to his stomach, slithering to the edge of the creek and descending into it. A trickle of water at the bottom shone black as he passed silently over it and climbed the other bank. Propping his HK416 rifle over the edge, he used its thermal scope to examine the settlement in more detail.

The scree-covered slope leading to it was steep, climbing maybe two hundred yards before reaching the lowest of nine visible buildings. All were constructed of stone—simple rectangular structures with flat roofs and one or two wood-framed windows. None appeared to contain glass and there was no sign of life at all.

"Looks good for our original incursion plan," he said into his throat mike. "No contacts and the layout's as expected. Advise when you're in position."

CHAPTER 2

"IT'S a wonderful exhibit," the young woman said in Spanish that suggested a privileged upbringing near Madrid. "You should take the time to see it if you can."

Damian Losa nodded with a barely perceptible smile. His people had perhaps done their job too well with this girl. Her dark hair played across shoulders so smooth that they seemed to reflect the light of the terrace and the city below. Her smile flashed easily, revealing perfect teeth completely unaffected by the thousand-euro bottle of wine she was sipping. Was there a trick to that? Some kind of chemical film? Probably.

The problem was that she was so compelling that she attracted the attention of the other restaurant patrons. Furtive glances from both men and women, carrying differing degrees of envy, desire, and fascination. The exception was his ten-strong security team spread throughout the elegant dining area. They'd been trained to pretend not to notice him but, in this case, their disinterest made them stand out. He'd have to remember to mention that to Julian at some point.

"I'm looking forward to the gnocchi. Did you see it? It's the third item on the tasting menu. I've never been able to perfect it. Italy's cuisine is simple on the surface, but it's all about the quality of ingredients and technique. In this case, the right potato combined with the right flour in the right proportion."

In their brief time together, she'd expertly covered subjects as diverse as politics, sports, art, and cooking in an effort to find something that elicited more than polite disinterest from him. His smile broadened a bit, so she ran with it. A moment later, he was being treated to very credible tasting notes on the wine he'd ordered and a description of the region that had produced it.

In truth, he didn't care one way or another about Italian food and only pretended to sip the wine in front of him. His increased engagement resulted from a memory she'd triggered of his mother making tortillas. The sunlight flooding through the window over the sink, the worn pots inherited from ancestors long dead. The earthy aroma.

Not that she'd had to make their food by hand or use those ancient implements. His mother had been a nurse and his father an accountant—members of a small middle class that had afforded him opportunities rare in that part of Mexico. He'd attended a modest private school and an even more modest university. He'd lived in a safe neighborhood and always had enough to eat. And he'd had his mother—a round and unwaveringly positive woman who woke up every morning with a heartfelt prayer of thanks to her God.

What would she think of what he'd done with the opportunities she and his father had worked so hard to provide? If she were to walk into the restaurant at that moment, would she even recognize the fifty-five-year-old man who had risen to become the most powerful criminal in the world? Would she be dazzled by the girl sitting across the table from him? A young woman he'd never met before that night and would never see again after tomorrow morning? Would the mansions, jets, and yachts impress her? Would she mistake people's fear of him for respect and social standing?

Doubtful. In retrospect, it was perhaps best that his parents had died young.

The Girl—he couldn't remember her name—sensed his mind wandering and moved with impressive ease to the subject of technology. Something about augmented reality that he tried to track on because it was indeed important. The world was changing at a dizzying pace and over the last few years he could feel himself losing his grip. On it and everything else. A decade ago, he would have allowed everything else to fall away during their time together. He would have been engaged in the conversation and sharing the bottle. He would have been wondering if her incredible breadth of knowledge extended to the bedroom and looking forward to finding out. He would have recognized that these moments were the culmination of everything he'd worked for. A life of wealth and power so limitless that he existed separate from—indeed above—the rest of society.

The fact that none of this had crossed his mind over the course of the last thirty minutes was worrying. It took more than cunning and experience to stay on top in the business he'd chosen. It took a certain amount of passion.

A waiter appeared and laid two small plates in front of them, describing in detail the exotic nature of the ingredients and the chef's motivation for selecting them. Losa gazed down at the elaborately decorated bite of fish contained on a single spoon. Not really the kind of food he gravitated toward, but he admired the artistry and precision of it. While perhaps not a connoisseur of Michelin-starred restaurants, he *was* a connoisseur of expertise. In his experience, it was perhaps the rarest thing in the universe.

Halfway through the explanation, he lost focus and turned his attention to the coastline and the city of Salerno that bordered it. The commercial port dominated, with a single cargo ship currently docked and in the process of unloading. Despite the distance and rain, he could discern individual trucks dropping their cargo and picking up new loads. Bringing the world to Italy and Italy to the world.

He lifted the spoon and slid the fish into his mouth, eliciting a smile from the Girl.

"Do you like it?" she said in a tone that suggested it was the most important question ever asked.

"It's delicious."

That prompted a charming story about her youthful penchant for stealing chocolate from a local restaurant's kitchen. The fact that it was almost certainly fiction didn't detract from its impact at all.

She was almost to the denouement of her tale when distant spotlights came to life over her perfect shoulder. He could just make out the urgent movements of a truck at their center and a moment later, the quiet pop of gunfire became audible, slightly out of sync with the corresponding muzzle flashes. Enough to furrow a few brows, but not enough to divert his fellow diners from their sea bass with asparagus. That took the explosion.

Everyone turned toward the percussive sound in unison. Losa thought he could see the flames reflected in the Girl's eyes, but it was likely that he was just romanticizing the moment.

"What do you think it is?" she said.

"I don't know," he lied. "Some kind of accident, I imagine. Maybe they were transporting something flammable."

"But there are police cars. And was that shooting I heard before?"

He shrugged. "I imagine it'll be on the news tomorrow."

"I wonder if anyone was hurt?" she said, drifting ever further from her script as she watched the fire spread.

"I don't know." Another lie. But after all these years, they came easy.

It was their most meaningful exchange of the evening, and the Girl used the opening to reach across the table and put her hand on his. She really would have been a pleasant way to spend the night, but he had too much on his mind.

She began chatting again as the people around them lost interest in the real world and settled back into the one provided by the restaurant. What happened on those docks—what contraband came in, who was injured, who died—had no bearing on their charmed lives. No effect at all on their families, future, or wealth.

Another seafood course arrived, and he watched absently as the Girl examined it with the aid of her fork. He allowed himself to enjoy her youthful enthusiasm for a moment before sinking into darker thoughts.

Three weeks ago, a member of his decimated network in Syria had sent him details about a shipment of reformulated captagon tablets leaving Tartus for Salerno. After a great deal of consideration, he'd decided to use his European contacts to inform the authorities. The hope was that the government would see the danger of this new variant and act with determination and competence.

A long shot, particularly in light of the fact that they'd largely missed the creation of an elaborate Muslim distribution network in their backyard. And to the small degree it had been noticed, it was being used solely as propaganda to keep the illusory threat of ISIS in Syria alive. The media-friendly remnants of that insurgent group allowed the world's governments to avoid facing the fragmented disaster that Syria had become.

Sadly, he could afford no such luxury. The network that had been built, and that this shipment would have put into full operation, was both surprisingly professional and shockingly well funded. The Syrian government's success at retaking control of its territory had combined with continued economic sanctions to transform the country into a narco-state. A potentially very successful one. Not only did they now have their European infrastructure in place, but they'd managed to develop a product that Losa's chemists couldn't reproduce.

Losing control of the European narcotics trade wasn't an option for him. He was the man who made people money. Who kept the peace and held the authorities at bay. The fact that he was now competing not against another cartel but against an entire nation would be taken into account by neither his enemies nor his allies. Any territory ceded would be seen as weakness and the fear he commanded would soften. Soon there would be whispers—leading inevitably to open discussion—of his advancing age. Of whom and what would come next.

He glanced past the Girl again, watching fire suppression vehicles arrive on the dock. The other machinery had fallen silent, and it appeared that a full evacuation was underway. He'd managed to draw first blood, but the war ahead would be long and brutal.

How would it play out? With such limited information, it was impossible to make intelligent moves on the chessboard. His life had been one of careful action based on hard data. It was what set him apart from the sadistic and impulsive men who made up the majority of his peers.

Normally, this would be a job for his renowned negotiating skills. He would fly to Damascus, sit down with Syria's leadership, and come to a mutually beneficial agreement. He had done that with great success in places as diverse as Colombia, Thailand, Morocco, and even the United States.

The government in Damascus was somewhat more complex. The speed and ruthlessness with which they'd dismantled his Syrian operation had been stunning, as had their move into Europe. He knew now that he'd underestimated them, counting on their corruption, internal tensions, and lack of regional experience. An uncharacteristically careless error on his part.

At this point, a personal appearance in Syria was far too dangerous. He needed someone to stand in for him. Someone with the ability to navigate the environment there and to survive long enough to gather the necessary information and contacts. Preferably a person from outside his organization who would be incapable of revealing anything sensitive if subjected to torture.

That left very few options.

The Girl touched his hand again, pulling him back into the present.

"I'm sorry," he said. "I've been distracted."

"It's all right."

He smiled, this time with a bit more sincerity. No decisions would be made that evening. It would take a few sleepless nights to sort all this out. And if that was the case, there was no reason not to enjoy himself.

"Don't be so understanding. It's an insufferable trait in a dinner companion. But from now on, you have my full attention."

CHAPTER 3

THE barely perceptible crunch of approaching footsteps became audible behind Rapp. Their rhythm was familiar and just as confidence inspiring as when he'd first heard them so many years ago.

"Still nothing?" Scott Coleman whispered, dropping to the ground and peering up at the starlit village.

"Completely dead," Rapp replied.

The former SEAL nodded and spoke into his throat mike. "Give me a sitrep."

Over his earpiece, Rapp heard their men respond. Joe Maslick was in position to the north and Bruno McGraw to the south. Charlie Wicker, debatably the world's top sniper, was still setting up in the high ground, but promised to be ready inside of one minute. There was no hurry, so Rapp waited a full three before giving the order.

"Move in. Hold your fire until you hear mine. After that, kick up some dust."

He and Coleman crept out of the ditch, with Rapp sweeping left and his teammate right. They passed through a band of trees that had managed to take hold in the harsh environment and started climbing.

The loose terrain eventually gave way to a rock face steep enough that Rapp had to sling his rifle and use both hands to climb. Once at the top, he found himself within twenty yards of the village's first building—a crumbling structure with an empty door frame. He took aim at it and fired a controlled burst before running toward a path to the west.

A moment later, gunfire erupted throughout the tiny settlement. Muzzle flashes overpowered the starlight and the peace that reigned just seconds before was broken so violently that it was hard to believe it ever existed. A rotted wooden door with a rudimentary latch appeared to Rapp's right and he kicked it open, spraying the interior with his rifle.

The layout of the village made it practical to divide into quarters and each of them kept to his section in order to avoid friendly fire. Wick would remain in an overwatch position to call out any potential mistakes and deal with any surprises. Not that Rapp anticipated either.

He turned his attention to an ancient animal trough and put a few rounds into it because, why not? It still held some water from recent rains, and splashes appeared in the unsteady light. Rapp crouched and slapped in a fresh magazine before emptying half of it into the window of a house that looked exactly like all the others.

Finally, he stood, turning full circle before toggling his throat mike. "They knew we were coming!" he shouted. The level of his voice wasn't necessary for their communications technology, but was instead for the benefit of any Afghans who might be within earshot. The goal was to put on a show, and he felt like they'd accomplished that.

"Let's get the hell out of here!"

The undisciplined gunfire ceased, plunging the village back into the darkness and silence that it had been mired in for at least a quarter century. His three teammates fell in behind as Rapp broke into the open and headed northwest toward a designated landing zone. Wick had been tasked with covering the majority of their retreat, but would soon start breaking down his kit to follow.

The dull thump of a chopper became audible as they maintained their heading, but it still wasn't visible as it angled in. Rapp continued to the extraction point at a pace that was set to allow his overwatch to reintegrate with the team. Still no resistance or any indication at all of human presence. Just as the Agency's analysts had promised.

The black outline of the helicopter finally appeared and began to descend. Rapp cut left and stopped, waving his men on. "Go! Go!"

Wick was straggling a bit and Rapp grabbed some of the diminutive sniper's gear to lighten his load. The doors in both sides of the aircraft were open and all five men arrived at roughly the same time, piling in as the rotors started to pick up speed again. When the skids began to leave the ground, they all jumped out the other side and slipped into a boulder field just beyond. A moment later, the chopper was airborne and banking toward their base of operations.

The actual target was a village about a mile to the north. The idea was that the men there would have seen the commotion and heard the helicopter, leading them to assume that the Americans had once again gotten hold of bad intel and attacked a settlement that hadn't been inhabited in decades.

If Rapp knew the Afghans—and he did—they'd get a real kick out of it. There was nothing they liked more than watching US forces screw up. It didn't happen often in combat situations, but when it did, the locals used it as proof of their mastery over the desert, the superiority of their way of life, and proof that God loved them best. It was human nature to embrace the inferiority of one's enemies. A bias so strong that it tended to prevent people from thinking too hard about the actual plausibility of it.

No one liked a killjoy.

CHAPTER 4

A SHRINK would probably be concerned that Rapp associated the smell of Afghanistan with home. Dust, stone, sweat, and food cooked over an open fire. The reason he'd been able to operate so successfully in the region was that to some extent he'd gone native. He'd never seen his time in-country as a tour. He'd rarely felt a compulsion to go "home," which, for much of his life, had consisted of a beat-up apartment with boxes that never seemed to get unpacked.

He looked up at the stars for a moment and then returned his attention to the path he was walking along. It led to the village where the two American hostages were being held, but went no farther. A dead end for him both literally and figuratively. He didn't belong there anymore. He belonged in Virginia. In South Africa. It still surprised him how clear that had become. He had a place, and it was with Claudia and Anna.

More and more, he felt like it was time to circle the wagons. To bring the few people he cared about inside and keep everyone else out. His enemies kept multiplying, but at the same time became harder to identify. No one cared about anything beyond creating sufficient theater to move up the rungs of power. And anyone who wasn't unwaveringly devoted to producing that theater—anyone who for a moment lapsed into reality or put country before ambition—ended up with a blade in their back.

Maybe that's what had originally attracted him to Afghanistan. Their family and tribal bonds were unbreakable, and the enemy was obvious. The people here didn't skulk around. They looked you in the eye when they tried to kill you. Not exactly Utopia, but there was an appealing honesty to it all.

Rapp adjusted the cloth sack slung over his shoulder and slowed his pace. He'd traded his combat gear for traditional Afghan garb and a pair of trail-running shoes that had been deliberately trashed to look like something left behind by an American soldier. The hope was that he'd appear familiar enough not to set off any immediate fireworks. Just because the war was over didn't mean the peace had begun.

Ahead, the flicker of firelight was quickly joined by the scent of smoke. A few hours ago, the village he was walking toward almost certainly would have been set up for an ambush. There were solid reasons to believe that factions high up in America's intelligence community had convinced these people to hold on to their hostages in order to facilitate a little side job. They'd likely been given the time of Rapp's arrival, his incursion plan, the size of his team, and a rundown on his weapons. All they had to do was lie in wait. Then, when he and his men were dead, it would rain American dollars.

The question of what to do about it had been the subject of spirited debate. The obvious answer was to roll in early with an overwhelming force, but that had drawbacks. Namely, a lot of corpses that would inevitably include the two hostages. When Rapp suggested they carry out the attack exactly as planned, but a mile too far to the south, everyone had thought he'd lost his mind. They'd eventually come around, though. Mostly because it was his ass on the line and not theirs.

Rapp made it to the edge of the village without any issues. The houses were all dark, with shutters closed and the women and children stashed safely behind them. Ahead, booming voices punctuated by intermittent bursts of laughter were audible. He continued toward them, listening to the conversation as it became intelligible.

Despite his Dari not being anywhere near as strong as his Arabic, he caught the gist. Strained jokes about the Americans not being able to read a map, needing glasses, or being led by women. The customary chest-thumping about what they saw as their overwhelming victory against the most powerful militaries in history. Alexander the Great. The Persians. The British and Soviets. Now the Americans. Beneath the bravado, though, there was always an undercurrent of fear. The realization that there could be a Reaper drone circling just overhead.

After what had happened in the abandoned village neighboring them, they'd be absolutely certain of their opponents' next move. When the Americans screwed up, they went back to the drawing board. They analyzed what had gone wrong, cleaned their weapons, revisited their strategies, and upgraded their technology. As far as the Afghans were concerned, there was nothing the Americans hated more than improvisation. But as predictable as Western forces could be, the Afghans were even more so. They'd been doing the same things the same way for the better part of a thousand years.

As Rapp closed in, the conversation became clearer, switching from light comedy to a graphic description of what they'd have done if the Americans had managed to find their village. Tales of heroics worthy of Greek mythology ensued, all with the requisite assurances of God's favor.

The bonfire and men huddled around it came into view a few seconds later. None of them were the enemy. Not anymore. The enemy now was the people in Washington and Langley who had set this up. To the Afghans, Rapp's death meant money for food and shelter. Maybe a little revenge on a former rival or bragging rights when it came to finding a wife. The betrayal wasn't here. It was back home.

He continued to grip the bag with his left hand, while extending his right in a way that would make it clear he wasn't holding a gun. The reaction was immediate when he entered the circle of light. Men who had been sitting leapt to their feet and ones who had weapons nearby snatched them up.

"Salaam," Rapp said, touching his free hand to his heart. While his Dari might be marginal, he had perfected the art of hiding his American accent behind an Iraqi one. That typically created enough confusion to keep everyone from shooting at once. But not always.

An old man who appeared to be in charge was the first to speak. "Who are you? Show yourself."

Rapp eased the bag to the ground and slowly unwound the scarf from his face. Again, the result would be ambiguous. Dark eyes, beard, and sun-damaged skin.

"I was sent for the people you're holding," he said, nudging the bag with his toe. "I brought money."

"Then it was a trick," the old man responded, pointing in the direction of the abandoned village Rapp had attacked. "You knew we weren't there."

"Yes."

"A warrior who fights with his head and not his heart."

"I fight with whatever weapons are necessary."

The old man turned his attention to the bag. "We've already been promised payment."

"From the politicians," Rapp said, spitting on the ground with disdain that he didn't have to fake. "Cowards waiting to betray you from five thousand kilometers away. I came here in person with money in my hands. Better than a promise from men with no honor, don't you think?"

"We aren't being paid to release our hostages," the man said.

Rapp nodded at the confirmation that his and Kennedy's suspicions were correct. "You're being paid to kill the man coming to rescue them."

"Yes."

"There's no reason for it anymore. Give me the hostages and take what I'm offering. Use it to make a better life for your families."

"No!" a kid on the right blurted. "Are you blind? It's Malik al-Mawt."

The angel of death. A nickname the Taliban pinned on him when he'd operated there.

"I haven't been that in a long time. And there's no reason for me to be it again. You fought for your country, and I fought for mine. I killed your brothers, and you killed mine. But that's over now."

"It's over for you," the old man said. "You go back to your rich country and live like a king while my people starve."

"We gave you every opportunity to build a future. You rejected it. You fought among yourselves, you fell back on tribal bigotry, and you cheated each other. If you want to blame someone for your situation, look in the mirror."

Rapp scanned the faces in front of him, trying to hold back the memories. He'd been in a similar position on one of his first trips to Afghanistan. But back then he'd had better knees and a hell of a lot more youthful illusions.

Scott Coleman lay on his stomach in the dirt, moving only his eyes. He hadn't understood the shouted statement coming from the center of the village, but the tone was clear. After a five count, though, still no gunshots. A second miracle happened a few seconds later. One of the two men guarding the stone building he was watching wandered off to see what the commotion was about.

This whole plan was nuts, but somehow it seemed to be playing out exactly as Rapp predicted. He'd said the men in the village wouldn't empty their rifles into him when he came waltzing into town. That at least some of the men guarding the hostages would abandon their posts to exercise their curiosity. And that everyone would get out of this with their skin. Of course, that last one remained to be seen.

He slid back and circled to the rear of the target building. Based on a brief flare from around the wall, the remaining guard had just lit a cigarette. A consolation for being left out of the party.

The former SEAL slipped along the wall until he could see around its edge. The guard was no more than seventeen, with a smooth face that illuminated every time he dragged on his smoke.

Rapp wanted this to all go off without breaking too many dishes. For better or worse, the war was over, and he didn't want to revisit it. Coleman was more ambivalent, but he had no desire to kill this kid.

Unfortunately, his nonlethal tool kit was nearly nonexistent. Improvising, he picked up a rock and eased around the edge of the ancient structure. The darkness was fairly deep in that corner of the village and the kid had blown his night vision with the cigarette, so things went reasonably smoothly. The rock contacted his skull with a dull crack that wouldn't carry very far, and he dropped to the ground. Not sexy, but effective.

After propping him next to the door, Coleman flipped down his night-vision monocular and entered. In the northeast corner, he could see the two Americans asleep on the dirt floor.

"Time to get up," he whispered.

They both immediately woke, but were slow to move. The reason was easy to see with the benefit of light amplification. One was wearing an explosive vest with various wires leading from it to his companion. An antenna was visible above one of the charges, but the location of the remote detonator and whose finger was on it were impossible to say. Probably one of the men currently being chatted up by the newer, gentler Mitch Rapp.

"Is someone there?" one of the men mustered the courage to say.

"Shh," Coleman warned. "I've come to get you out of here."

"There's a bomb," the other said. "They've attached it to us."

"I understand." The former SEAL crouched in front of them. "Don't talk and don't move. Let me have a look."

Sadly for him, it was actually a pretty workmanlike job. Wires snaked everywhere and, unlike in the movies, they were all the same color. The weakness in the system was a couple of simple combination padlocks that secured the vest to one man and the triggers to the other.

Each lock was wound with wires that appeared to be glued in place. He had a set of bolt cutters with him, but there was no way to get through the shackle without also cutting through the wires—something that wasn't going to end well.

Instead, he pulled out a satphone and selected a number from the list of people he had on call that night. Despite the cold desert air, he started to sweat when it got to the fifth ring. After the sixth, a male voice came on.

"Hang on a sec."

"Hang on?" Coleman whispered incredulously. "I'm in the fucking Hindu Kush staring at a bomb."

"Don't get your panties wadded up, man. I was just pausing my game."

Coleman could picture the man sitting in his basement, holding a game controller, surrounded by empty beer cans and Doritos bags. Unfortunately, there wasn't anything he could do about it. The puffy little prick was the best in the business. And not by a little.

"Whatcha got?"

"Sending it now."

The phone had an excellent camera, but still demanded a dim flash. The hope was that whatever light filtered through the ill-fitting door would go unnoticed or be taken for the lighting of another cigarette.

There was an excruciatingly long pause over the line, but finally Coleman got some positive news.

"That's a Fortress 1850D combination lock. I had basically the same thing on my locker when I was in high school. Did you bring a padlock shim?"

"A what?"

"Don't worry about it. We'll just do this the old-fashioned way. Turn the wheel three times to the right."

"Are you fucking kidding me? I've got two of them. How long is this going to take?"

"Stop busting my balls. I'm not the one who forgot my padlock shim."

Coleman swore quietly. The truth was that Rapp didn't have much more than thirty seconds of charm on his best day. The chances of getting these locks open before he got irritated and shot someone was right around zero. He could barely get in and out of a Walmart without shooting someone. And if that happened, Coleman was going to end his life as a flaming chunk of meat soaring over the desert.

"All right. Three turns. Done."

"Now pull up kind of gently on the shackle and keep going right until you hear a click."

"Okay. I got a click."

"Now turn it two more numbers."

"What the hell does that mean?"

"Like, if it's on thirty, turn it to twenty-eight."

"You're killing me, man. You're literally killing me."

"I didn't build the thing. Quit being an asshole."

"This isn't a video game, you know? There's no reset button on my life."

Coleman's heart was pounding uncomfortably in his chest and his palms were sweating enough that the dial was getting slick. The fact that one of the hostages was whimpering like a recently kicked puppy didn't help, either. He hated this claustrophobic, stressful shit. Give him some open terrain and a bunch of flying bullets any day. Precise fiddling in the dark while waiting to get blown into the next zip code sucked.

Having said that, in less than three minutes, both locks were open and he was gently extricating the men from their respective booby traps.

The swollen little jackass had done it again.

"So, we should just take your money and forget? Is that what you're saying?"

Rapp nodded. "Pretty much, yeah."

The kid on the right spoke up again. "Why not kill him and take the money he brought? Then we get paid twice."

"If you know who I am, then you know what I'm capable of," Rapp responded. "More of you than I can count have tried to kill me and I'm always the one who walks away. It won't be any different this time."

"All talk!" the young man shouted. "He's one man. He's—"

"Shut up, Hadi!" the old man said. "Don't be stupid. He's not alone! He—"

"Don't tell me to be silent! The end of the fighting has turned you into a bunch of old women!"

The tone and volume of his voice weren't a problem as long as all he did was run his mouth. Unfortunately, he was too young and proud for that. He jerked his rifle upward in an effort to sight along it, but before he could get it to eye level, he crumpled to the ground.

Other than the thud of the bullet and the impact of his body against the dirt, there was no sound. Charlie Wicker was too far away and using a suppressor.

The rest of the men possessed enough experience fighting the Americans that they remained frozen. All of them had understood the certainty of their companion's fate the moment he raised his weapon, and none were anxious to join him. Not yet anyway.

"Take the money," Rapp repeated.

Video sent of the hostages suggested that they were wearing explosives that could be set off wirelessly. That meant that someone had a detonator. And with the hierarchal tribal culture that ruled the region, a good bet would be the elder. Taking him out was tempting, but didn't come with any guarantees.

"You might kill us all," the old man responded. "Or we might finally be the ones who kill *you*. Either way, you won't get what you came for."

Rapp had guessed wrong. Both of the old man's hands were in clear view when the explosives blew.

• • •

Scott Coleman followed the hostages through the door and cut left just seconds before the detonation. The door and part of the jamb were transformed into projectiles, but the stone walls held. He was knocked to the ground, but with no injuries beyond some minor burns to the exposed skin on the back of his neck.

By the time he pushed himself back to his feet, the two men he'd freed were already disappearing into the darkness. Neither was particularly fit, but what they lacked in athleticism, they made up for with enthusiasm.

The Afghans seemed to decide simultaneously that they weren't going to let this go. They leapt to their feet, with two not even making it fully upright before Wick dropped them. Rapp crouched and sprinted left, trying to lose himself in the smoke blowing from the edge of the village and covering ground as fast as he could. Between the haze and darkness, it wouldn't take long for him to disappear.

He managed to pull his Glock from a holster in the small of his back and use it to take out the one man who'd decided to pursue. His lifeless body had barely hit the ground when someone began firing on full auto from the east. Likely Joe Maslick hosing down the bonfire area in order to give the Afghans there something more important to worry about than the fleeing Malik al-Mawt. Revenge tended to become a secondary concern when you found yourself caught between a random hail of bullets on one side and precision sniper fire on the other.

Rapp turned out of the smoke, crossing some loose terrain and scrub before regaining the trail that had led him there. The starlight was bright enough to allow him to keep a decent pace without much danger of breaking an ankle or diving off a cliff. He guessed about an eight-minute mile—a pace that few people could match given the conditions. Certainly not the men he'd just left behind.

Various bullets sped past, but nothing close. When he looked back, he could see the flames from the explosion spreading and intermittent flashes of gunfire, but no one in direct pursuit.

"Scott," he said into his throat mike. "You still alive?"

He felt a powerful sense of relief when his old friend's voice came over his earpiece. "No thanks to you, asshole. Weren't you supposed to turn on the charm?"

"That was the charm. Is the chopper inbound?" Rapp said, jumping over a narrow ditch. He'd been focused on off-road triathlon training for the past few months, and it seemed to be bearing fruit. Despite the relentless pace, he still had enough wind for a coherent conversation.

"ETA seven minutes. We're making a beeline west with no one following. They probably think the hostages are dead and don't want to take any more casualties."

"I'm not sure," Charlie Wicker interjected over the comm. "It might just be because they have bigger fish to fry. Men are pouring out of those buildings and everyone old enough to be out of diapers has a rifle."

"Mas, Bruno. Are you both okay?" Rapp said.

"Yeah, boss. They're not interested in us. It looks like they're putting together a posse that's going to be coming in your direction. We've got a drone overhead. Should we give them the go-ahead?"

Rapp thought about that while maintaining his speed across the desolate landscape. The men pouring out of those building weren't the only ones living in them. Their wives and children would be inside, huddled in corners wondering if the Americans were about to rain hell down on them.

"Any horses or vehicles?" Rapp asked.

"None I can see," Wick said. "What are your orders, Mitch? They're starting to move. You've got less than a minute before they're too scattered to take out with a missile strike."

"Tell the Reaper to stand down," Rapp said as the terrain opened up a bit. There was no way those men were going to catch him and there wasn't another inhabited settlement for at least thirty klicks in any direction. "I'm going to stay on this heading. Pick me up eight miles south in an hour. By then they'll be far back enough that you won't have to worry about taking fire."

"If you say so," Maslick responded. "Enjoy your workout."

CHAPTER 5

IT was well after midnight and the quiet neighborhood in the 16th arrondissement was completely silent. The homes visible outside the limousine's windows looked much like they had a century ago—dark, imposing, and exclusive. Damian Losa gazed at them as they passed, but his mind was lost in other places. Other times.

His driver finally pulled up in front of one of the grander structures, a neoclassical villa partially obscured by an iron gate and manicured grounds. He'd never seen it before and, after his stay, he'd never see it again. Such were the security measures necessary for a man like him.

"Sir?" his driver said hesitantly. "I'm sorry, but there's no parking on the property. You'll have to walk."

The men from Losa's lead and chase car stepped out onto the street, moving in various directions to secure the area. Once satisfied, one of them opened the gate and another led him to the open front door.

Losa passed through alone, entering a cavernous vestibule with spotless marble floors and abundant artwork that bordered on the grandiose. A young woman appeared at the other end, tilting her head inquisitively as he approached.

Isabella had come into his orbit shortly after her graduation from college in Venezuela. The collapse of the country and death of her family had happened almost simultaneously, leaving her alone and without much hope. Initially his housekeeper, she now managed what could loosely be called his personal life.

Humorless to the point of being robotic, she'd proved to be one of his better acquisitions. The loss of her country, her future, and her loved ones had stripped her of all desire. She'd concluded that the pain of loss was greater than the joy of having. It was an attitude that translated into steadfast reliability. Her work was all she had, and she aspired to nothing more.

"You're alone," she observed, a hint of concern visible on her normally expressionless face. Selecting the Girl had been her duty and she'd be concerned that she'd performed it inadequately.

"She was lovely, Isabella. I just have too much on my mind."

"Do you know how many days you've taken off in the last month?"

"I don't. But I'm sure you're going to tell me."

"None. You work fifteen hours a day, seven days a week. No one— not even you—can sustain that."

"Of course," he said as he approached. "You're right. Next time. But tonight, could you call Julian? I need to speak with him."

"Do you realize it's almost one in the morning?"

"I do."

She gave a short nod and pointed behind her. "You'll find what you're looking for at the end and to the right."

"Thank you, Isabella."

He followed her directions to a wood-paneled study dominated by a fireplace large enough to stand in. Because of the summer temperatures, a fire wasn't appropriate, but a series of flickering candles offered an adequate substitute. On a desk near the window, he found a bottle of Perrier and used an ornate knife to cut a slice of lime. It was something he preferred to do himself. Many of his associates speculated that it was out of fear of being poisoned but, in fact, it was just another reminder of his mother's kitchen.

Losa sat and focused on the tiny flames, sipping calmly from a cut-crystal glass. The older he got, the more he found himself thinking about how he'd become what he was. The violent early days as he broke into the business and tried to carve out a place in it. The increasing complexity and sophistication as his star rose. The rapid, sometimes uncontrollable, expansion that had made him a target of the dangerous men he was overtaking. And finally, the reversal of those roles as he fought to prevent someone younger, more motivated, and more merciless from doing the same to him.

Not that he had any right to complain about how his life had unfolded. Many of the people he dealt with had been born with very little hope. They had learned to kill or be killed while still in the cradle. He, on the other hand, had become the man he was for no better reason than that he was easily bored. And one day that conscious decision would be the end of him.

But not today.

His lieutenant arrived half an hour later, looking no more or less disheveled than he usually did. Seven years Losa's junior, Julian was in every way his opposite. He'd been born into a family of Mexican thieves that had put him to work in the street as soon as he was able. There had been no time for school or any thought of escape. Nor had there been any need. The man was brilliant, devoted, and had a ruthlessness that was much more calculated than most of his peers.

Thirty years ago, Julian had been one of Losa's first contacts in the criminal world, and the only one willing to take him seriously. He'd been a witness to the first man Losa had killed. To the first million-dollar deal he'd made. To his first meeting with a head of state and the day his net worth topped a billion.

What made them such a stable team, though, was Julian's self-awareness. He recognized his general lack of vision and the fact that he would never be able to move in the circles that Losa navigated so effortlessly. He recognized the weight of Losa's crown and preferred to hide in its shadow rather than risk trying to steal it.

"I thought your night was fully booked," Julian said, pouring himself a Perrier, but forgoing the pleasure of slicing the lime. "Is there a problem I'm not aware of? According to the news outlets, Salerno went about as expected."

"Casualties?"

"Initial reports are six police and one civilian killed in addition to the driver. There's no reliable count on the injured yet."

"Were our people on the dock able to get samples of the merchandise?"

"Seven tablets. A lot were burned too badly to be useful, and even more were blown into the water."

"And you've sent them in for analysis?"

"They're on their way."

Losa turned his attention back to the candles. "Six dead police officers and fifteen metric tons of a very new kind of drug. I wonder if that'll be enough to motivate the Europeans."

Julian laughed and took a chair across from him. "They'll shake their fists in the general direction of Syria, but no more than that. It's a quagmire they have no interest in getting dragged into."

"That makes two of us."

Julian's expression changed in a way that was all too familiar. He had something to say and had finally been provided an entrée.

"Then let's not. The Americans would call this situation a train wreck, but it's a slow-moving one. The Muslims have admittedly done an impressive job of building their organization, but it doesn't rival ours."

"Not yet. But all indications suggest that they have the resources."

"But that's the problem, isn't it? We both know that the Syrian government is behind this. Do we want to go to war with an entire country? Even a pariah one? Would it be wiser to organize an orderly retreat? Instead of playing to win, play to delay. We're not as young as we used to be, Damian. Maybe we should look at this as an opportunity. A reason to get out of the European drug trade. We make more in America and our position there is unassailable."

It was something that Losa had spent a great deal of time considering, but without arriving at any conclusion. The idea of a strategic withdrawal had its charms, but it was easier said than done.

"A few years ago, we'd have said our position in Europe was unassailable. Can we afford to have our enemies—and our allies—see us in retreat? Even an orderly one?"

"I think it's possible that you're overestimating how much people will blame us for backing away from an extremely costly and politically charged war."

"Really? Because I think you're underestimating it. But which of us is right? I don't know. We don't have enough information."

"I agree that more information is always better. But it doesn't seem to be on offer."

"It might be in Damascus."

Julian shook his head. "Syria is a graveyard for us, Damian. They've already subverted or destroyed most of our network there. We don't understand the players or the rules. Any contact we make with them is more apt to hurt us than help us."

"But if we had access to someone who *does* understand those things?"

"I can't think of anyone in our organization who fits that description."

"What about someone outside of the organization?"

"Who?"

"Mitch Rapp."

Julian laughed, but then fell silent when he realized Losa was serious. "You want to call in your marker with him?"

"Why not?"

"Why not? How much time do you have? He's a CIA operative completely loyal to his country. He's incredibly unpredictable, violent, and not afraid of us. He has resources that we don't understand and can't control. He—"

"But you agree he's capable."

"I agree that he has an ability to navigate waters that we don't, but he can't be trusted to do it on our behalf."

"I'm not so sure," Losa said. "I helped him when he desperately needed it and he's the kind of man who'll feel obligated to honor that debt."

"Maybe," Julian conceded. "But are you sure you know how?"

CHAPTER 6

WEST OF MANASSAS
VIRGINIA
USA

APP waited for the gate to open and then accelerated his
Dodge Charger onto a well-maintained road. His subdivision,
situated in a rural area well outside of Washington, DC, had originally
consisted of ten large homesites to be sold off at market price. As a gift,
his obscenely rich brother had bought them all up, leaving Rapp with a
hundred acres on top of a butte surrounded by farmland. It was a nice
gesture, but ended up being too remote. The 9th Armored Division
could roll through the perimeter fence and go unnoticed for a week.

Ever the idea man, Steven had quickly devised a solution. He sold
off the luxury lots to a select group of Rapp's friends for a dollar each.
Now, a few years later, he was surrounded by most of Coleman's team
as well as a number of former Secret Service, FBI, and CIA employees.
Some admittedly a little long in the tooth, but still not to be underestimated.

Even Maggie Nash remained, despite blaming Rapp for the death of her husband. The security and built-in support system was too good for a widow with four children to abandon. Also, Rapp suspected that deep down she knew Mike bore some responsibility for his own fate.

A barn appeared on the left and he actively ignored the ever-expanding farm operation spearheaded by Scott Coleman and Anna, his seven-year-old partner in crime. While it was unquestionably a maintenance nightmare, he had to admit that he liked the self-sufficiency aspect—a benefit that had gone beyond the theoretical during a nationwide blackout a while back. He slowed to allow a goat to wander across the street and then continued up a low rise.

At the top, the wall surrounding his house came into view against a sky just beginning to darken. The reenforced copper gate began to swing back as he approached, causing a slight clenching of Rapp's jaw. Claudia had activated it based on the security camera displays—something he'd told her a hundred times not to do. With the glare of the evening sun, it would be impossible for her to see through the windshield to confirm who was driving. In this case, though, it wasn't particularly risky. The large courtyard he entered was scattered with cars, including Irene Kennedy's Yukon, which would have arrived with two armed bodyguards.

No one was in evidence when he stepped out, and he took a moment to center himself. Claudia's idea of having a few of the guys over for some steaks and an informal debriefing seemed to have expanded into a block party. Not exactly a crisis, but crowds tended to bother him even when they were made up of people he knew. Particularly when he was returning from the empty desert.

Rapp scanned the vehicles, mentally matching them with their owners, and then turned his attention to the massive single-level house. It had been designed by his late wife, but she'd allowed him a wish list that included thick concrete walls and a near absence of exterior windows. Their architect hadn't been particularly happy with those caveats, but had done an admirable job of camouflaging the fact that the structure was fundamentally a bunker.

With Claudia and Anna apparently too busy with their guests to greet him, he hefted his duffel and headed for the front door.

Inside, much of the house consisted of floor-to-ceiling ballistic glass that looked into a landscaped interior courtyard. He crossed it, using a sliding door to access an expansive kitchen the architect had convinced him that he and his not particularly domestic wife needed. Thank God Rapp had been too indifferent to put up a fight because Claudia pretty much lived in it.

"You're back!" she said, craning her neck and giving him a broad smile that didn't require her to stop stirring a pot on the stove.

"Yeah. Sorry I'm late."

She switched to her native French. "No problem. You'd have just been in the way."

"Thanks," he grumbled, though it was true. Beyond scraping the grill, party prep wasn't his strong suit.

"I'm just teasing you. Everyone's out back. Go say hello and I'll be out in a minute."

He didn't see any reason to rush, instead grabbing a handful of peanuts and watching her cook. The cheerful demeanor and youthful appearance tended to belie her real story. Even for him, it was sometimes hard to believe that she'd once been the logistical genius behind one of the most successful private assassins in the world—a talent that she now used at Scott Coleman's company.

He wasn't crazy about her continuing to be involved in the business, but it would have been hypocritical for him to go to the mat on the subject. In truth, the fact that they both had so much baggage was part of the reason their relationship worked. They tended toward the same well-worn fatalism and neither had any right to judge. When they were together, their pasts felt like they canceled each other out and made the future a little clearer.

She glanced back at him again. "Why are you just standing there? The least you could do is go see if anyone needs a drink. And start heating the grill if Joe hasn't already done it."

"What happened to the debriefing?"

"Word got out that people were coming over. You know how it goes."

"You know I like to review ops when they're still fresh in everyone's mind."

"We can't always get what we want. Besides, everything went fine."

"Not everything. We should have—"

"Mitch! Quit stalling! Drinks! Grill! Go!"

Rapp got a few brief waves as he walked onto the lawn. People had separated into groups, speaking quietly and drinking copiously—both habits of people in their business. Irene Kennedy was near the south wall talking with a couple of the Nash kids. Apparently, Claudia had taken them in while Maggie was in Los Angeles on business.

"Dad!"

Rapp jumped as though someone had jabbed him with an electrical cable. Claudia's seven-year-old daughter had spotted him and was sprinting in his direction. She normally called him Mitch, but every once in a while, usually after he'd been away, the D-word slipped out. Why was it so panic-inducing? The problem wasn't her—she was a great kid. It was him. To say he wasn't father material would be a fairly epic understatement.

"I thought you were never coming back!" she said, wrapping her arms around his waist. The fact that everyone in the yard was now staring silently at him wasn't helpful.

"Let's not make a spectacle, okay, Oompa Loompa?"

"A what?"

Admitting defeat, he scooped her up and carried her toward the grill.

"The animals are all good," she reported. "But you need to start helping with them. Scott said so. Because he's got that big tractor now and he's doing the corn and stuff."

"We'll talk about it."

"And Mom won't let me ride my bike except on the streets around the neighborhood. You said you'd take me on trails."

"I feel like we have this conversation every time I come home. You're like a broken record."

"Because it's not fair! What's a record?"

"I think you might still be a little unsteady."

"Steadier than you!"

"Okay, maybe so. But I'm not sure your bike is going to work off-road. Why don't you let me do a little shopping and see if we can find you something better."

"Really? Like with shock absorbers and stuff like you got?"

"I don't know. They make bikes in extra small. But I'm not sure they come in Oompa Loompa."

She punched him in the chest.

"Go start the grill," he said, dropping her.

"Can I?"

"Do you remember how?"

"Open it. Turn the knob to the little lightning bolt thingy and push the red button."

"If you set your hair on fire, use the extinguisher."

She darted off just as someone slammed their hand down on his shoulder from behind. Undoubtedly Joe Maslick, because the force of it was nearly enough to buckle his knees. The former Delta operator was an inch taller than Rapp at six foot one and outweighed him by a good fifty pounds.

"I gotta do some work on Maggie's deck tomorrow," he boomed. "Build a door so Chucky doesn't fall down the stairs. I need an assistant and Claudia says your dance card is open."

"Sounds right up Scott's alley."

"Nope. He's in Estonia looking at a contract. The world gets crazier, we get busier. You want in on the action?"

"I don't know. What—"

"He does not!" Claudia called as she appeared with a tray of steaks. "It's a two-man job. Three at the most. Mitch needs some downtime."

"All right. As long as that downtime involves Maggie's deck."

Maslick spotted someone with a tray of nachos and made a beeline toward it. Rapp took advantage of the lull to retreat toward a cooler set up next to the kitchen door. He grabbed a beer and after draining half of it started to feel a little more centered.

"I suppose I owe you an apology," Kennedy said, approaching with a glass of wine in her hand.

"For what?"

"For sending you into a trap."

"It's not like it was a surprise."

She sighed quietly. "When I'm done cutting the cancer from the Agency, I'm starting to wonder if there will be any healthy tissue left."

"We knew that getting rid of President Cook wasn't going to be the end of it. But it was a good start. How's the new guy?"

Anthony Cook had been replaced by his vice president, Terrance Adams. Rapp had never met him, but he had the reputation of not being a complete scumbag. It was probably why Cook had chosen him. A mousy policy wonk with decades in Washington was just what he'd needed to soften his image.

"He's a decent man, but a bit naïve. Not a fatal trait in Congress, but less than ideal in the White House."

"Trainable?"

She shook her head. "He never wanted to be president. He took the job as VP in hopes of keeping the Cooks from running off the rails."

"I see what you mean by naïve. Still, though. An improvement."

"Definitely. And he listens. But only for the next three years, because he's made it clear that he won't run again. Hopefully, we won't find ourselves right back where we started."

Rapp nodded and took another swig from his beer. There was no question that US politicians were becoming increasingly autocratic, discarding all pretense of governing in order to focus entirely on clinging to power. But that was a problem for the Irene Kennedys of the world. Not for him.

Rapp strode down the hallway, peering into each bedroom as he passed.

"Anna! What's your status?"

"Teeth brushed! Pajamas on!"

"And your homework?"

"I did it all."

"I didn't hear you!"

"Done!"

"Okay, then. Get in bed. Your mother will be up to tuck you in momentarily."

Two of Mike Nash's sons were in the next room. The older was lying on the floor scrolling through something on his phone, while the younger was under the covers reading a comic book.

"Rory. Don't keep Jack up all night with that thing."

"I won't, Mitch."

He found Shannon, a teen like Rory, similarly enrapt by her screen.

"It's already after ten and oh-six-thirty's going to come pretty early," Rapp warned.

"Just one more video. I promise."

"One," he agreed, fighting against his true nature. Normally, the phones would already be confiscated and the lights off. But he found himself handling them with kid gloves. Children were resilient, but the loss of a father wasn't something you just walked off.

When Rapp arrived back in the kitchen, Claudia had opened another bottle of red from the cellar. There was a sway to her gait that appeared when she'd had a little too much.

"Join me?" she said in French. It was the language of the house now. He wanted to bring his level up from advanced to a native and they wanted the same for Anna. Unfortunately, she was resisting with a windmill-tilting obstinance inherited from her father. She'd literally taken to calling omelets *egg-pancakes-with-stuff-in-them*.

"In cleaning or drinking?" Rapp responded.

"Both."

"Why not?"

He poured himself a glass and started stacking plates in the dishwasher. Two-year-old Chucky Nash was asleep on the counter not far away, but seemed oblivious to the noise.

"So, are you bored yet?" Claudia asked. "No one's shot at you in almost two days."

"Nope," he said honestly. "I know you don't believe me, but I'm looking to be a little more selective about my beatings."

"With Cook gone, maybe America can enjoy a little peace."

"Or at least a lull between storms."

"Such an optimist."

"That's what they tell me."

"Irene wants to see you tomorrow. Did she mention it?"

"No."

"Eleven a.m. sharp."

Rapp despised going into Langley. Now more than ever.

"Tell her to come here. You can make her that thing she likes."

"I don't think it's going to work this time."

"Why not?"

"Because the meeting is at the White House. Apparently, the president wants to thank you personally for getting those men out." She smiled and raised her glass. "My little hero."

CHAPTER 7

RAPP squinted against the sun as he climbed a grassy slope that bordered Maggie Nash's house. He found Joe Maslick around back, pouring sweat as he put a fresh battery in his drill. Temperatures were only in the high eighties, but the humidity had spiked after a midday rain shower.

"Not finished?" Rapp said. "What've you been doing all day?"

"Humping wood and gear up that hill. By myself. You know, because a guy who looks just like you and goes by the same name left me hanging."

"I had to meet with the president."

"Well, la di da. How about you make it up to me by tossing me a beer?"

Rapp opened a cooler and dug a couple of cans from the ice. Maslick drained his in one long pull, crushed it, and tossed it toward a tree already littered with empties. Rapp pointed to a couple of bags of concrete next to a stack of lumber.

"I thought we were just putting on a gate."

Maslick shook his head in disgust. "Whole deck's sinking on the northeast corner. The door won't work right if it's not flat."

"You have a plan?"

The former Delta operator had no problem lifting the offending edge of the deck three inches off its support. "This is about straight. I was going to weld in an extension to the bracket and pour another footer to reinforce it."

Rapp studied the problem for a few seconds and shook his head. "I agree with the extra footer, but why not just epoxy some steel plates in there as spacers, then redrill the holes? We can dial it in by trial and error and you don't have to try to run your welder off an extension cord."

Maslick dropped the deck and stared down at it for a moment. "Hey. That's actually a good idea."

"You seem surprised."

"Your ideas are usually more like *If we swim in through the sharks, they won't see us coming.*"

"That wasn't my fault," Rapp said, opening his beer. "The biologists swore to me that species never attacks humans."

When the sun finally dropped below the horizon, the two men had retreated to their respective lawn chairs. A level with the bubble hovering dead center rested on the deck.

"Ready to get back to work?" Rapp said. "We've only got another half hour of decent light."

"We should let the epoxy dry," Maslick responded.

"It's quick set."

"Pays to be sure."

Rapp dug another beer from the cooler between them. "True that."

They sat in silence for a few minutes before the dull ping of an incoming message sounded in Rapp's pocket. Very few people had that number, and none contacted him without good reason, so he dug his phone out and glanced at the screen. Instead of Claudia looking for a progress report, he was faced with a somewhat more enigmatic message.

I'm in Paris. Can we talk? Damian.

Rapp stared at the text for a few seconds before returning the phone to his pocket.

"Supper ready?" Maslick asked, but he didn't get a response.

Damian Losa was unquestionably the most powerful criminal in the world and a man Rapp had hoped to never hear from again. Their lives had become entangled a few months back when an extremely vindictive Honduran cartel leader named Gustavo Marroqui discovered that one of the people involved in the assassination of his brother was still alive. Unfortunately, that person was Claudia.

Marroqui had sent a ten-man hit squad to their house in South Africa, and while Rapp managed to take them out, dealing with their boss was a bigger challenge. He pretty much controlled the government in his home country and had a gift for staying one step ahead of his enemies. Despite tens of thousands of man-hours and tens of millions of dollars invested, even the world's intelligence agencies had never been able to locate him.

What was known, though, was his level of motivation. This was a man who created public art installations by dismembering his competitors and sewing them back together with pig parts. There was no amount of blood or treasure that he wouldn't expend to see his brother's killer die a glacially slow death.

Faced with that, Rapp had to do what no one else had managed to pull off—find him.

The only plausible way to accomplish that had been through Losa, a man he'd met years ago during an operation in Mexico. And while the crime lord had been happy to help, he'd made it clear that one day the favor would have to be returned.

Apparently, that day had arrived.

"You all right, Mitch?"

"Yeah. Why?"

"Because you look like somebody just shit in your hat."

"I was just wondering if one extra footer is going to be enough," he lied.

"It'll be fine."

Rapp pretended to admire their handiwork, but didn't really see it. Regret wasn't something he tended to wallow in, but it was hard not to wonder if he'd turned to Losa too quickly. Maybe he could have figured out a way to find Marroqui on his own.

No. That was bullshit.

If the CIA, DEA, MI6, and countless others couldn't find the man, he sure as hell wasn't going to. But with Losa's help, the time between the attack in South Africa and Marroqui's incineration was less than two weeks. Claudia was safe and the world was a better place. A win-win.

Hell, probably all Losa wanted was one of his competitors out of the way. While not exactly sanctioned, one more cartel scumbag fertilizing the jungle wasn't exactly something that would keep him up at night. Maybe he'd take the family and they could combine it with a little beach time.

"Why don't we knock off?" he suggested.

"I hear that."

Rapp was about to stand when Claudia appeared from around the house with Chucky in tow.

"Just as I suspected. Sitting in lawn chairs drinking beer."

"What are you talking about?" Maslick said, feigning offense. "We got a ton done!"

She frowned in the general direction of the deck as Chucky took off across the yard. "It looks exactly like it did yesterday."

"But flatter. Look at that level. Perfection."

She shook her head. "Mitch is a bad influence on you. What about the gate?"

"We'll get on that tomorrow."

"*You'll* get on that tomorrow," Rapp said, standing. "I need to hop a flight to Paris."

"Paris," Maslick muttered. This time the offense wasn't feigned. "So, while you kick back in the Oval Office and Champs-Élysées, I get to sweat my ass off and suck sawdust."

"Paris?" Claudia said. "Why?"

He retrieved his phone and handed it to her. Not surprisingly, her expression darkened when she saw the text.

"This isn't good, Mitch. It isn't good at all."

"We knew it was coming."

"I know. I guess I just didn't think it would be this soon."

"Me neither, but I think it's too early for you to get worked up about it. He probably just needs someone to disappear."

"Who wants someone to disappear?" Maslick asked.

"You don't want to know."

Claudia reread the seven words as though there was something hidden in them. Some clue of what was to come.

"You're underestimating him," she said, switching to French. "I never worked directly for him in my prior life, but I know people who have. He's brilliant and polished, but beneath that, also incredibly ruthless. In a way, he's the Irene Kennedy of organized crime. There's no way he'd waste you on something he could get one of his people to do. He has a marker from Mitch Rapp, and I guarantee that he knows the value of it."

CHAPTER 8

Two hours after sunset, the heat had diminished enough that Rapp decided to walk to the address he'd been given. The street he found himself on was devoid of the normal crush of tourists and instead lined with imposing villas. A perfect neighborhood to create a veneer of respectability for people who made their livings at the edges of the law. Behind the iron gates and well-tended gardens, he suspected he'd find an interesting mix of Russians, South Americans, and Chinese who had abandoned their homelands in favor of something more befitting their newfound wealth.

The man he was there to see, though, was the standout. Damian Losa—almost certainly not the name he was born with—had appeared as if from nowhere about thirty years ago. Despite a modest start, he'd managed to build a criminal empire so extensive that his picture would be more at home on the cover of *Fortune* magazine than hanging in a post office.

Rapp found the gate he was searching for and stopped in front of it. There was no buzzer, but it turned out to be unnecessary. A man appeared from the shadow of a tree and opened it before stepping aside to let Rapp pass. Despite looking like a serious operator, he seemed to have been relegated to the role of greeter as he led the way to a mansion that dominated the manicured grounds. He neither spoke nor showed any interest in checking for weapons before passing Rapp off to a woman waiting on the porch. She wore a vaguely disapproving expression and gave the impression of being of Latin American descent—a hypothesis confirmed when she addressed him in strained English.

"Welcome. Please go to the back of the house. Mr. Losa waits you there."

Rapp started along the hallway, taking in the ornate portraits and general opulence of the place. Normally, he'd be assessing threats and looking for potential exits, but in this case, he wasn't particularly worried. Losa wanted him alive. The question was, for what?

He found the man in an elaborate conservatory. Walls and ceiling were constructed entirely of glass, with an impressive dome supported by iron lattice. Losa rose from a sofa and strode across the room with his hand outstretched.

He looked exactly the way Rapp remembered—mid-fifties, trim waist, perfect teeth, immaculate gray hair. Their last meeting had taken place in a Mexican jungle, where he'd been completely at ease. He seemed equally comfortable in this exclusive Parisian suburb. Cargo pants and boots had been replaced by wool slacks, a tailored shirt, and shoes that were probably worth nearly as much as Rapp's car. Fifty percent CEO, fifty percent wealthy European retiree, zero percent ruthless cartel leader. An impressive illusion.

"It's good to see you again," he said, clasping Rapp's hand firmly.

"I'd be lying if I said the same."

"And yet you came."

"I pay my debts."

"An admirable trait," Losa said, pointing to a chair. Rapp sat and the Mexican took a position on the opposing couch.

"What do you want, Damian?"

"I assume it goes without saying that everything we talk about is confidential?"

"Depending on what you want, I may need to use my contacts. But I'll keep your name out of it as much as I can."

Losa smiled. "I respect a man who's clear about what he's agreeing to. It inspires confidence."

Rapp just shrugged.

"Are you familiar with the terrorist attack that took place in Italy a few days ago?"

"Superficially. The media's calling it an ISIS attack, but my understanding is that it was actually related to a drug shipment originating in Tartus. They're saying captagon pills, but I don't think there's any confirmation of that yet."

"Your thoughts?"

"I'm not sure they'd be useful. I haven't operated in Syria in a long time. The country's a clusterfuck and it's hard to do anything there that doesn't cause more problems than it solves."

"I'm surprised. Your reputation is as an interventionist."

"Only when I can win."

"Still, you're familiar with the country. I'm interested in your take."

"My take is that ISIS is a pretty loosely defined organization in Syria and has limited capabilities and ambitions. But they're a good boogeyman and it's easier for the West to blame them than to admit that our policies have turned Syria into a narco-state. Damascus has taken back control of most of the country and now more than half their GDP comes from drug trafficking. Captagon accounts for the majority of that."

"So, you're familiar with the drug?"

"Sure. It's popular in the Middle East, but hasn't gotten much traction anywhere else. Little white pills. They're called *abu hilalain* in Arabic."

"I didn't know that. What's it mean?"

"The one with two moons. Back when ISIS was still a serious movement, they were the primary manufacturers of it. They made money selling it all over the region and gave it to their fighters to keep them going. The tablets themselves still have their symbol on them—two crescents. The Syrian government's kept that part to deflect blame and everyone's happy to go along."

Losa leaned back and folded his arms across his chest. "Interesting."

"Not really," Rapp responded. "I imagine you knew all that already. Is that why I'm here? Because if you're thinking about trying to import captagon into Europe, I'd advise against it."

"Really? Why?"

"It's cheap and it has a certain mystique in the Middle East, but I've tried it and it's not anything that's going to impress European drug users. They can afford better."

Losa nodded slowly. "What if I told you that what you know as captagon really isn't."

"Meaning what?"

"The captagon you've experienced is just a mix of easily obtained amphetamines and caffeine. Cheap to produce, profitable to sell, and with a good customer base and distribution network in the Middle East. What came into Salerno last week was more or less authentic."

"Authentic?"

"Precisely. Captagon is actually a brand name for a psychostimulant designed to treat attention deficit disorder and narcolepsy. It was originally manufactured by a German pharmaceutical company, but was banned in the eighties because it was extremely addictive and had significant potential for abuse. The active ingredient, fenethylline, tended to cause aggression, create sensations of euphoria, and suppress fear, among other things."

"So, you think Syria's using their pharmaceutical industry to create a drug that'll appeal to the West and cut into your market?"

"It's a bit more complicated than that but, in essence, yes. Over the past couple of years, a very effective Muslim-dominated distribution network has been constructed across Europe. To date, they haven't had much product to work with and they've concentrated on trafficking small quantities of the new captagon, mostly in Italy and Belgium."

"Working out the bugs," Rapp said.

"Exactly. But apparently that's done now. The shipment that was destroyed in Salerno weighed in at around fifteen metric tons."

Rapp glanced over at a well-stocked bar along the wall and pointed. "You mind?"

"Please."

Rapp stood and poured himself a twenty-five-year-old Glenlivet. "What's any of this have to do with me? I assume you still have better infrastructure in Europe than the Syrians—particularly now that they made such a mess in Italy. Why not just get one of your scientists to copy their formula and block their entry into the market?"

"You missed your calling," Losa said as Rapp sat again. "That was exactly what I intended to do."

"And?"

"The problem is that fenethylline is expensive and difficult to produce. Also, there are other compounds included in the pills that my people haven't seen before. Some appear to have been designed to make the drug even more addictive, but the purpose of the others is a mystery. So, while it's possible that we could create a reasonable facsimile of the drug, we can't do it at a viable price point. Every scenario we look at leads to a significant loss on every pill sold."

"And that's where I come in," Rapp said. "You want me to go to Syria to find out how they're doing it."

Losa nodded. "Not just how, but also who, why, and any other information you can get. I have some far-reaching business decisions to make, and I can't do that without data."

"I don't know anything about the Syrian drug trade, Damian."

"I disagree. You're familiar with captagon and you've been entangled to some extent with the Middle Eastern drug trade for decades.

You understand the local culture and you're reputed to speak fluent Arabic."

"It's a big country," Rapp said, taking a sip of his drink. "And the Agency's network there is almost nonexistent."

"I can put you in touch with the right people."

"Okay. But what then?"

"That's a question for you to answer. I'm not sending you in as a soldier, Mitch. I'm sending you as my representative. If you can figure out how I can replicate what they're doing, fine. If you can come up with a way to stop them, that works for me, too. But I'm also open to negotiation. Maybe even a partnership."

"More likely they'll kill me on sight."

"Possible, but I doubt it. On the surface, you pose no threat to them, and as my envoy, you have credibility. They'll want to talk and determine whether I have something valuable to offer."

Rapp stared at the cut-crystal glass in his hand, letting silence descend on the room. After about thirty seconds, Losa broke it.

"I don't think you should equate this with the missions Irene Kennedy sends you on, Mitch. There won't be any shooting or hiding in the desert. More like a couple of weeks living in palaces and meeting with government officials."

"Then why don't you go yourself, Damian?"

Instead of responding, the Mexican just flashed his thousand-dollar smile.

CHAPTER 9

RAPP crossed the Parc Floral's grass, admiring the colorful landscaping that made the place such a popular Parisian destination. A child of about four ran past him with his mother in pursuit, creating a burst of activity that contrasted with the classical music emanating from a bandstand on the other side of the central water feature.

He adjusted his trajectory, weaving through couples sitting on blankets toward a less frequented section of the park. Finally, he spotted Claudia setting up their picnic in front of a stone wall that was still within earshot of the music. The location had the drawback of being in full sun, but it was a sacrifice she'd made to ensure that he had something solid at his back. Perhaps unnecessary in his current situation, but old habits die hard.

She waved when she spotted him, grinning beneath the shade of her broad straw hat. The casual sundress she wore was sleeveless and printed with flowers that mimicked the ones next to her so well it almost qualified as camouflage. Otherwise, she was typically devoid of jewelry and her sandals had been cast aside to reveal tanned, dusty feet.

"You look amazing," she said, giving him a quick kiss as he took a seat next to her.

He didn't acknowledge the compliment, but she was right. Along with a portfolio of meticulously forged documents, Losa's people had reworked Rapp's image to fit that of a wealthy Canadian attorney named Matthieu Fournier. The Richard Mille watch alone ran north of half a million dollars.

The timepiece felt a little obnoxious strapped to his wrist, but it was hard to complain about the rest. The tailoring on the tan slacks and Egyptian cotton shirt was impeccable and both somehow seemed impervious to the damp heat that had settled over the city. The pièce de résistance, though, was the shoes. Also custom-made, they looked like a pair of five-grand Italian loafers, but performed like a set of trail runners.

After a closer inspection and a series of approving nods, Claudia retrieved a jar of pâté from her picnic basket. "Can I tempt you?"

"Absolutely."

She spread some on a piece of baguette and then dipped back into the basket for a bottle of champagne. He accepted a glass, its coldness suggesting that the traditional wicker container hid something more high-tech inside.

She scooted closer, running her fingers through hair that had horrified Losa's stylist and then down his carefully trimmed beard. "It's so soft. And your skin looks ten years younger."

"It took a four-person team two days," he admitted.

"And the cut of your shirt," she said, lowering her voice. "I can't see even a hint of your gun."

"That's because I'm not carrying it."

Her expression carried the expected amount of surprise.

"Apparently Damian's executives don't carry weapons. He thinks it's vulgar."

"It's Damian now?" she said with a hint of disapproval. "And you agreed to that?"

"Until I've repaid my debt to him, he's the boss."

She frowned as he polished off the bread and pâté, washing it down with some champagne.

"Maybe it's better that way, Mitch. You're just a lawyer representing his business interests. A noncombatant. Your shield is that there are very few people who want to make him angry. Certainly not over a simple negotiator. All risk, no reward."

"You could be right. But it might not be his enemies that are the problem. It might be Syria itself."

"An unpredictable operating theater to be sure. But you can't take on an entire country with a Glock and a couple of magazines. Better to focus on playing your role convincingly and let other people do the shooting."

"That's the goal," he said, joining in the applause as the symphony went silent.

"Try to achieve it."

He laughed. "Where's Anna? Don't tell me you gave up a chance to force her to speak French."

"Tempting, but not so much that I was willing to miss out on a little adult time in Paris. I left her with Scott. He just bought a new attachment for that tractor he loves so much and they're going to spend the weekend playing with it."

Rapp placed his champagne on the grass and leaned back against the wall. Coleman could never think of anything to spend his money on, so he'd recently bought a top-of-the-line John Deere that he'd then had painted by a local hot rod shop. When he wasn't involved in an operation, he liked nothing better than to drive it around his burgeoning agricultural empire.

"So, what do you have for me?"

She took the change of subject in stride. Their relationship was built on an inviolable division between business and personal. No matter what happened on one side, it was to have no effect on the other. Most people had bet against their arrangement working, but they'd managed to beat the odds.

"The Agency examined all the Canadian identity documents you've been provided and admitted that they couldn't have done much better."

"What about backup, though? If someone sends an investigator to Toronto, are they going to find physical evidence of Matthieu Fournier?"

"Definitely. Bank accounts, an upscale apartment with a Porsche in the designated parking space, gym membership, utilities, food delivery accounts with long histories, and so on. It'd take a lot of scrutiny to find a crack. Well beyond the capabilities of the Syrian intelligence apparatus, I think."

"What about the situation on the ground in Syria?"

She reclined, propping herself on one elbow to face him. "It's a mess."

"I was hoping for something more specific."

"Me too. I used to have contacts there, but I haven't been in touch with any of them in years. I suspect most are dead."

"What about Irene?"

"She's better connected, but still her resources on the ground are limited. She has a handful of reliable people, but for obvious reasons doesn't want to expose them for the benefit of your new employer. If you get in serious trouble, she might change her mind, but remember that *reliable* has its own definition in Syria. An ally on Monday could be your worst enemy on Tuesday."

"That's more or less how I remember it."

"The person with the most in-country resources is your new friend," she said, avoiding the use of his name. "But don't let him oversell you on his capabilities. His reach isn't what it once was there, and he's made a lot of enemies. There was a time when his network was useful to Damascus because it kept drug money out of the hands of the worst of the insurgents. Now the government mostly sees him as competition and they've done a good job of dismantling, absorbing, or chasing his network underground."

"What about the European intelligence agencies?"

"They're working on the Salerno attack, but at this point, they know less than you."

"Were you able to find out how the Italian police knew about the shipment?"

"Interestingly, it was an anonymous tip."

"Losa," Rapp said under his breath.

"A strong possibility."

"He says that the captagon in that container wasn't the crap that gets sold in the Middle East. It's actually a reengineered version of the original pharmaceutical-grade stuff."

"As far as we know, the Europeans haven't gotten around to analyzing the pills they recovered. I doubt they'd see it as a priority. If that's what he's telling you, though, you can rely on the information. In the field of narcotics, his chemists are the best in the world. Is that what he's concerned about? The Syrian government moving in on his European operation?"

Rapp nodded.

"And what exactly does he expect you to do about it?"

"My sense is he isn't sure. But I can tell you that he's sweating. He can't figure out their manufacturing process and he's impressed by the product. Right now, he's completely blind, so whatever information I can get will be an improvement."

"Again, why you? What little experience you have with the narcotics trade is from the enforcement side, not the distribution side. And negotiations aren't exactly your strong suit. You just proved that again in Afghanistan."

Rapp scanned the widely spaced people in front of them as the symphony came back from break. "I think he's more interested in my other traits."

"Such as?"

"I don't charge anything, I'm completely expendable, and if the Syrians interrogate me, I don't know anything. Even if I catch a bullet ten seconds after I land in Damascus, that's good information and he hasn't lost anything."

"That doesn't make me feel better."

"Me neither, but it is what it is. Hopefully, the Syrians will be smart and want to work with me. All they have to do is recognize that he's got a lot to offer, and this should be quick and civilized."

"And you can add supporting the Syrian government and the most powerful drug cartel in the world to your résumé."

"Not the worst thing I've ever done," he said, reaching for his champagne again. "Not even in the top five."

CHAPTER 10

GENERAL Aleksandr Semenov exited his private elevator and left the modern wing of the building. The dilapidated lobby was a reminder of the complex's past life as a hospital, but that area was no longer in use. Paint peeled from the concrete walls and a crumbling ceiling had deposited a layer of dust and debris on the tile floor. To his right, a set of cracked glass doors reinforced with duct tape looked onto an empty landscape.

He stopped to gaze through them, past the perimeter fence and guard towers, to the arid land rolling toward the horizon. In the distance, he could see bare stone mountains that seemed to have been melted by the relentless Syrian sun. Scattered clouds cast shadows across the baked earth before disappearing into a yellow haze.

Sun, dust, and exile. The three things that defined his time there.

Though *exile* was perhaps too strong a word. There was no question that Russia's president was envious of Semenov's successes and feared his influence among Kremlin insiders. And with good reason. Despite being barely fifty years old, Boris Utkin was in questionable health and as backward-thinking as men decades his senior. It was only natural that Russia's elite would be looking to what was next. Natural, but in Utkin's eyes, also extremely dangerous.

Banishing his most gifted general to Syria had admittedly been a clever move on the chessboard. Semenov had become too powerful to imprison or remove, and he was too cautious to succumb to an assassination attempt. The president had portrayed this assignment as an honor—a mission so critical to Mother Russia that it could be entrusted to no one else. It was an excuse that rang hollow to all ears that mattered, but that hadn't been enough to save Semenov from spending his last two years in this hellhole.

On its surface, Moscow's involvement in propping up the Syrian government was a rare triumph. Russia's military support had crushed the insurgency and had kept the rest of the world on the sidelines. Beneath that victory, though, was the same rot that had plagued his country for nearly half a century. The contracts to rebuild Syria had never materialized and plans to exploit its natural resources had never been pursued. Instead, the idiots in Moscow had turned their attention to a confrontation with the West. A confrontation that, inevitably, had evolved into one of the greatest disasters in Russian history.

The former president had been a prodigy at exploiting the memory of Soviet power. Working only with a third-rate military, silos full of nonoperational nuclear weapons, and an anemic economy, he'd managed to get Russia a seat at the table. To interact with Europe, America, and China as equals. When he slammed a fist on his desk, the world trembled the same as they had when the Soviet Union was at its peak.

Now that spell was broken. Russia had been revealed for what it was: a starving old woman lashed by the Siberian wind. The world had been given a glimpse behind the Potemkin village that his countrymen had been building since the time of Catherine the Great. And once revealed, there was no going back. NATO powers would never again fear his country's conventional military capability. The Europeans would wean themselves completely from Russian energy, and sanctions would remain in place.

Of course, the men in power—those responsible—were unwilling to face the destruction they had wrought. But there were whispers. In dark corners of the Kremlin, the next generation of leaders yearned for a man capable of rebuilding Mother Russia for the modern era. Of making the world once again cower before it.

And he was that man.

He'd been only thirty years old when they'd given him command of Russia's asymmetrical warfare unit in St. Petersburg. At the time, it had been a backwater project laughed at by ancient generals still enamored with technologies used in World War II. That laughter had gone silent when he'd transformed the division into an offensive weapon that no country in the world could match. A weapon that didn't just sit in a silo or rust away on some military base. One that could be *used*.

Hacking, ransomware, election interference, social media disinformation, the support of fascist and terrorist groups, blackmail. It had all been his doing. Even the Syrian refugee crisis that had sparked nationalist movements throughout Europe had been his vision. Once seen as nothing more than a convenient by-product of Russia's involvement in the country, it was now recognized as the only tangible benefit.

The era of conventional wars between great powers was over. The projection of power now had to be done using stealthier and, in many ways, more effective strategies.

His strategies.

The idea that the West could be defeated by conventional military means was nothing more than a bizarre fantasy. A dangerous delusion that had led to Russia's current sorry state and blinded its leadership to the fact that victory was indeed achievable if they were willing to embrace the modern battlefield.

Not that this was a simple matter. The terrain constantly shifted, new technologies appeared and then faded into obsolescence almost overnight, and the West became more proficient at defending itself. Innovation had to be constant, creativity trumped discipline, and boldness was rewarded.

It was precisely his gift for bold innovation that had landed him in the Middle East. His latest strategy was seen as too dangerous to be carried out from within Russia's borders. President Utkin had insisted that plausible deniability was critical and used that as cover to send his potential rival to Syria—a place where he would be cut off from his Kremlin allies.

When the heat of the sun penetrating the damaged glass became uncomfortable, Semenov began moving again. The steel door at the far end of the space had a keypad lock that lacked the sophistication he was accustomed to, but was sufficient for the task at hand. Few of his prisoners wanted to escape and, even if they did, there was nothing but dry, open terrain for seventy-five kilometers in every direction.

The corridor he entered was significantly cooler and Semenov picked up his pace. The wall on his left turned to glass, providing a view of an interior courtyard that was empty at this time of day. The room that was his destination was guarded by a single uniformed soldier. The young man stiffened when he noted his commander's approach, firing off a crisp salute before opening the door and standing aside.

Semenov entered an expansive space that featured a floor-to-ceiling chain-link construction that acted as a funnel. It wasn't unlike the system used by livestock operations, but in this case the livestock was human. Or at least a close approximation.

He scanned the eighteen dark, dirty faces behind the wire, but they were no different from the ones that had come before. Not surprising, since they'd been taken from the same places. The men were courtesy of a prison that housed captured ISIS fighters and other antigovernment insurgents. In contrast, the women had been plucked from a refugee camp northeast of Damascus. Most were the wives of foreign jihadists who had been either killed or captured.

Five Russian soldiers kept the group moving, dealing efficiently with the level of resistance they'd come to expect. Some of the men jostled and shouted meaningless demands in Arabic, while the women tried to make themselves as small as possible.

Semenov watched a girl pass through the narrow gate at the tip of the funnel. He focused on her youthful eyes and the vague outline of her body beneath her chador. She followed the orders of a translator and lowered herself onto a stool near the wall. There, a woman dressed as a nurse selected a syringe and indicated that the girl should expose her arm. After the injection was administered, a soldier grabbed her beneath the arm and led her through a door at the back.

The procedure had been refined over the years to minimize violent incidents, but no amount of tinkering could prevent them entirely. It seemed that there was always one and this time was no different. A young man feigning meekness as he passed through the gate suddenly attacked the nurse. In the early days of this project, troublemakers had been summarily executed, but later Semenov had thought better of it. The most interesting subjects were the strong ones.

He watched as the man was slammed to the concrete floor and held there by three soldiers. His sleeve was torn off and the rattled nurse inserted a needle without the benefit of sterilization. He looked a little unsteady when they got him to his feet, but the remaining prisoners would attribute that to the violence and not the injection.

Semenov committed the man's bearded face to memory before he disappeared through the door. It would be a pleasure to watch him break. The initial defiance. The unanswered pleas for God's salvation. And finally surrender. It was the path they all took eventually.

Boris Utkin would soon discover that banishing Russia's most valuable asset to Syria was yet another in a long line of disastrous decisions. The work Semenov had accomplished during his exile would do nothing but add to his legend. The president wasn't the only powerful man in Moscow. There were others and they would be taking notice.

• • •

Semenov stepped from the elevator into an opulent suite that included both his office and living quarters. It was part of the new wing of the complex, built by Syrian slave labor, but finished by Russian craftsmen. A reminder of where he came from. And to where he would one day return.

He'd barely settled in behind his desk before his assistant appeared in the doorway. Leonid had been with him for five years and had proved to be a capable lieutenant. Originally from the FSB, he was smart enough to understand that Semenov was the future—both his own and Russia's.

"What do you have for me?" Semenov asked.

"Excellent news, sir. Our informants believe that Damian Losa is sending a representative to Syria."

"A representative. He's not coming personally?"

"No, sir."

"So, good news. But hardly *excellent*."

"No, sir. I'm sorry, sir."

"And?"

"The few people Losa has left in Syria are laying the groundwork for meetings that they hope will lead to the presidential palace."

Losa was undoubtedly aware of the Muslim distribution network that had sprung up in his territory. It was also likely that he'd acquired samples of the new captagon formulation in circulation. Maybe even the ones from the failed shipment to Italy. And if that was true, the Mexican would have many questions about the drug's chemical structure and how it could be produced profitably.

"So, he wants to join us, does he?"

"He's likely recognized that competing with an entire country—even a pariah state like Syria—will be extremely difficult. He'd also see his European network as superior to the one we've created. His reputation is as a clever businessman who uses violence only as a last resort. Partnership is always more profitable than a war."

Semenov drummed his fingers on the desktop. Damian Losa

wasn't a man to be underestimated, but there was also no reason to mythologize him. He'd built a multibillion-dollar criminal empire and an almost supernatural mystique, but, in the end, he was just a criminal.

"Can we get to this representative?"

"I don't see any significant obstacles. But do you want to move against him immediately? Or do we want to hear what he has to say first?"

There was no need. In return for a cut of the profits, Losa would offer up his expertise, influence, and access to his European network. Valuable for sure, but nowhere near what Semenov wanted from the Mexican. No, he'd accept nothing less than everything.

CHAPTER 11

R APP woke to a quiet ping and immediately reached for his
phone. Claudia stirred next to him, and he went still until her
breathing evened out again. It was just past three a.m., but the lights of
Paris were still powerful enough to penetrate the shades and illuminate their hotel suite. Claudia slid closer, throwing an arm across his
torso, reminding him how little he wanted to cross into Syria. Particularly in the service of Damian Losa.

He finally looked at the text on his screen.

THERE WILL BE A LIMOUSINE WAITING FOR YOU DOWNSTAIRS IN
THIRTY MINUTES.

Rapp managed to ease out from beneath Claudia's arm and pad
silently to the closet. After pulling on a pair of jeans, a cotton shirt,
and a stylish pair of boots also provided by Losa's shoemaker, he retrieved a hanging bag with his dress clothes. When he turned around,
Claudia was sitting up in bed, her body silhouetted by the window
behind.

"It never lasts long, does it?" she said.

"Once this job's done, I'll be in a position to pick and choose."

"Really?"

"I know you don't believe me, but all I want to do is stay here a few more days with you and then go back and find Anna that bike I've been promising her."

"Don't trust him, Mitch. No matter how reasonable he sounds, remember what he is."

"I don't trust anybody," he said, scooping some things off a dresser and into a duffel fitted with backpack straps.

She stood and walked across the room, wrapping her arms around him. "What I hate about this most is that I feel so helpless. There's almost nothing I can do for you there."

"You worry too much. The Syrian government wants money and Damian Losa knows how to make it. I'm going to take his jet to Damascus, get wined and dined for a few days, and work out a deal."

She looked up at him, her almond-shaped eyes almost black in the semidarkness. "Liar."

Maybe he wasn't so much a liar.

The limo was as plush as any he'd been in and the jet it was pulling up to bore little resemblance to the Agency's increasingly threadbare G5. Unless he missed his guess, it was a brand-new Global 8000.

So far so good.

They glided to a stop and Rapp grabbed his bag before stepping out. The aircraft's door was open, so he climbed the steps to find Damian Losa sitting on a sofa in the middle of the cabin. The Mexican rose to shake hands and indicated a chair across from him.

"Can I offer you a drink?" he said, holding up the glass in his hand.

Rapp just shook his head. Claudia was right about him being slick. It was difficult to imagine him being involved in anything more violent than a spirited debate about French wine vintages. In this case, appearances were deceptive. Rumor had it that there was a time when he hadn't shied away from getting his hands bloody.

"My plan to fly you into Damascus to talk with decision-makers— maybe even the president—hasn't worked out as well as I hoped."

"Meaning?" Rapp said, unsurprised, but interested in how Losa would spin it.

"The feedback I'm getting is that trying to go straight to the top wouldn't be useful or safe."

"So, the government isn't in a negotiating mood?"

"I don't think they understand how helpful I could be to their interests, and I'm concerned that you might not be treated with the respect you deserve."

Rapp smiled at the elegant turn of phrase. *Might not be treated with the respect you deserve* translated to *will use a blowtorch on your balls.*

"So where does that leave me?"

"I'm going to put you in touch with people who can make lower-level introductions and provide reliable security. You just need to state our case and gather as much information as you can. The hope is that it'll be enough to move you up the chain."

"Can I assume I won't be taking this plane?"

"No. It makes sense for you to go in more quietly. The best way to do that is on foot with an organization that traffics people across the Turkish border."

"If I remember right, that border's heavily patrolled and there's a wall."

"It won't be a problem. The authorities aren't concerned about people crossing from Turkey into Syria. For obvious reasons, the flow tends to go the other way."

"And when I get there?"

"You'll be met by someone who'll take you to Idlib, where you'll be able to connect with what's left of my organization. I assume you're familiar with the region?"

Rapp nodded. It was one of the last rebel strongholds in Syria, though "stronghold" might be overstating the actual situation on the ground. With the help of Russian forces, the government was doing a good job of strangling the residents.

"Unfortunately, the few Syrians still loyal to me have been forced to take refuge there."

"Loyal," Rapp repeated. "How loyal?"

"Obviously, my operation there has been badly degraded, but I still have enough influence to get you into the hands of men who won't turn on you."

That sounded a little optimistic to Rapp, but there wasn't much he could do about it.

"And to be clear, no one knows my real identity."

"Only me and my lieutenant, who is completely above suspicion. To everyone else, you're a Canadian attorney who represents my interests. And that's what you're going to do, correct?"

"The fact that I'm here proves that."

"Suggests," Losa corrected. "The fact that you're sitting here *suggests* that. You've spent your life in the service of America. How are you finding redirecting that loyalty to me?"

"The US has very few interests in Syria."

"That's not much of an answer."

"I'm sure you'll find a way to live with it."

CHAPTER 12

"YOU can just see it . . . There!"

Rapp peered through the side window as the Fiat bounced along the gravel road. Down a steep, moonlit slope, he could see a vague line that ran east into the hills. The border wall that divided Turkey from Syria.

"This is nine meters tall," his driver continued in heavily accented English. "It is made of many sections, each fourteen tons. Yes? Very heavy. Very strong. On the top is sixty centimeters of wire with . . . Thorns? Spikes?"

"Barbs," Rapp said when he realized his new companion wasn't going to stop guessing until he stumbled upon just the right word.

"Yes! Barbed wire, no? It has seventy watchtowers and many hundreds of kilometers, but this section is dark. This wall is the second-longest construction in the world. Do you know what the first is?"

Rapp didn't answer.

"The Wall of China! This one covers almost our whole border. It is very good because we have many, many refugees from the war. My country has taken most of them. Three million. But now it is very hard for them to cross." He slapped the peeling dashboard joyously. "Unless I help them, of course. I am an expert!"

He kept talking nonstop, but it was more a release of nervous energy than an effort to impart information. It was something Rapp was accustomed to, but this time he wasn't what was scaring the man. It was the specter of Damian Losa. The Turkish smuggler knew that his life—and perhaps the life of his family—depended on Rapp getting safely to Syria.

"There!" he exclaimed again. "Do you see the lights?"

Rapp did, two dots moving west. Still miles away.

"These are the headlights of a Cobra II patrol vehicle. Do you know what this is?"

Rapp nodded. Turkey's answer to the Humvee.

"Very dangerous," his driver went on. "But we know their schedule and have people watching."

"How much longer?" Rapp asked, not anxious to be caught in the open by daylight. The flight from Paris to Kilis had taken longer than he'd anticipated, and dawn was starting to break.

"We are almost there. You can see." His driver pointed through the filthy windshield at a hilltop that loomed over the border. The concrete house perched on top seemed kind of obvious, but Losa had assured him that the men who operated from it were the best in the business.

The dirt driveway was nearly too steep for the vehicle, but they finally crested, surrounded by hazy dawn light and the stench of the burning clutch. Rapp stepped out with his backpack, but his driver remained.

"Good luck, my friend," he said, not bothering to hide his relief as he let the car roll back down the hill.

Rapp scanned the empty terrain for a moment, focusing initially on the road that paralleled the border wall and then on the scrubby hills beyond. From that vantage point, Syria looked deceptively peaceful.

The house's front door was yanked open the moment his foot landed on the porch. The man who stepped out was no taller than five eight, with a barrel chest and bare, leathery scalp. He called over his shoulder in Turkish, revealing various blackened teeth beneath an impressive mustache.

A second man appeared a moment later, shook his head in disgust, and initiated a brief verbal exchange. Rapp didn't speak the language, but their tone and body language suggested they weren't impressed with the man they'd been sent. Undoubtedly, they were used to desperate, war-hardened Syrians who would do anything for a chance at a new life.

"It is hard, this journey," the one with the mustache garbled. He pointed to the wall just starting to glow pink in the dawn light. "Have to climb in dark and cross mountains."

Rapp was about to push past him into the building, but then remembered that he was no longer a CIA operative. He was a Canadian attorney.

"I can do it. I have no choice."

That statement had the desired effect. Like them, he was just a man trying to avoid the wrath of Damian Losa. Whatever he might lack in physical ability, he could be counted on to make up for in motivation.

They finally let him pass and Rapp tossed his bag on a disintegrating couch before taking a seat next to it. "What's the plan?"

"We go tonight," Mustache Man said.

"What about the patrols?"

"There will be none. We've paid them."

"Reliable?"

"Not always. But this time yes. They don't care about you. Because you go the wrong way. No one wants to go to Syria. They want to leave."

"What's the problem then?"

It seemed implausible that Losa would get smugglers involved when a ladder and a map would suffice. Ladders and maps were one hundred percent reliable and didn't have mouths to run.

"Problem?"

"Why do I need you?"

That prompted another brief exchange in Turkish.

"The other smugglers. This is why we are important. There are many in this area because the border commander here can be bribed. But it means great competition. It would be dangerous for you without protection. It is a war."

Rapp wasn't sure if they were referring to the Syrian civil war or the war between the smugglers, but at this point it didn't matter. He was going over that wall with or without them, and with was probably marginally better than striking out on his own.

He moved his pack to one end of the sofa and lay down, closing his eyes. "Let me know when it's time."

"You understand what you have to do?" Nijaz—Mustache Man—asked.

Rapp nodded in the darkness. It was one in the morning and skies were clear, bathing the landscape in colorless light. The concrete wall was surprisingly prominent, with the undulating terrain behind cast in more subdued tones.

"Ahmet, he go first. You second. I go last."

"I heard you the first three times," Rapp said.

"The heights. This is not a problem, yes?"

The Turk was once again reeling through everything that could possibly go wrong. Annoying, but understandable. Rapp did the same thing when he was running an op that involved people he didn't know.

"I'll be fine."

A Turkish voice drifted up from below. The man next to Rapp glanced at his watch and translated. "Ahmet sees the patrol. Once it goes over the hill, we must move quickly."

"Okay."

The glare of headlights became visible a few minutes later and another five passed before the armored vehicle came fully in view. Rapp turned away, protecting his night vision from the powerful light bar mounted on top.

"Now!" his guide said when the taillights disappeared over a rise.

Rapp shouldered his pack and jumped off the porch, taking a zigzagging route down the trailless slope. By the time he reached the road, the Turk had fallen well behind. His partner was faster, having already set up a purpose-built ladder and climbed to the midpoint.

The bottom section had normal rungs and was lashed to spikes hidden in the brush. Where the ladder met the razor wire about ten feet up, it was covered in plywood with two-by-four handholds. Not a fancy solution, but perfectly functional.

Ahmet climbed to the junction between the concrete and wire, then flipped a hinged piece of plywood over the top, creating a kind of teepee over the dangerous section. A thick rope with regularly spaced knots was attached and he tossed it into Syrian territory before continuing.

By the time Rapp started to climb, the wind was kicking up enough dust to provide a little more cover. Not that it was necessary. The Cobra II patrol was long gone, and his guides assured him that budget problems had forced the Turks to cancel plans for electronic surveillance.

Still, he stayed low when he reached the top, slipping over with one hand on a rung and the other on the rope. A few moments later, he'd descended hand over hand to the ground.

"Where's Nijaz?" his guide asked, waving him over to where he was crouched in a bush.

"Not far behind."

The least athletic of the three, Nijaz huffed audibly as he climbed. Finally, he made it over, and at that moment all three of them had achieved something no one in their right mind would attempt—to smuggle themselves into Syria.

"Come! We hurry!"

They started south, with Ahmet in the lead and Nijaz puffing away at the back. Rapp made it a point to move a bit unsteadily over the terrain, trying to counteract his display of athleticism on the ladder. These men likely would do their best to forget this night ever happened, but still it made sense to stay in character. Not only would it be catastrophic for him to be identified, but he was also eager to be labeled the effete Canadian lawyer. After spending most of his career living in the long shadow of his accomplishments, he was looking forward to being written off as harmless.

The air felt unusually heavy as they climbed. Usually slipping across borders was a bit anticlimactic. They were nothing more than lines drawn on a piece of paper that didn't have much meaning on the ground. Syria seemed different.

Maybe its long history gave it a weight that many other places lacked. This was the home of one of the most ancient civilizations in the world. It had been controlled at one time by just about everyone who was anyone in history—Sumerians, Persians, Greeks, Romans. Alexander the Great had fought there. As had Rome's Pompey.

After breaking away from French rule following World War II, it had become a relatively secular state built on a foundation of iron-fisted government control. Supported by the Soviets and later the Russians, Syria had managed decades of the kind of oppressive peace that people tended to confuse with stability. Beneath the surface, though, it had been boiling. Building pressure until the smallest spark could cause it to explode.

That spark came in the form of an anti-government slogan painted on a wall south of Damascus. The schoolboys responsible were quickly rounded up and tortured by the secret police, causing citizens to take to the streets in protest. The government pushed back hard—a strategy that had always worked for them before. For reasons that historians had yet to fully grasp, this time was different. The country exploded.

It was part of a series of uprisings across the Arab world, each feeding off the other. Strongmen were deposed and their subjects, intoxicated by their sudden freedom, attempted to rebuild based on democratic principles.

The problem was that they quickly discovered that democracy is hard. It's a political system built around the idea that people you hate will inevitably have their turn at the reins of power. In countries with deep sectarian divisions and entrenched corruption, chaos ensued. The West tried to help, but its institutions had never been good at discerning the difference between an underdog and a good guy. Americans and Western Europeans tended to think that oppressed people just wanted to shake off their chains and breathe free. The truth was a bit darker. Most had no interest in freedom or peace. They just wanted to be the ones inflicting the pain as opposed to the ones feeling it.

Movement to the east pulled Rapp back into the present. Still distant, he couldn't quite make out what it was. At first, he assumed a small group of people being smuggled toward the border. Their movements seemed a bit random, though. Individuals huddled together and dispersed. They proceeded hesitantly through the moonlight and then reversed themselves. For a moment he considered the possibility that it was a herd of unattended livestock, but that didn't seem right, either.

Rapp grabbed the pack of the man in front, forcing him to a stop.

"You tired?" he said. "Do need water? Five kilometers more and need to—"

"What's that?" Rapp said, pointing into the shallow ravine next to them.

"What?" Nijaz said, coming up behind. "Why are we stopping?"

Rapp reached out and turned Ahmet's head so he could use his light-sensitive peripheral vision. A moment later, the Turk grunted his understanding.

"Many smugglers here. This is why we walk the ridge. The territory below is for criminals. We have many problems with them. They do not do business correctly. They harm their people and steal from them. They want this entire territory alone even though there is enough for everyone. They have killed for it."

The group stopped again, this time breaking in two with about half starting back the way they'd come.

"They look lost," Rapp pointed out.

"They are idiots," Nijaz said. "And too far to be danger for us."

Ahmet nodded. "A man is waiting for you and we are slow. We must—"

"What do you mean they're idiots?" Rapp said.

"I do not understand," Nijaz responded.

"They traffic people through that corridor regularly, right?"

"Yes."

"How often do they get lost?"

"Why does this matter? We have been paid to take you to your people. We must go."

Rapp didn't budge. It mattered because these two dipshits were falling into the same trap that he'd laid in Afghanistan the week before. They wanted to believe their enemies were morons despite all evidence to the contrary.

"If those people are lost, their guides aren't with them. And if their guides aren't with them, where are they?"

Nijaz still seemed confused, but Ahmet was starting to show a glimmer of understanding.

"We're exposed up on this ridge," Rapp continued. "If I spotted them down there, they sure as hell spotted us up here. What's your relationship with them? Is it possible they see this as an opportunity to get rid of some of their competition?"

The answer came in the form of a gunshot that echoed off the steep terrain. Both Turks froze, and Rapp was forced to pull them to the ground. Nijaz offered a little confused resistance, but Ahmet went down easily. Too easily.

Rapp dragged him behind a berm as more shots rang out. The muzzle flashes suggested that their opposition consisted of two men about fifty yards to the south. If Rapp hadn't seen the people they'd left behind, he and his two guides would have walked into an ambush.

Blood bubbled black from Ahmet's mouth, and his eyes had rolled back in his head. He gripped Rapp's arm for a moment and then went completely limp. Nijaz had retrieved his pistol and was firing blindly over the low ridge they'd taken refuge behind. Rapp grabbed his wrist and yanked it upward, relieving him of the weapon.

Nijaz shouted something in Turkish that was easy to interpret by the tone and the fact that Ahmet's name figured in it. Rapp clamped a hand around the smuggler's throat and slammed him to the earth. "Calm the fuck down! Do you understand me?"

The combination of Rapp's words and the impact with the rocky ground succeeded in shutting him up.

"Listen to me, Nijaz. What weapons do we—" Another shot rang out, ricocheting off a nearby rock outcropping. Rapp fell silent until the echo died. "What weapons do we have?"

"I don't—" Nijaz started, but Rapp slapped him across the face. His cover as a soft Canadian lawyer had suddenly turned from asset to liability. What he needed now was respect and obedience. Nothing else.

"*What weapons, Nijaz?* You have this Sarsilmaz B6. What about spare magazines?"

"Yes," he stammered. "One."

"Ahmet?"

"The . . . The same."

Rapp moved quicky. If these assholes were committed enough to set up an ambush, they were committed enough to try to go for position. He pulled the pistol from Ahmet's blood-soaked hip and then searched his pack, coming up with a combat knife and spare mag. When he turned back around, Nijaz was raising up to peer over the top of the berm. Rapp yanked him back just as a shot struck a few inches away and showered them with dust.

"Listen to me, Nijaz. I need you to engage these pricks while I get behind them. Do you understand? Every minute or so, shoot from a random position behind this hill. We need them to think Ahmet's still alive and I'm just a helpless client."

"You're not?"

Rapp ignored the question. "Just do what I say, and we'll both get out of this alive."

While the Turk seemed skeptical, he wasn't prepared to contradict someone who worked for Damian Losa. He reached over one side of the berm and pulled the trigger. Rapp did the same from the other side and then immediately slithered to the west. While he was dressed as a civilian, he'd chosen clothing that blended in with the terrain. Not so important in the celestial light, but critical in the illumination of muzzle flashes.

He made it to some scrub brush about twenty feet from where Nijaz was following instructions with surprising diligence. Rapp remained motionless, watching the return fire and noting that the enemy wasn't playing their game. It was clear that only one man was shooting now. That meant there was at least one more out there.

But where?

If someone wanted to approach Nijaz's position, they were almost certain to take the same route Rapp had used to move away. It sloped gently upward, offering high ground, and a combination of bushes and medium-sized boulders provided decent cover.

Action was etched deeply in Rapp's DNA, but sometimes it was best to take a breath. Combat was often about patience. He switched Ahmet's knife to his dominant hand and relegated his pistol to the other. Quieter was always better when feasible.

Time passed slowly, as it always did in situations like these, but it allowed him to familiarize himself with the rhythm of the battlefield. Nijaz continued to alternate firing from opposite ends of the berm he was hiding behind, though in a suspiciously predictable way. A shot from the west. Forty-five seconds. A shot from the east. Repeat. Not particularly convincing, but in the heat of the moment, likely good enough.

His opponent was putting forth even less effort—firing from roughly the same position, usually in direct response to Nijaz. Not surprising because the enemy's position was the stronger of the two. The berm he was barricaded behind was similar, but higher and shaped like a crescent. Farther back, the terrain fell away into a steep, loose slope that would be impossible to climb quickly or quietly.

Getting to him was going to take some creativity.

A few more minutes passed before Rapp heard the expected crunch of footsteps to his left. He couldn't risk moving anything but his head, and even then, only with glacial slowness. By the time the man crossed into his line of vision, he was less than ten feet away.

Crouched and holding a pistol in his right hand, he was prioritizing stealth over speed in his attempt to flank Nijaz. It was a reasonable strategy, but one that was going to work against him in this instance. Eventually he'd be attracted to the bush Rapp had taken refuge beneath. Its location and size were impossible to resist.

It was almost time for Nijaz to fire from the east side of the berm and Rapp partially closed his eyes, concerned that the muzzle flash might reflect off them. The approaching man had calculated his opponent's timing, too, crouching before the landscape was briefly lit. He waited for his comrade to return fire before creeping forward again.

It took only a few seconds for him to reach the bush and dip down behind it, so close that Rapp could hear his breathing and the creak of his boots. Still poorly positioned to get off a reliable shot at Nijaz, he crawled forward, planting a hand only inches from Rapp's head. Once he'd passed, Rapp abandoned his gun and rose, clamping his empty hand over the man's mouth and nose, and ramming the knife into the back of his head.

It was a maneuver that Stan Hurley had taught him early in his career at the CIA. The old bastard guaranteed that with careful placement there would be no sound from the victim and no muscle contractions that could cause an inadvertent trigger pull. And while Hurley had been wrong about a lot in life, his advice on the subject of killing was impeccable.

The man's body went slack, and Rapp lowered it before crawling in the direction of Nijaz. If there was someone else out there watching, he wouldn't have seen anything more than his comrade briefly duck behind a bush and then continue on.

After another two careful minutes, Rapp managed to bring Nijaz into view. Now came the interesting part.

He lined up the weapon he'd taken from the man he'd killed and squeezed off a shot that struck the berm a few inches from Nijaz's head. As planned, the Turk spun and returned fire. Rapp reacted by running toward the enemy shooter dug in to the north. He fired randomly behind him as Nijaz dove to the ground and got off a few wild shots in Rapp's general direction.

The hope was that the man ahead would see only what Rapp wanted him to—that his companion had missed his opportunity and was now running for cover with bullets flying.

A muzzle flash lit up just ahead and Rapp tensed, waiting for the impact. It didn't come, though. The man had bought the illusion. He was shooting at Nijaz, trying to cover his comrade's retreat.

A bullet from behind came a little too close for comfort and Rapp threw himself over the crescent-shaped berm, landing hard and rolling across the rocky ground. The man ensconced there didn't bother to look back, instead focusing on the threat posed by Nijaz. He never saw the gun barrel line up with the back of his head or felt the bullet that killed him.

A quick search turned up only two backpacks. Not a guarantee that they were in the clear, but a pretty decent indication. A more in-depth search with a dim red penlight turned up only two sets of footprints, one of which had a tread pattern belonging to the corpse.

"Nijaz! Can you hear me? It's Matthieu!"

"Matthieu?" came the hesitant reply. "Where are you?"

"Behind cover right in front of you. There were only two men, and both are dead now. Do you understand?"

"Are you sure?"

Rapp let out an exasperated breath. "Yes. I'm sure. Now I'm going to stand up and come over to you. Don't shoot. Did you understand me? *Don't shoot.*"

"Yes. I understand."

Rapp rolled over the berm and ran to where the Turk was hiding. Ahmet's body was lying next to him along with two spent magazines and Rapp's pack.

"How long will the man I'm supposed to meet wait?"

"Not long," Nijaz said, staring down at his fallen comrade. "There are patrols and bandits in this place. Sometimes shelling. I have no way to contact him, and I think now we cannot arrive in time."

"You can't, but I can. Is the rendezvous point hard to find?"

"No. You just follow this ridge. It changes to flat and crosses a road. There you must turn east. He will be waiting two kilometers away."

Rapp put on his pack and then pressed the barrel of his gun to Nijaz's chin. The Turk froze, wide-eyed, and staring straight ahead.

"Listen to me very carefully, Nijaz. I didn't have anything to do with this. We were ambushed and you and Ahmet fought back while I hid. You finally killed the men who attacked us, but Ahmet died in the process. Then you guided me to the rendezvous point and left me there. Are we clear?"

"Yes."

"You're sure? Because if Damian Losa hears you telling stories about his lawyer shooting smugglers, there are going to be problems. Do you understand the kinds of problems I'm talking about?"

"He will make me watch my family die before he lowers me into a container of acid with them."

A much more specific answer than Rapp was expecting. Once again, the Mexican's reputation preceded him.

CHAPTER 13

R APP moved through the gully as silently as possible. The peeling sedan was parked on a dirt road to the east, having climbed as far as its tires and suspension would allow. It was as described and where it should be, but based on Rapp's experience in Syria so far, caution was in order.

A reddish glow inside suggested someone smoking and, as he approached, the form of a lone driver gained definition. Finally, an arm appeared from the open window and the butt arced into the night.

Rapp reluctantly dropped the knife and gun he was carrying before climbing from the gully. He approached slowly, staying in the center of the road and raising his hands. The headlights came on a moment later and he squinted against the glare as the man stepped from the vehicle.

"I'm Matthieu Fournier!" Rapp called in what would pass for a desperate tone. "Did you hear me? Matthieu Fournier!"

"Are you alone?" came the lightly accented response.

"Yes. We . . . We were attacked. By smugglers. Ahmet was shot.

Nijaz brought me to about half a kilometer from here and then went back to help him."

The man lit another cigarette, working his old-fashioned lighter with a deft, one-handed motion. Despite the glare, Rapp could see the reason for the man's dexterity. He was missing his left arm. A souvenir from Syria's civil unrest.

"Get in the back."

Rapp did as he was told and waited until they were underway to ask how long the journey would be. He got no response beyond a cloud of cigarette smoke. Clearly the man didn't feel the deference toward Damian Losa's representative that the smugglers had. It wasn't surprising. In war, exhaustion eventually supplanted fear. The result was an entrenched indifference that was almost impossible to overcome.

The sun was up when they reached the rubble that had once been a suburb of Idlib. Midmorning temperatures were already over one hundred degrees Fahrenheit, making the rolled-down windows a mixed blessing. The breeze helped with the heat, but the dust it carried permeated everything.

Idlib was at one time the epicenter of the resistance, but had now devolved into a hornet's nest of criminals, jihadists, and rebels. Electricity was intermittent at best, and many people lived in bombed-out buildings exposed to the elements. Rapp leaned closer to the window, the scent of pulverized concrete becoming overwhelming as he studied a group of dirty children climbing on the burned carcass of a pickup. Above them, a number of balconies hung precariously, threatening to collapse and end their lives almost before they'd started.

His driver reached for the pack of cigarettes on the dash and shook it with the same frustration as he had the first three times. Finally, he found the fortitude to admit that it was empty and threw it out the window. The wind caught it and sent it swirling down a side street made impassable by debris.

With nothing left to smoke, the man finally broke his hours of silence.

"Have you been here before?"

"No."

Technically a lie, but it was hard to equate what he saw with what he'd experienced prior to the war.

When the government lost control, the country had fractured with a speed and violence that had surprised even him. Part of the reason, of course, was that power vacuums tended to be filled by the worst possible actors. ISIS, Hezbollah, and myriad other terrorist organizations flooded in from neighboring countries or formed organically from the local population. They came and went, shifted alliances, dissolved and re-formed, always unleashing the violence and suffering that was their specialty. Now that the government was regaining control, many of those men were dead or imprisoned, leaving families trapped in overcrowded refugee camps. And then there were the bigger players—primarily Russia, but also Iran, Turkey, and Saudi Arabia. Even the US had dipped its toe in the waters with the hope of keeping ISIS from becoming a regional power again.

"We wanted freedom," his driver said. "To live in a country that serves a purpose greater than to quench one man's thirst for power. It was something worth fighting for and so we did. We fought for the right to control our futures like you do in Canada."

"But your president fought back," Rapp said.

"Yes. He fought back. There was no amount of misery he wouldn't inflict to keep his privilege. But it wasn't enough. He was losing. And then the Russians came. They said everyone who was against the government was ISIS and used this as an excuse to murder us. And the world believed it and looked the other way."

In truth, the world hadn't believed it. Certainly not the intelligence agencies. This man's problem wasn't ignorance. It was indifference. Sure, the refugee crisis was more far-reaching than anyone had predicted but, beyond that, Syria wasn't a country worth getting bogged down in.

"More than five hundred thousand of us are dead. Half of my countrymen have been driven from their homes and ninety percent of us live in poverty," he continued as he steered around a downed chopper covered in anti-government graffiti. "I was an English teacher. Now I'm a criminal to feed my wife and children. And even with everything I've done, my family barely has enough. When I die—when they finally kill me—what will happen to them?"

Rapp met his eye in the rearview mirror and shook his head. "I don't know."

The building they finally arrived at wasn't what Rapp anticipated. Instead of a remote safe house, it was in the middle of town, an imposing white stone structure that mixed Arab and modern architecture. The east side of the roof had some damage that looked like it had happened sometime ago, but a more extensive collapse to the west looked fresh. The flow of rubble had snapped off one of the four palm trees in the courtyard and come to a stop at the iron fence surrounding the grounds. There was a sign outside, but it was so faded that Rapp could barely make out what was left of the Arabic script.

The Idlib Museum.

His driver stopped in front and pointed to the gate. Rapp grabbed his pack and stepped out into the sun, looking around him at the light pedestrian and vehicle traffic. No one seemed particularly interested in his arrival, focusing instead on going about the business of surviving Syria's new reality.

The exception was the man opening the gate and waving him over. He looked to be in his late fifties, with a gray-streaked beard and an expanding waistline that suggested prosperity in a region where food was hard to come by. His clothes told a similar story. A bit threadbare now, but in their heyday, they would have been stylish and of high quality.

"Please follow me," he said in a nearly native British accent.

Rapp did, entering the gloom of the building and stopping almost immediately when the man took a seat in a ticket booth.

"One thousand Syrian pounds, please."

Rapp's brow furrowed a moment but, to be fair, the entry price was printed clearly on the window. Arguing the point seemed counter-productive, particularly in light of the man who had just appeared at the other end of the reception area. He was dressed all in black, with a scarf wound around his head that left only his eyes visible. The AK-47 wasn't yet pointed in Rapp's direction, but it didn't seem like it would take much to change that.

"Do you take euros?"

"Of course. One."

A five was the smallest thing Rapp had and he handed it over.

"Thank you, sir. I'll just put the other four in the donation box. For repairs. Very generous of you."

"My pleasure."

"My name is Dr. Ismail Faadin," the man said, coming out from behind the booth and offering his hand. "Please join me."

He led Rapp through the building, pointing out various empty rooms as though they still contained exhibits. His explanation of the region's history contained an undercurrent of genuine passion, while his description of the damage recently caused by Uzbek jihadis was delivered with tired fatalism.

"So, you're the caretaker of this place?" Rapp asked before the man could start waxing rhapsodic about the mosaic floor they were crossing.

"In fact, I'm the museum's director and its only remaining em-ployee. We reopened some time ago and stayed open despite the Uz-beks. Unfortunately, recent bombing by the Russians have made the place structurally unsound. We had to move everything to an under-ground location outside the city. It will be safe there."

Almost as if on cue, a series of explosions became audible. Distant, but not so much so that the vibration didn't dislodge some dust from the ceiling. Faadin stopped and listened for a few seconds, trying to determine if they were going to be vaporized by whatever government or faction happened to be playing with explosives that day.

Silence descended again and they continued, eventually entering an office that seemed untouched by everything happening outside of it. The window was both intact and clean, and shelves were still lined with reference materials. Faadin took a seat behind a polished desk and pointed to the chair in front of it. Rapp nodded politely and settled in. Maybe Losa would turn out to be right. Other than the shelling, this seemed pretty civilized.

"Now, what is it I can do for you, Mr. Fournier?"

"You haven't been told?"

"Damian Losa's people contacted me and asked me to put you in touch with the government forces that now control the narcotics trade in my country."

The juxtaposition between the man Rapp saw in front of him and the words coming from his mouth was, at a minimum, stark. Losa, for all his slickness, still had a criminal aura, while this guy really did come off as an academic.

He seemed to pick up on Rapp's curiosity.

"The museum closed at the beginning of the war and stayed that way for almost a decade. Like everyone, I needed money for my family to survive. What choice did I have but to turn to enterprises like narcotics, weapons, and smuggling?"

"And that's how you got connected to Losa?"

He nodded. "I was well educated and discovered that I had a talent for making money, so people began to follow me. Eventually—"

He fell silent when another explosion sounded, this time closer. The shelves behind him shook and the lamp hanging over his head swayed gently. After about ten seconds, he continued as though nothing had happened. "Eventually, I became successful enough to be noticed by your employer."

"And you've remained loyal to him?" Rapp said. A naïve question befitting a pampered lawyer.

"Loyal? It's not a word that has meaning in Syria, Mr. Fournier. Mr. Losa's network here isn't what it once was. Many of my people are having to look for other opportunities in order to survive. Some have joined the government's trafficking efforts, while some are still fighting against Damascus. Others have fled the country or are in the process of doing so. Because of the museum, my options are narrower. For the moment, my interests and those of Mr. Losa's are still aligned."

"For the moment."

The Syrian nodded.

"Then you'll put me in touch with people who can help me?"

"I've made inquiries."

"And?"

Faadin leaned back in his chair, examining Rapp for a moment. "As little as the word *loyalty* means in Syria, it means even less in the world of Damian Losa. He used our desperation to strengthen his position here, and now with the government regaining control, it seems that we're no longer useful. Other than to help him move on to a more profitable partnership."

"That may be the case. But Losa isn't one to turn on his people. It's bad business."

"Bad business? Perhaps. But sacrifices must be made, no? And it occurs to me that I and my men might be a convenient bargaining chip. The government would like very much to shut down our enterprises here and he could help them accomplish that. A demonstration of his goodwill that I doubt would hurt his reputation in the outside world."

"We're both expendable, Dr. Faadin."

"Yes, but you chose this path. I was forced onto it."

"It doesn't matter how we got here. What matters is how we get out. If you make these connections for me, you'll be well paid. Or, if you prefer, you'll be given safe passage for you and your family to Europe. On the other hand, if we can work out a deal with the government, we could potentially get you a position with them. Mr. Losa wants stability and peace, because those things translate into profitability."

"I want weapons to fight the government."

"Were you not listening to what I said about peace and stability?"

"And profitability," Faadin reminded him. "The true god of the West."

Rapp motioned with his head toward the open door. "If you go outside and look around, you'll see that our god's worked out better than yours."

The flash of anger in the man's eyes was inevitable, as was the sound of the man in the doorway shouldering his AK. Rapp had assumed he didn't speak English. In the end, though, that wasn't his most serious mistake. His problem was that he'd forgotten that he wasn't here to win confrontations. That was Mitch Rapp's vocation. Matthieu Fournier was here to make friends.

"That was rude," Rapp said. "I hope you'll accept my apology."

"You can't imagine what I've lost, Mr. Fournier."

"You're wrong. I *can* imagine it. And I understand that you want revenge. But that's all there is left here. Hundreds of factions probing for weakness, attacking, retaliating. You can't build a country on that. You can't preserve your heritage. Someone strong has to be in control, and for now that looks like the government. Otherwise, Syria will spend the next hundred years like this. Let Mr. Losa give you and your family a new life."

Ismail contemplated that for a few moments before responding. "The money Damascus makes in the narcotics trade is all that's keeping the government from collapsing."

"I'm specifically interested in the captagon that's being shipped to Europe."

Faadin's eyebrows rose. "Then you've found the one exception."

"Exception? I don't understand."

"That sector of the business is handled by the Russians. My understanding is that the Syrian government has no involvement at all."

Rapp turned on his satphone as he passed a series of ancient columns that had apparently been too heavy to move. He dialed a number from memory and the call was immediately picked up by Losa's lieutenant, Julian. A moment later, the man himself was on.

"I'm happy to hear your voice, Matthieu. My understanding is that your crossing didn't go as smoothly as we'd hoped. Have you made contact?"

"Yes."

"And?"

"It seems that your problem isn't with the Syrians. It's with the Russians."

There was a short pause over the line. "Interesting. That piece makes the puzzle a bit clearer."

"How so?"

"They would have the expertise and financing to create a designer drug like the one we're seeing. And with the current geopolitical landscape, they need to diversify away from selling energy. Narcotics—particularly if done from the shadows in Syria—makes sense."

"Mission accomplished, then," Rapp said.

Predictably, Losa didn't see it that way. "Questions remain, I'm afraid. How are they making their product cheaply enough to generate a profit, while I can't? And why the novel compounds that don't appear to enhance either the high or the addictive qualities?"

"By-product of the manufacturing process?" Rapp said.

"No, it's not an accident. According to my people, it's been specifically produced and would add even more to the cost."

"The Russians have never been all that good at making money."

"Agreed. But they're better than this. I think it's worth sitting down with them and seeing what they're open to. Obviously, they've made strides in creating a European distribution network, but it'll take a lot of time and money to transform it into one that can rival mine. Particularly if they're relying on Muslim immigrants. I think the window has closed on stopping the flow of captagon to Europe. But the possibility of a collaboration still exists."

"You can't collaborate with the Russians because their goal is power, not profit. You'll spend ten percent of your time doing business and the other ninety trying to keep them from stabbing you in the back."

"Perhaps. But I want to know what my options are, and it never hurts to talk. You knew when you asked for my help with Gustavo that I'd eventually call in the favor. Can I still count on you to repay your debt to me?"

It never hurts to talk was something people said when they were sitting in a Parisian mansion sipping Perrier. The reality on the ground in Syria was different. But Losa was right. Rapp had made a deal with the devil and the devil had held up his end of the bargain.

CHAPTER 14

THE Russian soldier performed the salute that General Aleksandr Semenov insisted on, but never returned. He enjoyed the mindless subservience of the gesture and, even more, he enjoyed the irony. Strictly speaking, he'd never been a member of the armed forces. The rank bestowed on him by the Russian government with great pomp and circumstance was just a convenience. A way of garnering the unwavering obedience of the men assigned to him.

Even more ironic was the fact that there was perhaps no category of human he disdained more than soldiers. While many had no choice but to join for a relatively brief mandatory service, those who made it their career were clearly defective. Men who lacked the intelligence, creativity, or strength to do anything more meaningful than offer themselves up as Moscow's cannon fodder.

Even worse than the common foot soldier was their leadership. One would have thought that Russia's failures on various battlefields would have caused a light to dawn, but the opposite was true. Every defeat entrenched them deeper in the conviction that they needed to continue along the same path, but with greater resolve. And then there was the corruption. Left to their own devices, his fellow generals would issue their men guns made of cardboard and sell the real ones to pad their already swollen Swiss bank accounts.

Soldiers, by their very nature, were slaves. To their superiors. To their ideologies. To their illusions of glory and honor. Having said that, it was undeniable that they could occasionally be useful idiots.

Semenov continued the length of the hallway and pushed through a door at the end. The man sitting behind the desk that dominated the office leapt immediately to his feet. He was in his early sixties, with unkempt gray hair and a lab coat that identified him as something much more deadly than a soldier. A scientist.

"Give them to me," Semenov said simply.

Dr. Konstantin Novikoff retrieved a plastic bag of white pills and handed it over.

"They're larger," Semenov said. The round shape stamped with two crescent moons was familiar, but the visual and physical weight had changed.

"Yes, sir. We've solved the physical withdrawal problem, but the compounds necessary added a bit of mass. Still, they continue to be smaller than most over-the-counter pain relievers."

"When you say you've solved the withdrawal issue, define *solved*."

"We're using something similar to xylazine. Severe withdrawal symptoms last an average of three times longer than they do for users of heroin and fentanyl."

"What about pharmaceutical interventions like methadone?"

"Completely ineffective."

Novikoff turned his computer monitor and started a video that depicted a whitewashed cell containing a single prisoner. It ran at five-times speed as they watched the twitchy, almost comical motions of a man in agony. He threw the blankets to the floor, glistening with sweat, and then immediately retrieved them to shiver beneath. The act was repeated a number of times before he lunged for the toilet to vomit violently into it. According to the timer, he spent almost a minute convulsing there before sinking to the concrete floor and shouting up at the camera in the ceiling. There was no audio, but the pain and desperation on his face suggested that he was pleading for the narcotic that he'd become so dependent on.

"How much does the new formulation increase cost, Doctor?"

"About fifteen percent."

Semenov nodded silently. Still far cheaper than a tank. And far more effective. It could flood across the borders of NATO states with only token resistance. No Javelin missile could destroy it. No surveillance drone could track it. And no embargo could starve it of fuel, ammunition, or spare parts.

"It was the last piece we needed to get one hundred percent voluntary uptake," Novikoff added hopefully.

The scientist had been told that when he accomplished his scientific mission, he would be sent home to his family. And despite his undeniable intelligence, he actually seemed to believe it. In reality, he would eventually end up in the same mass grave as his many victims.

"I want to see."

The observation area was on the top floor and had been created by replacing the windows looking into an interior courtyard with open railings. Even out of the sun, the heat was oppressive, but it did provide an excellent view of the fifteen or so prisoners below. All were wearing similar orange jumpsuits and all were being denied the gender separation customary in the region.

They were crowded into the shade on one side of the ten-meter-square space, with occasional skirmishes breaking out as men jockeyed for position and women tried to stay clear. Despite having access to far better food and medical care than they'd enjoyed in their prisons and refugee camps, all had a similar pallor and unsteady gait.

This was the cream of the many crops they'd run through the

facility. They were the ones who, despite being forced to use ever-improving captagon formulations, had maintained their ability to refuse it when use became optional. For some it appeared to be a simple genetic resistance to addiction. For others it was the depth of their religiosity. Still others relied on their unusual reserves of willpower or hatred of their captors. Now iteration 64XZ had broken through those defenses. Or so Novikoff said.

There was a large digital clock on the wall and as it crept closer to time for the pills to be distributed, the group's agitation increased. With two minutes to go, the most desperate braved the sun and began to form a line in front of a barred window beneath Semenov's position. The hierarchy was one that had formed organically numerous times— the strongest men at the front, descending to the weakest women at the back. A few shoving contests broke out between participants who were too evenly matched to have their positions completely codified. No damage was done, though. All had been denied their fixes for more than twenty-four hours and were now significantly weakened by withdrawal symptoms.

At precisely 1400, the window opened, and a woman dressed as a nurse began passing single doses through the bars. Semenov watched in silence as every one of them took their allotment, slammed it in their mouth, and swallowed without the aid of liquid.

The effect manifested much more slowly in pill form, but he was happy to wait as the test subjects became increasingly dazed. At the twenty-minute mark, a number of them—including one of the women—began stripping their clothes off. Others wandered aimlessly, losing their place in space and time. One man seemed frozen at the center of it all, staring directly into the sun. It was an interesting compulsion that left around seven percent of test subjects blind.

If this group of hardened resisters could be broken, what hope did drug users in Europe and America have?

Semenov turned toward his lead researcher. "And the psychoses?"

"We have no new data. Our hope was that the Italian shipment would allow us to expand our knowledge of real-world effects. Obviously, that didn't materialize."

"But the addition of the new compounds won't affect the level of damage."

Novikoff shook his head. "The compounds work independently. Confusion, paranoia, and aggression will set in after around six months of use. Those tendencies will intensify with continued uptake and won't diminish even if access to the drug is cut off. The damage is structural, and once it's done, it can't be reversed."

Semenov didn't like to show emotion in front of the staff, but it was impossible to fully suppress his smile. The drug that caused the permanent brain injury had originally been seen as a glorious victory for the Soviet pharmaceutical industry. It had been developed to treat schizophrenia and was believed at the time to be a breakthrough that would bolster the country's prestige and be a source of much-needed hard currency.

Initial indications had been extremely promising, relieving the symptoms suffered by the majority of test subjects. But as the trials continued, issues began to surface. At first, researchers thought the drug lost its efficacy over time, prompting them to increase the dosages. This, as it turned out, was exactly the wrong thing to do. The issue wasn't that the patients' mental problems were resurfacing, it was that the drug was causing new ones. And once those new psychoses manifested, they were permanent. None of the people in the high-dose group were ever able to rejoin society, with the last of them dying in a mental institution a decade ago.

For obvious reasons, the program was quietly shut down and largely forgotten until he'd stumbled upon it.

The drug's potential as a weapon should have been obvious to anyone willing to open their eyes. In recent years, the West had developed yet another chink in its tattered armor: an exploding taste for opioids. The target was soft enough to be irresistible. Converting demand from heroin and fentanyl to his captagon was an entirely achievable goal.

The formulation was similar in its effect, but with an even more immersive high. Further, it was virtually impossible to overdose on and could be subsidized by Moscow to be the cheapest narcotic in its class.

The West would find itself in a desperate battle against a drug with a destructiveness that far exceeded anything before encountered. The Europeans wouldn't end up with a handful of casualties like the Soviet pharmaceutical industry had. They'd end up with millions. The burden would overwhelm their already strained health care systems. Politics would become even more polarized and nationalistic when authorities came to believe that Muslims were responsible. Conservatives would demonstrate little sympathy for the addicts and their long-term care. In contrast, liberals would expend unsustainable levels of resources on them, while fighting against a rising tide of xenophobia.

In combination with his other asymmetrical attacks, it would be enough to tear the European Union apart and leave its components turning to authoritarianism to provide the stability that freedom no longer could.

When Semenov returned to his office, he found his assistant waiting. The man was wearing a smug expression that he thought he hid well, but in fact was entirely transparent. It was a weakness that would prevent him from rising much beyond his current station.

"What do you have for me?" Semenov asked, taking a seat behind his desk. The rest of his day was fully booked, but this evening a celebration would be in order. He'd finally get to taste a treat that he'd been saving for just such an occasion.

"Our informants have identified the group that Damian Losa's man is going to meet with: Syrian smugglers who used to work for his organization but now work for the Syrian military's Iraqi drug operation. The details of the meeting are still being negotiated, but in all likelihood, it will take place in Saraqib two days from now."

Losa undoubtedly viewed this as a straightforward situation. The narcotics business was about making money and he would assume that there was a path forward in which everyone benefited. It just had to be found. What a man like him couldn't possibly understand was that sometimes financial gain wasn't the goal.

Further, Semenov didn't need him for his European venture. Cheaper, better merchandise combined with the continent's endless supply of disaffected Muslims would be enough to eventually outcompete him. Losa's usefulness related to something much bigger.

America.

While far more powerful than Europe, the US was just as vulnerable. Its citizens suffered from the same addictions, its society was just as polarized, its health care system was similarly overextended, and it had at least as strong an anti-immigrant sentiment. Even more convenient, the Latinos who were the target of ever-intensifying hatred were the key to Damian Losa's operations there.

Semenov was confident that if he could get control of the Mexican's network, America would fall even faster than its allies across the Atlantic. Its democracy was old and tired. Its citizens were sick of the responsibility it demanded.

They thirsted for something new.

CHAPTER 15

D R. Ismail Faadin was gripping the tattered steering wheel with knuckles blanched white. Whether the color was due to his current state of mind or the failing dashboard lights was hard to say. Rapp decided it wasn't worth worrying about and turned back to the warm air flowing through his open side window. This part of Saraqib had taken too much shelling to sustain much population and the only evidence of habitation was the flicker of a few campfires. All were too distant to see detail, but in his mind's eye, he could picture the people huddled around them. Enraged insurgents plotting revenge. Widows wondering where their next meal was going to come from. Children who didn't know anything else.

"The men we're going to meet used to work for me," Faadin said. "But now they smuggle narcotics for the Syrian army. Their specialty is creating packaging designed to avoid detection. It's rumored that they were involved in loading the container of captagon that was discovered by the Italians."

They'd already been through this, but Rapp understood that different people dealt with fear differently. Some went silent, others talked nonstop. Faadin was in the latter category, but there was no reason to hold it against him. He was a museum director, not a SEAL.

"So that's what brought them into contact with the Russians?" Rapp prompted.

"With a few degrees of separation. They work for Syrian army officers who, in turn, work for generals who work directly for the Russians. If they're impressed by what you have to say, they can pass it up their chain of command. With luck, that will eventually get you to the decision makers."

"I assume that none of them are trustworthy?"

"Not in the least. That's not to say that our parting was adversarial. It wasn't. But their alliances are for sale. Make no mistake about that."

"Everyone's for sale," Rapp responded. "It's just a question of how much."

"Yes. And in Syria, the price is cheap."

As they progressed deeper into the city, the stone and concrete buildings got larger and the destruction more selective. Virtually everything was damaged from the war, but now collapsed buildings shared space with ones that were more or less intact. Many streets had been cleared and previously empty lots were filled with concrete debris blooming with rebar.

Eventually, signs of permanent human habitation also began to reveal themselves. Families weaving purposefully through the streets. Circles of illumination fed by jury-rigged cables. Vendors knocking off for the night and pushing their carts to wherever home was now.

"Saraqib is somewhat disputed territory," Faadin continued. "Technically, it's held by the Syrian government, but only barely. They keep a low profile, and the Russians stay out. It is a powder keg waiting for a spark to ignite it."

"But relatively neutral."

"Yes. I would use the analogy of two men standing in the middle of a minefield. No matter how much they hate each other, both recognize a fistfight is in no one's best interest."

"And the people we're meeting share that philosophy?" Rapp said. "Everyone understands that this is just an informal get-together to lay groundwork for talks? I'm just a messenger and that message is cooperation."

"All explained," Faadin assured him.

The building they pulled up to didn't have much to set it apart from all the others on the narrow street. Consisting of five levels, the first four had suffered serious damage, with missing walls that exposed the slabs and pillars that kept it precariously upright. The top floor appeared to be in somewhat better shape, but the tenuous light made it difficult to pick out detail.

Rapp stepped out and Faadin did the same, followed by his three bodyguards in the back.

"One man on each of the first three floors," he said in Arabic that Rapp pretended not to understand. "We agreed that the fourth would remain empty. I'll go with Fournier to the fifth."

His men retrieved their assault rifles and started across the street. Rapp followed, but moved slowly, searching the buildings around them. Faces peeked from empty windows, around corners, and through tattered tarps. The rhythm of the city had been broken and its inhabitants were taking notice. Their lives depended on the détente they'd managed to form, and all would be aware of how delicate it was.

"The name of the man we're here to meet is Rahim Suleiman," Faadin said as they entered. "He has an equal number of men as we do. Don't be alarmed. It was part of our agreement."

They found the first one just inside. Despite being little more than a shadow, he looked serious and was holding an AK-47. One of Faadin's men stopped near him and they did their best to stare each other down—but no more than that. Not yet.

What was left of the concrete staircase hung largely unsupported and was covered in graffiti shouting out to the various factions controlling the city. They left men to counter Suleiman's on the second and third floors before climbing to the fourth. It was little more than an open deck with barely enough structural support to keep it from collapsing. At first glance the space appeared to be empty, and Faadin didn't seem interested in confirming that impression. His gait became increasingly jerky as they ascended the last set of steps, nerves fraying with each one.

The top floor had various sections of missing wall, but the roof was more or less intact. Before crossing the rubble-strewn expanse, Rapp paused to smooth the suit he'd worn for the occasion. It was impeccably tailored and the dress shoes Losa's cobbler had made continued to perform beyond all expectation. Not only did they look good enough to bring a tear to Claudia's eye, but they also possessed a sole that was both grippy and silent on every surface he encountered. Confidence-inspiring, but hopefully only the aesthetics and not the performance would be tested today.

Ahead, a heavy blanket hung in place of a missing door. Light from inside bled around the edges, dim enough to be barely visible even to the dark-adjusted eye.

"It'll be over soon," Rapp whispered as he coaxed Faadin forward. "Maybe Mr. Losa could make a nice donation to your museum. A couple of million euros ought to get it up and running again."

The possibility seemed to fortify the former academic and he called out in English when they were still fifteen away. "Rahim! It's me. Ismail. We're outside."

"Enter!" came the shouted answer.

They pushed through the blanket into a room that was smaller than Rapp expected, but contained only two men, as had been negotiated. One had an AK and a scarf-covered face, while the other was wearing a threadbare suit and sitting at a low table with an empty stool in front of it. Light was provided by a single candle that was also warming a teapot.

"It's a pleasure to meet you, Mr. Fournier," the man said, standing and offering his hand. His accent was thick enough to be nearly incomprehensible, adding another layer of complexity to what Rapp was there to do.

"Mr. Suleiman," Rapp said pleasantly, taking the man's hand in a firm but not overly domineering grip. "Likewise."

"Please! You sit."

Rapp nodded his thanks and took the stool offered. He'd never been particularly good at these kinds of interactions. In his experience a bullet to the kneecap tended to move things along faster than a pot of tepid tea.

Despite that, he accepted a cup with over-the-top gratitude.

Behind him Faadin put a hand near his gun and moved to what a museum curator would consider a strategic position.

"I appreciate you agreeing to meet with me," Rapp started. "Mr. Losa believes that we can put any misunderstandings behind us and create a profitable relationship."

The man leaned forward a bit, taking a few beats to decipher Rapp's words. "You want to talk to people very powerful, yes? Why? We have much respect for Mr. Losa. But my bosses are very shy. You must understand, yes?"

Rapp reached into his jacket, moving slowly enough to not concern the man with the AK. His hand reappeared a moment later with a pack of cigarettes and a silver lighter. Technically, he didn't smoke, but in Arab countries with limited access to quality tobacco, it was a surprisingly effective bonding strategy. He offered one and leaned over the tiny table to light it before taking a second for himself.

"You've been very successful in your business, Mr. Suleiman. The amphetamines and hashish you distribute across the Middle East is high quality and, based on our understanding, extremely profitable. Obviously, Mr. Losa has nothing to offer you on this front."

Rapp paused to let the man catch up before speaking again.

"However, it appears that now the men you work for want to access the European market with a captagon formulation that's very different than the one you traffic in the Middle East. Again, Mr. Losa offers his compliments."

Suleiman nodded sagely, though it was obvious that he wasn't fully tracking on the conversation. Whether it was because of his limited English skills or the fact that he understood nothing about the Russians' new enterprise was hard to say.

"Your manufacturing process is clearly very efficient, and your product is very appealing. But you're held back by your distribution network in Europe. That was proven in Italy, and now you have a serious situation on your hands. Your people have been identified as terrorists and that will allow authorities to draw on virtually unlimited resources to capture them. They're already starting to raid Muslim areas where your people live and operate."

"You can do better than this?" the man challenged.

"Yes. We pay high-level people in Europe's police forces, intelligence community, and docks. For instance, we would have known that the authorities had discovered your shipment well before it arrived in Italy. Maybe even before it left Syria. Further, when you finally do get a significant amount of product into Europe, Mr. Losa has a much larger and better-established distribution network that extends from Spain to Finland. Yours is active primarily in Italy, Germany, France, and Belgium. Isn't that correct?"

In truth, it was unlikely that he had any idea where the network was active. But he knew people who did. All Rapp needed from this man was to accurately convey to his superiors what was discussed in this meeting.

Suleiman leaned back in his chair, examining Rapp while he savored his cigarette. "Why do I trust you? Losa wants everything. And he sends a Frenchman? One of the colonialists who enslaved my people? Is this an insult?"

"I'm Canadian, not French. And those things happened a century ago. Before our grandfathers were born. You and Syria have more serious problems than the colonial era."

"God has a long memory," he said. The smoke rolling from his mouth swirled in the candlelight.

Rapp held up a cautionary hand. "Let's not speak of God. He has nothing to do with this. We're just two drug dealers trying to make money destroying the lives of our fellow man. I doubt either of our gods approve."

"You know nothing of Allah. We fight the infidels that desecrate his name. First the Crusaders. Then the French. You come here with your arrogance..."

Rapp stopped listening and instead looked around the room. This asshole hadn't said anything substantive the entire meeting and now he was waxing rhapsodic about the Crusades? He was stalling. But for what?

Better not to wait around and find out. He stood, but despite the slowness of his movements, the man with the AK stiffened.

"Perhaps it would be better if Mr. Losa came here personally," Rapp said. "I think I can convince him that his presence would make negotiations more productive."

If he could dangle the possibility of Losa showing his face in Syria, maybe he could stave off whatever this prick was planning. Probably not, though. He was too low on the food chain to make decisions on the fly.

The guard suddenly swung his rifle in Faadin's direction, causing the academic to claw clumsily for the gun in his waistband. The muzzle flash was as blinding as the sound was deafening. Faadin jerked ninety degrees to the right and dropped to the concrete floor. The impact sent his weapon clattering across the floor before coming to a stop near the wall. A moment later, gunfire became audible throughout the building as the men on the levels below faced off.

Rapp ignored the pistol and charged straight at the guard. It seemed almost certain that these men had orders that he not be harmed. A dead negotiator served no purpose at all. A thoroughly interrogated one, on the other hand, could be quite valuable.

His theory proved correct, and he managed to use the rifle to pin the man against the wall. The weapon's sling was still around his body and Rapp reversed himself, jerking back on the weapon instead of pushing. The man stumbled forward, and as he began to fall, Rapp wrenched the weapon from his hands, twisting it in a way that wound the canvas strap around his neck.

"Stop!" Suleiman shouted, causing Rapp to look up. He was much bigger than he appeared while seated—at least six one and carrying two hundred and thirty reasonably solid pounds. Of more concern was the pistol in his hand.

The Syrian's expression suggested well-warranted confidence, but also a little confusion about how a man in a five-thousand-euro suit had gotten the better of his guard. Rapp decided to amplify his confusion by putting a foot in the struggling man's back and snapping his neck.

"I said stop!" Suleiman raised the gun and sighted along it at Rapp. An obvious bluff. If he were going to shoot, he'd have already done it. Failing to bring his prisoner out alive would carry a penalty far worse than anything Rapp could do to him.

Rapp charged and, instead of firing, the much larger man tossed his gun aside and began his own charge. A collision wasn't going to go well for Rapp's one hundred and seventy-five pounds, so he side-stepped at the last moment, grabbing the back of the man's shirt and driving him toward the wall. The impact wouldn't be violent enough to put him down, but it would be enough to provide a brief advantage.

Suleiman hit the wall face-first, but the impact was even less than Rapp had predicted. It almost felt as though the wall was padded—that the man's momentum hadn't been fully arrested. It took only a split second for Rapp to comprehend what was happening, but even that was too slow.

The weakened concrete had given way and the Syrian was going through it. He turned at the last moment, making a successful grab for Rapp's tie, only to learn that it was a clip-on.

As Suleiman pitched out into the night, Rapp couldn't prevent himself from following. His luck finally seemed to have run out when the upper part of the wall came raining down on him, but then he saw a line of rebar jutting from where the floor had met the now-collapsing wall. His hands clamped around two of them and both held, leaving him dangling more than fifty feet above the street.

He pulled himself back into the building, reasonably confident that no one had seen him. After collecting Suleiman's pistol and checking the magazine, he crouched next to Faadin. Searching for a pulse was pointless—the man was clearly dead.

Rapp felt a pang of regret as he stood. He'd meant what he said about coercing Losa into sending money to repair the museum. Faadin hadn't chosen this life and he'd deserved a second chance. The problem was that *deserve* didn't mean shit in Syria.

CHAPTER 16

GENERAL Aleksandr Semenov poured another vodka and then turned to look out over a moonlit desert. The massive windows were only one of many luxurious touches he'd included in his top-floor flat at the facility. The rich wood, sumptuous carpet, and priceless artwork from his homeland were meant to be a reminder of who he was. And who he would become.

He pulled the silver lid from a tray to expose the dinner that had been prepared for him by his personal chef. Spaghetti carbonara, greens grown on-site, and fresh-baked bread. Likely better than what his counterparts in Moscow were enjoying.

Over time, he'd taught himself to see his posting in Syria as a respite. A period of reflection before returning to the Kremlin and starting a political battle that, once begun, had to be won. Neither retreat nor surrender would be an option. There could be only glorious victory or abject defeat.

Euronews was playing on a television to his left and he turned when it switched to a story developing in Germany. There was still very little information, so the station just looped a short cell phone video while a commentator babbled nonsensically over it. Taken by a tourist, the footage started as an innocent depiction of a crowded Munich shopping street. At the five-second mark, a bearded man at the edge of the frame began screaming something in Arabic. The person holding the camera centered on him just as he pulled an assault rifle from his coat and began firing at the people around him.

The feed lost its coherence as the person holding it tried to get to the woman and young girl who were the intended subjects of the video. Panicked people screamed and darted in every direction, the strong and fast pushing past—and sometimes over—anyone in their path. All to the static-ridden soundtrack of gunfire.

Semenov raised his glass when the newscaster announced that the perpetrator had been identified as a Syrian refugee named Adham al-Numan, but that no further information was yet available.

Semenov, in contrast, possessed a great deal of further information. Al-Numan had initially been recruited to his captagon distribution network in Berlin, but was deemed too unstable for the job. It had seemed a shame to waste his temperament and religious fervor, though. People with his level of impotent rage were as rare as they were useful.

The planning and financing of the attack had been trivial. Not much more than ensuring he couldn't be traced back to the men who had rejected him and providing a weapon, a time, and a target. He'd happily done the rest. Ostensibly for Allah, but in truth for Mother Russia.

Germany had a vibrant fascist movement that was perhaps the most vigorously suppressed in all of Europe. Incidents like these were critical to creating an environment in which it could take its first hesitant steps from the shadows.

The knock on the door was precisely on time and elicited a rare smile from him. There were few things to recommend this godforsaken country, but he was about to enjoy one of them. A fitting end to a very successful day.

"Come."

By the time the door had swung fully open, the guard was already receding toward the stairs. What remained commanded Semenov's attention in a way that few other things could.

His people had identified the girl a year ago in a shelter near Jibrin. She'd only been fifteen at the time, but her beauty had already been startling. After the discovery, it had been made clear that she wasn't to be touched or married off and, in return, she and her mother were provided upgraded housing, food, and medical care.

That arrangement remained in place until three months ago, when she'd been brought to the facility for grooming, a proper finishing diet, and a strict exercise regimen. Even more important, she'd gone through the captagon program and was now hopelessly addicted to the ever-improving product. His on-site psychologists assured him that there was nothing she wouldn't do to get her fix.

Finally, it was time to test that theory.

"Alea," Semenov said, standing. Normally, he wasn't particularly good with foreign names, but hers was burned into his mind. "Please come in."

She didn't speak Russian, but his body language was sufficient to communicate his wishes and she complied. Her dark eyes darted around the lavish space in a way that suggested she'd never seen—or even imagined—anything like it.

He walked past her and closed the door, turning to admire her motionless outline. She'd been dressed in a sheer white gown that hung loose enough to only hint at her youthful curves. But those hints shimmered hypnotically in the light. He approached and touched her long hair, letting it run through his fingers as he circled to face her.

In front, the fabric clung a bit more suggestively and he took a moment to admire her long legs, flat stomach, and firm breasts beneath the material. Her pupils were a bit dilated from the drug, but it also relaxed her—keeping fear from turning to terror.

That was assuming she even understood what was happening.

Between the repressive Arab culture, the realities of the camp where she'd been raised, and the watchers he'd assigned, she'd led quite the sheltered life. A life with no future. No past. No hope. Her months in this facility—in the embrace of his narcotic—had undoubtedly been the best of her life.

Of course, the psychoses would eventually start to manifest, but that was of no importance. By then he'd have moved on to a new toy. For now, though, he was enthralled.

"This way," he said, putting a hand in the small of her back and guiding her to a bar at the back of the room. Next to his open bottle of vodka were two captagon tablets resting in a glass dish. Her withdrawal symptoms wouldn't start for another hour or so, but she understood very well the suffering they would bring. Her hand immediately shot out, but he caught it before she could reach the pills.

"Not yet, Alea. There are things you need to do for me first."

Similar to the living area, the west wall of Semenov's bedroom was dominated by glass. The filtered moonlight flashed dully off the vodka in his hand and in the half-closed eyes of the girl on the bed.

He sipped his drink, feeling it go to his head as he gazed at her naked body. She'd gotten what she wanted and now her mind was floating in the warmth his captagon was uniquely capable of providing. Sitting there watching the compounds he'd developed take control of her began to arouse him again and he put his glass down.

This time there was no resistance. Or even awareness. A bit of a shame, but there was plenty of time to play with his new doll. And so many interesting games.

He was still inside her when the shrill ring of his phone broke the silence. The girl didn't react beyond a subtle change in the rhythm of her breathing, but he swore aloud. His assistant knew full well that he wasn't to be disturbed. If Leonid had summoned the courage to do so, it was undoubtedly a matter of importance.

Semenov slid off the girl and retrieved his phone, feeling his irritation grow as his erection faded.

"What?"

"I'm sorry, sir, but we're getting reports of shots fired at the meeting in Saraqib."

"My understanding is that we expected that. Losa's man brought guards, no?"

"That's correct, sir, but the information we have suggests an ongoing battle."

Semenov's irritation turned to anger. How hard was it to capture a lone Canadian attorney?

"Tell the Syrian forces to move in."

"I'm in contact with them, sir, but they're reluctant. They maintain that Suleiman's people have the situation under control."

"They maintain?" Semenov said, the volume of his voice rising to the point that the girl twitched noticeably.

If he wasn't dealing with crushing incompetence, it was crushing cowardice. Losa's people had picked Saraqib because its instability made Damascus reluctant to run overt operations there. Clever, but the future of Saraqib and its citizens was of absolutely no importance to him or to Russia.

"If Matthieu Fournier escapes or dies, I'll make sure that every one of the men who refused to enter that building is executed and their families are put out in the street. Is that clear?"

"Crystal clear, sir. I'll convey the message."

CHAPTER 17

RAPP snuffed the candle, extinguishing the only source of light in the room. It could call attention to his position and was no longer necessary due to the spotlights now raking the building. Ismail Faadin's body was partially blocking the exit and Rapp had to straddle it in order to peer around the blanket hanging over the doorway.

The swirl of illumination gave the space a video game feel, but revealed no sign of human presence. Outside, bursts of gunfire were audible at random intervals. Nearby, but probably not directly related to him. More likely locals reacting to the sudden appearance of Syrian security forces. That wasn't necessarily a positive development for him, though. A full-scale battle erupting in Saraqib wouldn't be in anyone's best interest.

He eased out of the room, keeping his gun hand low and close to his leg. The longer he could maintain his image as a noncombatant, the better. The fact that the goal here seemed to be to capture and not kill him was a significant improvement over his normal operating environment, where *everyone* wanted to kill him.

He moved from pillar to pillar, doing his best to stay in shadows that were moving targets as more spotlights ignited below. Muzzle flashes became visible in the building across the street, confirming his suspicion that the city's inhabitants were getting involved.

He'd been in situations like this before and they tended to get out of hand pretty quickly. Best to trade the expensive European suit for something more local and slip away in the coming chaos.

The sound of someone sprinting up the stairs became audible and he eased behind a pillar. Peering around it, Rapp saw that the breathless man who appeared on the landing was one of Faadin's. Whether that was a good or bad thing was hard to say. While it was possible that he'd just been quicker than the man assigned to kill him, it was also possible that he'd switched sides.

Rapp moved a little more to the right, allowing his arm to briefly catch a beam of light. The wind had kicked up a bit, creating a haze of concrete dust that reduced visibility and surrounded him with a scent that he'd come to associate with war zones all over the region.

"What's happening?" he said, affecting a panicked tone. "They killed Ismail!"

The man jerked around to face him, raising his AK-47 instead of coming to his aid. "Don't move!"

The words were in Arabic—easily understood by Mitch Rapp, but unintelligible to the Canadian attorney he was impersonating.

"Don't shoot!" he shouted, keeping his left hand in darkness as he raised it. The man never saw the gun, and with the searchlights it was doubtful he even noted the muzzle flash that killed him.

Not cleanly, though. The round hit him in the left pectoral, causing him to stagger back and clench his trigger finger. The rifle was pulled upward as it fired on full auto, raining down ricochets whenever a round found solid concrete above. Rapp hugged the pillar as the force of the bullets leaving the AK carried the man toward the edge of the floor slab. He teetered over the precipice for a moment, finally tipping into the gap between the building they were in and the ruin of the one next to it.

By the time Rapp released the pillar, the situation had further deteriorated. Voices were now audible below, along with running feet that had gained the floor directly beneath his position. Meanwhile, the gunfire outside was becoming more frequent and widespread, punctuated by two distinct explosions that weren't as distant as he'd like.

Rapp ran to the edge of the floor and looked down, spotting the body of the man he'd shot lying on a slab three levels below. An unknown number of men were on the stairs leading to the fifth floor, ascending fast with no attempt at stealth. Undoubtedly, they calculated that he was less of a threat than the fighting intensifying around them. The goal would be to capture him as quickly as possible and be long gone from Saraqib before the shit fully hit the fan.

Rapp estimated the gap between him and the partially collapsed fourth floor of the adjacent building at about fifteen feet, with a drop of about ten. Not ideal, but doable unless the whole thing gave way when he landed.

He backed up as far as he could without revealing himself to the men ascending the stairs and then sprinted forward. The edge was hard to discern exactly, but he got it more or less right. The stellar traction of his dress shoes launched him from the dusty surface and a moment later he was airborne.

The landing was more wrenching than he'd hoped, making it impossible to stay upright. Instead, he found himself rolling through the jagged debris, finally getting lucky when he came to a stop just short of a series of holes dropping to the level below.

Next door, he could hear chatter in Arabic and see the beams of rifle-mounted lights sweeping the area he'd jumped from. They'd found the bodies of Faadin and the man who'd killed him and were fanning out. One called out the name Matthieu Fournier and promised not to harm him if he showed himself.

Rapp slid on his stomach to the edge of the floor slab and looked down at a swarm of military vehicles that kept growing. Six men leapt from an armored personnel carrier and ran toward the building next door while taking fire from above. They made it safely inside thanks to the cover of a tracer-spewing chain gun that was pulverizing any position that looked even vaguely accommodating to a sniper.

The thirty or so men taking part in the operation were almost certainly the cream of Syria's spec ops crop and their vehicles looked like they'd just rolled out of the army's showroom. Clearly, the government was interested in having a sit-down with the infamous Matthieu Fournier, but not in the spirit of cooperation that Losa was promoting. If there was anything that the Syrians and Russians had in common, it was their insistence on doing everything the hard way.

A number of soldiers remained on the street, trying to set up a functional perimeter while a mob of locals inched closer. Their shouts were largely unintelligible, but their tone wasn't. They'd mistaken this operation for an attempt by the government to close its fist around Saraqib and they weren't going down without a fight.

Rapp slid back and dropped through a hole in the floor to the level below. Finding the stairs there more or less intact, he descended them. The walls of the space he found himself in were almost all missing, giving him a solid view of the hunt for him next door. Teams were moving systematically upward as they cleared their assigned areas, allowing him to peer down into the gap between the buildings without being seen.

Below, the man he'd shot had gone unnoticed and was still laid out on a concrete block jammed between support pillars. Rapp climbed down through the gap, with Syria's ubiquitous exposed rebar once again making his life better.

It took a couple of minutes to free the corpse, but he finally managed to get the body into a fireman's carry and climb back to the second level. Outside, the situation continued to deteriorate. To the east, the crowd now numbered as many as a hundred people and included everything from old women to young children. The west side had a similar group, maybe half the size, but growing. Sniper fire from surrounding buildings had been suppressed for the time being, but the Syrian forces were in danger of being surrounded.

Someone bounced a rock off a soldier's body armor, prompting him to fire a warning burst over the heads of the crowd. Anywhere else in the world that would have caused people to scatter, but in Saraqib it just made the mob angrier. More rocks flew, many thrown by kids caught up in the moment. Likely not much different than the spray-can-armed ones who had started the war in the first place.

Rapp removed the AK from the body and checked the magazine. While he was doing so, a sniper opened up from a building near the end of the street. Once again, the chain gun erupted and once again people who should have been running their asses off were instead emboldened.

The crowd closed in, backing the soldiers into a tight group with weapons pointed outward. Rapp had seen similar scenes play out in various countries across the world. All it would take was one solid hit on a soldier and they'd open up on the crowd. If the government forces didn't move on soon, this was going to turn into a bloodbath that the women and children in the mob would take the brunt of.

The problem was that they couldn't move on. Not until they'd captured Matthieu Fournier.

Rapp's jaw clenched and he stood motionless for a few seconds. Finally, he dropped the AK and backed up to give himself another running start. The gap between buildings wasn't as long at this level— maybe ten feet—and the debris in his landing zone was significantly more diffuse. Not that it made his reentry any more palatable, but escape no longer seemed like an option. This wasn't an Agency mission where collateral damage was an unavoidable by-product of pursuing the greater good. He was there representing the interests of a criminal cartel. He'd made the deal with Losa, and it wasn't these people's responsibility to pay for it.

Rapp managed to achieve a somewhat more graceful landing this time, jogging to a stop before tossing the pistol stuffed down the back of his pants.

"Don't hurt me! I'm unarmed! I swear!"

The randomly sweeping lights visible on the landing above froze for a moment and then refocused on the steps leading down to him.

Rapp tried to decide how a Canadian lawyer would behave in a situation like this and opted to drop to his knees. A little spit on his finger allowed him to create streaks in the dust beneath his eyes that would approximate the path of tears. Overly melodramatic? He'd soon find out. At least three Syrians were already charging down the stairs, blinding him with their rifle-mounted spots.

Rapp shrank from the glare, raising his hands. "Please! I don't have a gun! I swear! Don't hurt me!"

Apparently his performance was credible because he was immediately grabbed beneath the arms and dragged to the ground floor. Five men surround him as they broke into the open, protecting him from the rocks, chunks of concrete, and the occasional bottle arcing through the air.

He was hustled toward a Russian Tigr infantry vehicle parked across the street. They'd almost reached the rear doors when a single shot sounded from the east and one of the soldiers to his left went down.

Rapp was lifted completely off his feet and propelled forward at a full sprint as the men around him began shooting blindly into the mob. The Tigr was already starting to move when he was thrown in the back, followed by two operators. The driver floored it and the 4x4 surged into the street while one of the Syrians struggled to close the rear doors. He lost his grip when a dull thud rocked the vehicle, but managed to get hold of it just as the body of a civilian was spit out from beneath the rear tires.

The sound of gunfire was constant now, and one of the soldiers rose through a hole in the roof to man the machine gun there. He managed to get off a short burst, but then jerked left and sank back into the vehicle with a hole in the side of his head.

The driver made a hard turn and Rapp was slammed into one of the steel sides, ending up with the body on top of him.

"Stay down!" the surviving man shouted before taking control of the weapon.

Rapp was content to follow orders, lying on his back and holding the bleeding corpse on top of him to protect against any rounds that might penetrate the vehicle's armor. For the moment, everyone seemed to have the same goal: keeping Syria's favorite Canadian attorney alive.

CHAPTER 18

THE Tigr was a perfect example of Russian technology: all brute force and no subtlety. The massive wheels made short work of the badly rutted road, but the suspension felt like it had been pulled from a covered wagon. Every impact created a symphony of grinding rattles that suggested the entire thing was about to fall apart, but it muddled on.

The sun had cleared the horizon and was heating the steel enclosure at the back of the vehicle. In another hour or so, it would turn into an oven, but they didn't have that much longer. A shouted conversation between the driver and the surviving man in the back with Rapp suggested that they were running out of gas.

The space in front of the wheel well seemed to provide the smoothest ride, so Rapp and the Russian staring at him had commandeered one each. The body of the first gunner had been left to bounce around near the rear doors, where the blood still leaking from him could escape through a gap. Rapp finally averted his eyes, remembering that his situation would be downright traumatizing for Matthieu Fournier. A little meekness was in order.

They'd abandoned the paved highway at least an hour ago, when an RPG had detonated close enough to rock them onto two wheels. Potentially an indicator that word was out about what had happened in Saraqib. Insurgents would be organizing to harass fleeing government forces and see if they could set the country alight again.

Rapp turned and gazed through the tiny windows in the vehicle's rear doors. It was hard to see through the dust beyond, but sharp detail wasn't necessary. He'd operated in wastelands like these for his entire career.

Escape was certainly doable at this point. Kill the man across from him, take the AK-9 he was holding, and go through the open hole in the roof used to access the machine gun. Unfortunately, that course of action created more problems than it solved. He wasn't sure the 9x39mm rounds would penetrate the top of the cab and, even if they did, he had no water, no knowledge of the area, and apparently no gas.

Not ideal and not his mission. To the degree that *mission* was the right word for this shit show. Patience wasn't his strong suit, but for now exercising it seemed to be the best option. Claudia would say it was a good opportunity for a little self-improvement.

"We're stopping!" the driver yelled through the grate at the back of the cab. Rapp pretended not to understand and didn't react when the vehicle coasted to a halt. He heard the driver jump to the ground, and a moment later, the rear doors were pulled open.

They were parked about fifty feet from a single-story cinder-block building with an intact roof, empty window frames, and a front door with an improbable amount of red paint still clinging to it. About sixty yards to the south was a significantly larger building dominated by bay doors and a roof that had collapsed onto the second floor. Not from shelling, though. From neglect. The place looked like it had been abandoned for decades.

Rapp examined the fallow farmland around it, committing important details to memory. An irrigation ditch. A section of stone wall that looked like it had been raided for materials numerous times over the years. Clusters of dead trees with trunks too narrow to provide much in the way of cover.

As the man in the back with him jumped over his dead companion to the ground, Rapp realized that he'd been wrong about the place being abandoned. The red door in the house swung open and a moment later a malnourished family began walking hesitantly through it. The man in the lead had his hands out to demonstrate that he was unarmed and was saying something that Rapp couldn't make out. The woman in second position wore a dark abaya and was struggling to keep a curious toddler behind her.

From his position in the truck, Rapp was helpless to prevent what he knew would come next. The driver, armed with a suppressed AK-9, had moved left and was now out of sight, while his similarly armed companion had gone right. There was no way to get to them in time.

A muffled shot hit the young man and he immediately crumpled. His wife reacted by spinning toward her son, but pitched forward when the back of her head exploded. The blood-spattered child began to scream and run awkwardly across the broken ground, unsure what had just happened or where he should go.

Rapp's stomach clenched when the kid took a bullet between the shoulder blades. He landed face-first in the dirt, and then there was nothing. The sound of the breeze, the faint stench of gunpowder, and the creak of metal expanding in the sun.

The two men disappeared inside with one covering the other. They emerged a few moments later and jogged toward the other structure, clearing it in the same efficient, professional manner. The lack of gunfire suggested the young family had been the only people there—possibly having found it empty and deciding to take refuge there as they tried to survive what their country had become.

The soldiers motioned for Rapp to get out. It didn't seem like Matthieu Fournier would be anxious to do so under the circumstances, so instead he pressed himself up against the back of the cab, hiding his anger behind feigned fear. The driver jumped in, shouting angrily in Arabic before grabbing him by the hair and dragging him into the dirt.

Rapp assumed he'd be led into the house, but his luck wasn't that good. Instead, the driver pointed to the three bodies and began barking orders in individual English words, each less intelligible than the last. With the addition of an elaborate pantomime, it was made clear that Rapp had been charged with the task of disposing of the bodies. He let his expression slowly evolve from confusion to comprehension to horror, but didn't move until he was staring down the silencer of one of the AKs.

He made a point of huffing mightily as he dragged the woman's body toward the barn. Despite the intensifying heat, the Syrian driver followed alongside, unleashing every insult he could come up with that even vaguely related to Rapp, his family, or his country. His diatribe suggested that he was afraid the incident in Saraqib would reignite the war and that he'd end up right back on the front line.

The family's state of hunger made their corpses fairly light, and it wasn't long before Rapp had both the man and woman lying neatly in the shade of the barn. Dragging the boy's lifeless body would have been more in character for a Toronto lawyer, but he couldn't bring himself to do it. Instead he scooped him up and carried him through the heat to his parents.

Rapp's next task turned out to be to pull the Tigr into the barn, which he did with the appropriate amount of gear grinding. They weren't exactly in a high-traffic area, but his captors figured an abundance of caution was warranted. Support for government forces in this region would be spotty at best.

When Rapp finally was allowed to enter the relative cool of the house, he found the other man in the process of disconnecting a call on his satellite phone.

"The Russians are sending men in a civilian vehicle," he said in Arabic.

"Are they going to bring us enough fuel to get back?" the driver asked.

"No. They say that's our problem."

"Our problem? How many men did we lose in Saraqib? And how many more will we lose when the jihadists get another taste of our blood? The city's going to burn and do you know who's going to have to go in there and put it out? Not those old women from Russia. Us." He spat on the dirt floor. "If they wanted this Canadian bastard, they should have gotten him themselves."

The other man just shrugged, unimpressed by his comrade's outburst.

"So, we wait?"

"Yes. We wait. They say two hours."

Both looked in Rapp's direction, but he just stared blankly back at them.

"We should kill this piece of shit," the driver said. "Tell the Russians that he got hit on the way out."

The other man shook his head. "I just told General Khalaf that he's unharmed."

"Then we just sit here babysitting him for the next two hours and then walk home?"

"It's never that easy."

"What do you mean?"

"Damascus wants to know why the Russians are so anxious to get their hands on him."

"We . . . We get to interrogate him?" the driver said. Unlike his companion, he seemed to think his day had just significantly improved.

"Don't get too excited. We can't leave any marks on him. He belongs to the Russians."

"But *he* doesn't know that," the driver said, pulling his sidearm and pressing it to Rapp's forehead.

Rapp blubbered a bit as the other man started a recorder on his phone. It turned out his English was quite a bit better than his counterpart's.

"Why are you here?"

"My name is Matthieu Fournier! I—"

"I didn't ask your name, idiot! Answer my question or my friend here will pull his trigger."

"I represent Damian Losa. I'm here because he wants to help your government distribute captagon in Europe. Please! Don't kill me. I'm a lawyer. I'm just here to negotiate. I swear! I'll tell you anything you want to know. Just ask me."

The man nodded approvingly, and his comrade returned the MP-446 to his shoulder holster, indifferent to the fact that it was unsecured and within Rapp's reach.

Rapp didn't even bother to move quickly, reaching for the weapon and shooting its owner in the solar plexus before putting a round in his companion's forehead.

They both dropped, but the driver was still alive, gasping from the impact of the round against his light body armor.

"I'll give you the same chance you gave the kid," Rapp said in Arabic. "Run."

He didn't need to be told twice, immediately pushing himself to his feet and going for the door in a hunched sprint. Rapp walked to the threshold, watching him angle toward the crumbling stone wall that could cover his escape.

Rapp switched the weapon to his left hand and just stood there. With every step, the Syrian would see his odds of survival increasing. By the time he made it to the wall, he'd believe the shot was impossible—a moving target wearing body armor at a significant distance. Maybe he figured that Allah had smiled upon him and caused the gun to misfire. Or that his companion had miraculously survived and attacked the man stalking him. Either way, he'd be increasingly certain that he'd see his wife again. His children. Maybe even grow old.

The pistol was unfamiliar to Rapp and his first round went low and right, extracting a visible puff of pulverized rock from the wall the man was climbing over. His movements became more desperate as hope turned from motivator to tormentor. Rapp adjusted his aim and squeezed the trigger again. This time, he was rewarded with a subtle jerk of the man's head. He slumped over the barrier and went still just a few inches from salvation.

CHAPTER 19

R APP stood in the threshold to the house's back room examining its windowless interior. The crumbling walls and dirt floor were partially swallowed by shadow, as was the occupant of a straw mattress on the floor. The body wasn't one of the soldiers, but instead the man they'd murdered. Chest wounds were significantly easier to obscure than head wounds and a plastic bag stuffed in the bullet hole was all that had been necessary to stop it from seeping.

The corpse was bound, wearing Rapp's expensive suit, and lying on his back with his head turned toward the wall. Even in the tenuous light, he looked pretty dead, but it would be good enough. The Russians had been told they were here to pick up an uninjured prisoner and, in Rapp's experience, people saw what they expected to see.

Satisfied that the stage was set as well as it could be, he adjusted the Syrian army uniform he was wearing and returned to the house's living area. There he raked some uncontaminated earth over the bloody mud left by one of the men he'd killed. It didn't have to be perfect. The Russians weren't going to be studying the floor. The real problem was the smell. Blood in the heat of a poorly ventilated building was unmistakable. There was an outhouse in the back where he could find plenty of material to overpower it, though. Then it would just be a matter of waiting.

Rapp saw the dust plume well before the engine hum reached him. He rose from the overturned bucket he was sitting on, improving his view while still remaining in the sliver of shade clinging to the front of the house. Details became sharper as the SUV approached—sun-faded paint, windows tinted enough to obscure the people inside, a missing front bumper. The Russians were even less popular than the Syrian military in this part of the country and they'd wisely decided to keep a low profile.

Rapp leaned casually against the building's façade as the vehicle skidded to a stop and three men stepped out. All wore desert camo and flak jackets, and all were fairly bulky. The driver actually went beyond bulky and bordered on fat. His forearms were thick and tattooed where they were visible below rolled-up sleeves, but a little formless. Not Russian regular army or Spetsnaz. Almost certainly mercenaries.

Two were carrying AK-74s, while the man with the tattoos had only a sidearm strapped to his right thigh. One of the riflemen hung back behind the vehicle, eyes sweeping the scene confidently. The other two approached, not acknowledging the hand Rapp had raised in greeting. They seemed to have zero interest in him. Exactly as he'd hoped.

"Where is he?" one of them said in Russian-accented English.

Rapp waved them inside and pointed to the empty door frame at the back. The man with the pistol strode toward it with Rapp trailing. As expected, the other merc held back. They'd see the threats as being external, so it made more sense to post a man at the window than to hang together.

The fact that the mattress was positioned so that it was invisible from the living area didn't seem to bother the Russian as he crouched next to the corpse. Once clear of the jamb, Rapp slipped a knife from the sheath on his belt and came up behind the merc as if to help. Instead, he clamped a hand over his mouth and nose, and then buried the blade into the base of his skull. His body went stiff and then immediately slack, allowing him to be easily lowered to the dirt floor.

"Yes," Rapp said loudly, using the man's sleeve to wipe the blood from his knife. "The well has water. I will get some."

He hurried into the living area with a quick, nervous gait. The man posted there was positioned in a corner that gave him full view of both the room and the window. His rifle was slung across his chest with his right index finger resting just above the trigger.

Through the open front door, Rapp could see the man standing behind the vehicle, still sweeping in a way that let him take in both the buildings and the land around them.

"Do you want water?" Rapp asked, taking a few steps toward the man in the corner.

His brow knitted in a way that suggested he didn't understand, and Rapp used that as an excuse to continue his approach while pantomiming taking a drink with his empty hand. The other held the knife tucked out of sight against his forearm.

"Nyet."

Rapp continued to casually close the distance between them despite the fact that there was now no reason to. The man stiffening noticeably. When his finger started to slide toward the trigger, Rapp used his left hand to thrust the knife and his right to flip the AK's safety lever.

Frontal assaults tended to be messy, and this was no exception. The knife hit the man in the throat, but didn't incapacitate him. Very much the opposite. He lunged forward in a spray of blood, yanking the rifle to the left and desperately trying to fire. Rapp extracted the knife, increasing the flow of blood, but it wasn't enough to generate a quick death. The sight of the arterial flow created a violent physical reaction from the man. His strength multiplied, but his ability to use it intelligently deteriorated.

Rapp managed a foot sweep that put the man on his back before he could move into the sight line of the man outside. After that, he focused on keeping him there and staying close enough to diminish the leverage of his blows. The total time before the Russian finally went limp was less than a minute, but it felt like ten. Worse, Rapp ended up looking like he'd just butchered a cow with a chain saw.

Not ideal for part three of his admittedly half-assed plan. He'd hoped to walk casually to the well and get an angle on the man out front before he suspected anything. Casual strolls were definitely off the table and the remaining Russian was positioned in a way that made a kill shot from the house impossible.

Still, the clock was ticking. It wouldn't take long for the surviving man to notice that his comrades were missing and call out. Rapp didn't speak enough Russian to credibly respond, leaving him without any other option than another reckless frontal assault.

He picked up the AK and held it at eye level as he swung it around the jamb. His target was faster than he looked, immediately spotting the threat and dropping to the ground as a burst shattered the vehicle's side windows.

Rapp immediately charged from the house, sprinting toward the low wall to the east. Hopefully, he'd have more luck than the Syrian soldier whose body was stashed behind it.

The Russian started shooting, firing on full auto in generally the right direction, but finding it impossible to aim accurately. A few rounds got close, but by then Rapp was diving over a three-foot section of stacked stone. He hit the ground rolling, immediately coming up on one knee and aiming over the barrier. The Russian flattened himself against the SUV's door, his face covered in blood from the shards of glass embedded in his forehead.

Lucky, but not decisive. He was slipping toward the back of the vehicle and if he got there, he'd be in a good position to regroup. At that point, the battle could devolve into a stalemate. He'd have time to clear his vision and could keep moving in a way that kept the vehicle between them. Even worse, he might be able to circle to the driver's side and get inside. If the keys were in it, he could plausibly escape and leave Rapp with transportation options that consisted of a nearly empty Tigr and a pair of extraordinarily comfortable dress shoes.

With no viable alternative, Rapp leapt back over the wall and ran for a position where he could get a clean shot. The Russian heard the footfalls and panicked, turning to fire instead of continuing to circumnavigate the vehicle.

It was a fatal mistake. Rapp dropped to his stomach, lining up a shot as he skidded through a patch of dry weeds. When he finally came to a halt, he squeezed off a quick burst that hit the man in the center of his ballistic vest. The impact caused him to fall backward against the SUV's rear fender and his rifle barrel rose, sending rounds harmlessly into the sky.

Rapp steadied his weapon as the man tried to get his feet back under him. The sights had been dialed in nicely and his next shot struck the Russian just under his right eye.

CHAPTER 20

THE helicopter followed the contours of the arid land below, maintaining a velocity near its limit. General Aleksandr Semenov was its only passenger, sitting in a thick leather seat that would have been more at home in a private jet than the Mil Mi-24 gunship. He'd isolated his headphones from the chatter of the pilots and was instead listening to Tchaikovsky's Third Symphony at a volume loud enough to nearly drown out the thump of the blades.

Through the widow, he could see the sun sinking toward the horizon and it infuriated him. He should have been in his living quarters enjoying a fine meal and looking forward to another intriguing evening with his new toy, Alea. The fact that he was being forced to involve himself personally in this situation was yet another reminder of how rare competence was in the modern world.

In the distance, two columns of smoke became visible, twisting together and then dispersing in the deepening blue of the sky. Semenov sank a little farther into the leather cradling him and focused on enjoying his last few moments with Pyotr Ilyich. Time to conjure some semblance of calm and remind himself that his influence was still limited. Some level of cooperation with the locals—no matter how distasteful and frustrating—was necessary. Until he had the power to clear the board, the game had to be played.

His chopper described a wide arc around the source of the smoke, allowing Semenov to study the scene. Two smoldering buildings, blackened and largely collapsed. A mix of no fewer than ten military and civilian vehicles with a commensurate number of men. Those wearing silver fire suits were sifting through the remains of the structures and operating construction vehicles in close proximity. Others, identifiable by their uniforms as Syrian security forces, were combing the nearby land, occasionally planting flags to denote some discovery. Beyond that, there was no sign of human habitation for kilometers.

They set down at a distance that wouldn't disturb the operation and a jeep immediately approached. Semenov didn't return the salute of the Syrian colonel, instead climbing in the back of the vehicle and allowing himself to be whisked to the center of activity.

Kifah Atfeh, the head of the Syrian Intelligence Directorate, had chosen a business suit over his uniform and didn't seem any happier to be there than Semenov himself. The dust and smoke clung to him as he approached, but he didn't seem to notice. Not surprising. After all, he'd grown up in this shithole of a country.

"Good afternoon, General," he said in English.

"What happened here, Kifah?"

A flash in the man's eyes suggested that he registered Semenov's dismissiveness, but he was unwilling to further react to the slight. Intelligence directors were the same all over the world. Backstabbers, liars, and bootlickers.

"Our men in Saraqib came under heavy attack, but they managed to get your man out of the city safely. One was killed during the operation, but the other two brought him here to turn him over to your people. It appears they were ambushed."

"By whom?"

"We're still investigating. The bodies have been burned beyond recognition. I think we can say with some confidence that three of them are the men you sent and three are our people. The other three are a matter of speculation and one appears to be a child. Perhaps they were part of the trap or perhaps just bystanders."

"How did the insurgents know our people were coming?"

Atfeh shrugged. "It's possible they were able to decrypt our communications. Or they followed the vehicle with drones or spies. Or perhaps one of your men or mine was being paid. If you are so interested in this man Matthieu Fournier, is it possible that other powerful parties are as well?"

Obviously, the answer was yes. Damian Losa was both interested and powerful. But this powerful? Did he have the Syrian resources to orchestrate something like this?

"As you can see, we have more work to do," the Syrian continued. "But already the events of the day are becoming clear." He pointed to a low rock wall. "We found a number of spent cartridges there and also to the north under the cover of a tree. Melted casings were also found in both buildings. Any vehicle pulling up would have been in a very disadvantaged position. The moment the passengers stepped out they would have found themselves in a cross fire with no practical place to take cover. We suspect that our men were immediately taken out and then the same happened to your men when they arrived."

"Why?" Semenov asked, doing his best to hide his impatience and frustration. For the time being, he needed this idiot.

"Why what?"

"Why would these attackers wait to do battle with my men? After rescuing Fournier, why wouldn't they leave?"

"The most plausible explanation is that they needed your people's vehicle for transportation. It's missing, but the Tigr my men arrived in was burned inside one of the buildings. It was nearly out of fuel and, as you can see, there are few places to conceal something that large."

While it was indeed plausible, Semenov was wholly unsatisfied by the explanation. Anyone clever enough to pull off this rescue wouldn't leave something like that to chance. They'd have had transportation arranged before the first bullets flew.

"Damascus might be willing to accept that theory, but I'm not. It's my understanding that you've been given a description of the SUV my people arrived in. If it's not here, where is it? Are you doing anything to try to find it?"

The Syrian intelligence chief shook his head. "We don't have the manpower. Particularly now that the operation you demanded has caused the security situation in Saraqib to collapse. If we don't allocate all our resources there, we could lose the entire city."

"Then you're going to lose the city!" Semenov shouted. "Why did you have any control over it in the first place? Why do you even have a country? If it weren't for Russian support, the corpses of you, your family, and your president would be swinging from light poles. But we don't have to stay. If you prefer, we can leave you to the mercy of your people and to the international criminal courts."

Atfeh affected a smile with the appropriate amount of subservience. "Of course, we have nothing but love and gratitude for our Russian brothers. But I'll have to get authorization from my superiors."

"Then do it, Kifah. Do it now."

CHAPTER 21

RAPP hung his arm out the SUV's window as he wove through a light mix of cars, pedestrians, and bicycles. Night had fallen sometime ago and the bombed-out buildings on either side of the road were completely dark. The only lights not attached to vehicles were the ones set up to illuminate incongruously well-tended billboards depicting Syria's president.

He glanced at the sky, first through the windshield and then through the glassless side window. Nothing but stars, as near as he could tell, but it was impossible to be sure. Both the Syrians and Russians seemed dead set on finding him and would be armed with a detailed description of the Toyota he was driving.

Having said that, there were a few things working in his favor. First, he'd gone to great lengths to create the illusion of a battlefield at the farm he'd been taken to. Based on the shell casing distribution, bloodstains, and blackened bodies he'd left behind, the obvious conclusion would be that Damian Losa had sent a team to rescue him. And while the evidence wouldn't hold up under close scrutiny, it would be deemed more plausible than the alternative: a blubbering Toronto attorney taking out five armed operators.

Rapp's second advantage was that it sounded like Saraqib was literally blowing up. Based on some gossip he'd overheard at a food stand an hour ago, government forces had both taken and inflicted significant losses during their hasty retreat. Now violent protests were spreading through the country, threatening to reignite the civil war. Damascus and their masters in Moscow would have every reason to put the matter of Matthieu Fournier on the back burner for the moment.

Traffic became heavier as he entered the city of Aleppo and habitable buildings replaced the ruins farther out. To the west, one of the largest and oldest castles in the world hovered in the beams of a handful of still-functioning spotlights. It turned out to be a useful landmark in a city that had been transformed since his last visit. Even in areas that were more or less intact, roads had been rerouted, off-ramps had collapsed, and neighborhoods had been leveled. Overall, though, it felt surprisingly vibrant. People strode instead of shuffling, restaurants were in full operation, and locals milled around open squares, laughing and occasionally even breaking into song.

What hadn't yet returned were the sophisticated surveillance cameras favored by dictators worldwide. Countries like Saudi Arabia and China were becoming impossible to operate in anonymously, but here he didn't have to be quite as concerned. Further, he'd found some clothing belonging to the man the Syrians had murdered, and it turned out to be a passable fit. Combined with his dark complexion, beard, and native-level Arabic, there was no longer much to distinguish him in this part of the world.

He passed through the center of town and continued through to the other side. It wasn't long before the darkness closed in again and he found himself surrounded by the familiar collapsed façades and hastily cleared rubble that he'd come to associate with Syria. When he was reasonably certain that he was alone, he turned the SUV onto a carpet of shattered concrete leading into a building with a roof that was still hanging on.

A small cloth bag contained his Canadian passport, the ID of the Syrian soldier who'd looked most like him, and all the cash he'd collected from his attackers' bodies. After retrieving it from the back and stuffing it down the front of his pants, he tossed the ignition key on the dashboard and stepped out into the breezy evening.

By morning, the SUV would be gone and by afternoon it would be chopped up for parts that would be shipped all over the country. At that point, Matthieu Fournier would cease to exist.

Rapp took a position at the back of a line snaking across one of Aleppo's largest squares. Not far away, a group of kids were playing drums and belting out an English-language pop song with a level of enthusiasm that made up for their lack of skill. They were a diverse group, with boys favoring jeans and T-shirts emblazoned with Western brands, and girls wearing everything from bulky dresses with headscarves to knee-length skirts with tights. Another reminder of Syria's baffling complexity.

When his turn at the food stand came, he bought a grilled cob of corn and then wandered to a less popular vendor specializing in pre-paid cell phones. After a bit of haggling, he managed to get three for forty dollars and the elated seller threw in a hot-pink case that didn't fit any of them.

Rapp took a seat on a wall between the singing kids and a group of men arguing about everything under the sun. The noise would cover up his conversation and the commotion would make him fade into the background. He finished his corn and tossed the empty cob into a trash can before unwrapping a phone. After dialing a number from memory, he listened to it ring a few times before Damian Losa's assistant answered in English.

"Yes?"

"I'm still alive, Julian. Is he in?"

"One moment. I'm putting you through."

Rapp glanced in the direction of a distant explosion, but was the only person in the square who seemed to care. Losa came on a moment later.

"It's good to hear from you. My understanding is that your meeting went poorly."

"You could say that."

"My people are dead?"

"Faadin is for sure. I can't say for sure about the others. At least one switched sides."

"Difficult to avoid in Syria. Even for me. I was told you were captured."

"That's right. By Syrian forces working for the Russians. They took me to a safe house with the idea of turning me over. Three mercs came to pick me up."

"But you had other plans."

"Yes."

"Were you able to question them?"

"It wasn't practical. And they wouldn't have known anything. Just muscle."

"But presumably they would have taken you to someone who *did* know something."

Rapp smiled at the veiled reprimand. "Probably. But I don't think that would have gone all that well for me."

"So, what you've managed to accomplish is to get some of my people killed, cause Saraqib to collapse back into open hostilities, and kill a handful of government operatives from two separate countries. A busy day, but not a particularly productive one."

"I disagree," Rapp said as the kids stopped singing and entered into negotiations about what their next number would be. "The Russians aren't people who play to win. They play to make everyone else lose. They don't do anything useful. They don't make anything useful. If you gave a Russian a Ferrari, he wouldn't drive it. He'd use the key to scratch the paint on everybody else's car. Even under the best circumstances you don't want to get in bed with these pricks. And they just made it clear that these aren't the best of circumstances."

"No?"

"No. They could have negotiated in good faith and heard you out. But they didn't. They rolled in with the calvary and tried to snatch me. Why? I can't think of any reason other than to interrogate me about you and your operation."

There was a lengthy pause before Losa responded. "I agree that the Russians are less than ideal partners. They tend to seek power for the sake of power even when it's counter to their interests. Having said that, I've managed to forge profitable relationships with them in the past. It's just a matter of convincing them to resist their nature."

"My gut says walk away," Rapp said. "And my gut's usually pretty accurate."

"I don't think we're in a position to make that determination yet and you haven't fulfilled your obligation to me. I gave you Claudia's life and you've given me nothing in return. If you're right and one of the most powerful countries in the world wants to destroy my European operation, I need to know how, where, and when. Without that kind of information, I have no way of defending myself."

"I understand what I agreed to," Rapp said. "But you're going to have to give me a little more direction. I can't just wander around Syria waiting to bump into a Russian who wants to do business with you. That wastes both our time."

"Point taken. I still have a few reliable people in Syria. Let me re-tool a bit and see what I can come up with."

Rapp powered down the phone and stood. When the kids started singing again, he started diagonally across the square.

CHAPTER 22

D AMIAN Losa put his phone down on the sofa, while Julian remained glued to his chair, staring intently at his laptop and manipulating a detached mouse. Through the glass walls of the atrium, the shadowy outlines of security personnel melted from the carefully tended landscaping and then disappeared again. The dogs were a bit harder to pick out—low and sleek, they seemed to instinctively stay in the shadows.

Even combined with the state-of-the-art electronics that he'd had installed, it suddenly felt insufficient. Particularly while sitting on display in the elegant glass cage he'd come to favor. During the violent years of his rise to power, he'd valued security above all things. Later, his unprecedented success had allowed him to relax those protocols somewhat. He made so much money for so many people, potential threats tended to be exposed and dealt with long before they posed any real danger.

Was that still true?

"He didn't return to Saraqib," Julian said, breaking him from his trance. "The call was made from Aleppo."

Not surprising. Based on the reports they were receiving, no sane person would return to Saraqib if they were lucky enough to have escaped. Aleppo was a logical choice. It was reasonably stable, had functioning infrastructure, and was bordered by abandoned areas that someone like Rapp could disappear into.

Losa walked to an ornate sideboard to refill his Perrier. As he began slicing a fresh wedge of lime, Julian spoke up again.

"What do the Russians want?"

"People have been asking that for centuries and I don't think anyone's come up with a satisfactory answer."

"Money?"

"No. The men who matter there already have it. By some measures, I imagine that President Utkin is the wealthiest man in the world."

"Respect then? The destruction of their perceived enemies?"

"The destruction of their enemies, yes. Respect might not be the right sentiment, though. Fear."

What he'd told Rapp about his interactions with the Russians was only half true. Many years ago, he'd done business with the Russian mob. The partnership had been less about money than expanding his contacts across the globe, but even then the cost had been greater than the benefit. The men he'd been forced to collaborate with—even the ones in the higher echelons—had been beset by substance abuse problems, mental instability, and sometimes outright death wishes. Violence for them wasn't a means to an end, but a way of life. Fleeting entertainment for men who woke up every day expecting that it would be their last.

In many ways the Russian government was no different. Grander in scale for sure, but at its core just another dysfunctional crime family. Antiquated, inefficient, and unpredictable.

"So how do they plan on achieving those goals?" Julian asked, glancing over the top of his laptop.

"Rapp was right when he said the Russians play to make every-one else lose. Did you know that Boris Utkin wrote his master's thesis on how his country was squandering their natural resources by using them for economic benefit? In his mind, they were much better allo-cated as a weapon against the West. Make the Europeans dependent on Russian energy and then use that dependence to dominate them."

"Meaning?"

"Maybe this drug is the same. Not a business designed to provide profits—"

"But a tool to inflict damage on Europe," Julian said, finishing his thought.

Losa nodded. "One of the few tools they have left. Their conven-tional military capability has proven to be third-rate and Europe is well on its way to permanently replacing Russian energy imports. Utkin has doomed his country to irrelevance, and with no way out of the hole he's dug, his only option is to drag the West down with him."

"So, they release a highly addictive narcotic in Europe at a finan-cial loss to overburden their social services. And they use a Muslim distribution network to try to feed authoritarians and nationalists who tend to support the breakup of the European Union."

"I wonder if it's even worse than that. Now that we know that the Russians are the ones developing the new captagon formulation, I'm suspicious about the compounds we can't identify. They're too expen-sive and difficult to manufacture to not be intentional. And since the Russians' only purpose is destruction, we have to assume they exist for that reason. Further, it's hard to imagine that they won't want to ex-tend this operation to the US. While Europe might be their geographic enemy, America is their existential one."

"And our US network would be perfect. Not only because of how extensive it is, but because it has such a strong Latino component. Like with Muslims in Europe, the xenophobia against migrants already ex-ists in America. Russia just needs to further fan the flames."

Losa lowered himself back onto the sofa and stared into his crystal glass for a moment. "Interesting, but at this point nothing more than speculation. If Rapp had been able to sit down with them, we'd know more."

"More likely they'd torture him for information that they could use to get to us and our American assets."

"Agreed. But Rapp doesn't know anything. There's nothing particularly useful he could give them under duress. At worst he dies. At best he learns something valuable and then does what he does best: kills everyone involved and escapes."

"You told him you were going to contact reliable people who could help him," Julian said, starting to look worried. "I'm not aware of us having any reliable people left. And we certainly don't have contacts inside Russia's Syrian command."

"True."

"You want to betray him."

"What I want is for him to meet with the Russians like he agreed. If we have to facilitate that meeting, then so be it."

"Dangerous," Julian observed. "If he lives, he might try to retaliate against us. And if he dies, we could have Irene Kennedy to deal with."

Losa shrugged. "He's a lone man in a country he has limited experience operating in. The Syrians were willing to destroy Saraqib to get to him. With that kind of motivation, it's certainly plausible that they could find him without our help. In light of that, it seems like any retaliation would be aimed at Moscow or Damascus. Not us."

"I can turn over what we have on Rapp's location to the Syrians," Julian said. "But I'm not sure I agree with your strategy. The risks are clear. But the rewards are less so."

Losa nodded. "I'm afraid that's where we've landed, my friend. On a path where every turn leads to disaster."

CHAPTER 23

THE restaurant was about as informal as they came, but still packed many hours after sunset. The owners had taken advantage of an abandoned ruin by shoring up its remaining floors and converting them into balconies. A few hundred feet of fairy lights had been placed around the missing façade for ambience and to illuminate the charcoal grills that were the establishment's draw.

And for good reason, Rapp reflected as he gnawed a chunk of lamb from a wooden skewer. Great food was one of the things he'd always associated with Syria. Oddly, the other was stability. While unquestionably brutal, the government had managed to create a Middle Eastern country that didn't take Islam too seriously and let people find their own path unmolested. Unless that path was political opposition, of course. In that case, they and their families would be on the fast track to an early grave.

Rapp pointed to one of the smoke-enshrouded grill masters and held up a couple of fingers. His request was answered by a thumbs-up and he soon had two more skewers on his plate. This time chicken. It was all about the marinade and this place had it dialed.

He dug in, keeping an eye on the pedestrians picking their way through seating that had sprawled all the way across the street. A beer would have helped put a little perspective on his situation, but it turned out not to be an option. While Syria was in some ways known for its cultural flexibility, that rarely extended to alcohol.

Not that it would have made much of a difference. It would take something a lot stronger than an IPA to make him any less suspicious of Losa's new plan. He would have led with his best people, and finding a reasonable Russian to negotiate with wasn't likely. In Syria, they'd be about as plentiful as unicorns.

Claudia's description of Losa as an evil reflection of Irene Kennedy kept turning over in his mind. What would Kennedy—unbound by sentiment, loyalty, or patriotism—do in this situation? How would she view an utterly expendable operative with no information that could be useful to the enemy?

It wasn't a difficult question to answer. She'd throw him to the wolves.

Worst-case scenario, Rapp would be tortured for everything he knew about the criminal mastermind—essentially nothing—and end up dead. Best-case scenario, he would manage to make a case for a business partnership or escape with intel on the players and their plans. If the latter played out, it'd be hard to prove that Losa had betrayed him, so Rapp would end up just handing over what he'd learned and calling it even.

If Losa's plans did indeed include handing him over to the Russians, Rapp saw that as well beyond the parameters of the debt he owed. While it was true that he was good at withstanding torture and making improbable escapes, it wasn't exactly his favorite pastime. And if Losa decided to go one step further and bargain away Rapp's true identity, things would get exciting fast.

In light of that, an experiment was in order.

With his sixth skewer stripped clean, Rapp lit a cigarette and studied a man who had just appeared around a corner to the north. They were about the same height and had the same longish hair, but the approaching Syrian wore a much longer beard and carried a prominent gut. Not bad, but something better would come along.

It took another fifteen minutes and two more cups of tea, but Rapp finally spotted what he was looking for. The man was a bit younger than him and appeared to be a rough customer, but he had about the right build, hair, and beard. Even better, he seemed somewhat oblivious to the canvas bag he had slung over one shoulder. An insurgent whose appearance would be enough to dissuade pickpockets and other ne'er-do-wells. Rapp, however, wasn't so easily put off.

He turned on the phone he'd used to call Losa and slapped some cash down on the table before standing to follow the man. When the crowd thinned a bit, Rapp picked up his pace, coming alongside his target. At that point, it was a simple matter to drop the phone in his bag and veer unnoticed down a side street.

Rapp held his surprisingly durable dress watch to his face, barely managing to make out the hands. Four in the morning. Temperatures had dropped into what he guessed were the low sixties, causing the cold to sink into him more deeply than he'd like. Not surprising in that he'd been lying motionless in a pile of rubble for hours now, keeping vigil over a bullet-pocked building across the street.

Inside, the man now in possession of his phone appeared to be asleep. He'd entered through the front door a little after midnight, and less than a minute later a light had gone on in a second-floor window. It stayed lit for only a short time, suggesting that he'd gone to bed without discovering the addition to the contents of his bag. What that meant was yet to be seen.

There was no activity on the narrow street and there probably wouldn't be until sunrise brought the city back to life. Rapp was in a good position to watch the building without being spotted, but once daylight broke, he'd have to retreat. Not only because he would be visible from the street, but because the icebox he'd spent the night in would quickly turn into a furnace.

After that, he wasn't sure. Being separated from Irene Kennedy and her army of eggheads created an intelligence black hole that he despised operating in. Who was the man he'd chosen purely because of their superficial resemblance? Did he go to work every morning? Where? Did he have a wife and children in the building? Other family? Did he have electronics that could be hacked or associates that could be bribed?

No way to know. It was Losa's move. Would he make it?

Rapp had to wait only another twenty minutes for that question to be answered. He'd sunk into a half doze, when he spotted movement with his partially closed right eye. Just a shadow at first, it quickly morphed into a human outline as it approached. An early-rising local? No. The movement was too quiet and purposeful.

His analysis was confirmed when the figure dropped to one knee and began working to open the door Rapp was watching. A couple of minutes later, he stood and pulled a pistol from a holster hidden in the small of his back. The movement prompted five more men to materialize, two from the east and three from the west. Whether they were Russian or Syrian was impossible to tell, but they weren't making the same mistakes as were made in Saraqib. All were silent, wearing civilian clothes, and had forgone rifles in favor of handguns. Night-vision gear didn't go on until right before they entered.

It was a smooth, but not particularly quick, operation. While his phone could be confidently traced to the building, there would be no way to drill down on which apartment. The team would be forced to systematically clear them until they found their target.

Eventually, two men reappeared in the doorway, guiding a third with bound hands and a bag over his head. They'd barely set foot in the street when a car glided up with the back door already open. Also silent. Rapp recognized it as an electric model made by the Chinese company BYD.

The prisoner was shoved in the back, followed by his two chaperones, and the vehicle pulled away. The remainder of the incursion team appeared a few seconds later, melting back into the darkness they'd emerged from.

Despite the fact that the temperature continued to fall, Rapp felt a strange warmth spread through him. He leaned his head back against a concrete block with a smile playing at his lips. There could be no doubt about who had given up the existence of that phone. Only one call had ever been made from it. To Damian Losa.

Rapp had agreed to help the cartel leader with his Syrian captagon problem. Not to be betrayed and handed over to the Russians. As far as he was concerned, his debt was now paid.

He stood and picked his way back to the street before turning toward the city center. It wouldn't take long for an experienced interrogator to figure out that the man they'd captured wasn't Canadian, wasn't a lawyer, and had never heard of Damian Losa.

Best to be safely home before that happened.

CHAPTER 24

FLUSH with cash from his Russian and Syrian victims, Rapp had chosen a reasonably upscale clothing shop. The bathroom in back also served as a dressing room and he took full advantage. Using the shirt he'd spent the night in as a makeshift washcloth, he cleaned up with water from the sink and then used a pair of scissors to cut his hair into what he'd determined to be the most common local style. An electric clipper he'd bought completed the job by bringing his beard in line with the minimalist look favored by Syrian men.

After putting on a pair of tan slacks and a loose-fitting cotton shirt, he examined himself in the mirror. Not exactly a miraculous transformation, but also not bad. He was now about as generic as he could reasonably get. Neither short nor particularly tall. Average build. Not wealthy, but also not wondering where his next meal was coming from. In the context of Aleppo, a man who would be easily forgotten and difficult to describe.

The only article of the clothing remaining from his entry into Syria was the shoes. He couldn't bring himself to give them up and justified that decision by telling himself that they were now too beat-up to draw attention.

Rapp tossed his old clothes in a garbage can and emerged to the approving expression of the shop's owner.

"A significant improvement!" he said, circling Rapp to check the fit of his pants. "This is what I do in this shop. It's what my father did. As they say, clothes make the man. You are once again a respectable member of society."

But not for much longer if Rapp had anything to do with it. The plan was to put this country in his rearview mirror as soon as possible. Forty-eight hours at the most. Twenty-four would be better.

He pulled the appropriate amount of cash from a leather bag slung across his body and the man exchanged it for a piece of notebook paper.

"This is what you were asking for. The woman's name is Cala, and the address isn't far from here. Easy to find—I drew a map on the back. Her husband was killed in the war, and she makes money taking in boarders. Her house is not luxurious, mind you, but her prices are fair, and I understand it's clean and well equipped."

Rapp thanked the man and exited onto a busy thoroughfare that bisected one of Aleppo's main retail areas. Donning a pair of sunglasses against the morning sun, he found a less trafficked side street and continued along it until he reached an uninhabited area. Once satisfied that he was alone, he unwrapped a new phone from its packaging and turned it on. The number he dialed was from well-worn memory, almost as familiar as the voice that answered.

"Hello?"

Irene Kennedy's greetings tended to be purposely generic when picking up the line that only they knew existed.

"How've you been?"

There was a short pause before she responded. "Better now that I hear your voice. Since I don't recognize this number, can I assume that you're not at home?"

"Still in-country. My new friend sold me out to the Russians."

"The Russians?"

"That's who's behind the new captagon trade in Europe. It's worth looking into. The formulation's apparently not normal and if the Russians are involved, I think we can assume they're going to break some dishes with it."

"It is what they do best," Kennedy agreed. "I'll see if my European counterparts have any information. But, in truth, your new employer is in a better position to collect that kind of intelligence than they are."

"He can do it without me. I didn't sign on to be set up."

"Are you looking for an exit?"

"Yeah. Any chance you can give me an assist?"

"For obvious reasons, I can't involve myself or America in this, Mitch." She paused for a few seconds. "The Israelis on the other hand . . ."

"Quneitra?" Rapp said, referring to a crossing between the Syrian- and Israeli-controlled parts of the Golan Heights. It was managed by the UN Disengagement Observer Force with only nominal US participation.

"That was my thought. Can you get there?"

"Shouldn't be a problem."

"I'll call Ben and see if we can set something up."

Rapp frowned. Ben in this case was Colonel Ben Friedman, the head of the Mossad. Unquestionably dedicated and competent, but also a bit of a prick who got off fanning the flames of hatred between Israel and its neighbors. Years ago, he'd unilaterally ordered the destruction of a nuclear research facility in Iran, creating the potential for a confrontation that could have dragged in half the countries in the region. Rapp had managed to convince the Iranians and the rest of the world that the explosion was the work of an internal resistance group, averting a potential war and pulling Friedman's fat out of the fryer. But it had been touch and go.

Kennedy correctly interpreted Rapp's silence as reticence.

"He owes us."

"I wonder if he sees it that way."

"It would have been better if you hadn't shot him in the leg."

"He had it coming."

"I don't disagree, but sometimes a little restraint goes a long way."

"That was restraint. I wanted to aim at his forehead."

Kennedy's sigh sounded like digitized static over the connection. "I don't see a better option. Let me talk to him and I'll get back to you. I assume this number won't work?"

"No. I'll call you."

"Do you still have that Canadian passport?"

"Yes."

"Give me a few hours."

Rapp disconnected the call and used a rock to destroy the phone.

He would have time for a proper shower and a little home-cooked food before setting out for the Israeli border. With a little luck, he'd be spending the night at the Royal Beach Hotel in Tel Aviv before catching the first plane back to the States. Or maybe he'd book a suite and fly Claudia and Anna over. The kid had never seen the Holy Land and he knew people who could open a lot of interesting doors. She'd crush the other second graders in her What-I-Did-on-Summer-Vacation report. And while Claudia would undoubtedly argue that it wasn't a competition, flying over Masada in a fighter jet seemed like a guaranteed A.

CHAPTER 25

DAMIAN Losa gazed distractedly at the interior study's heavy wood paneling. In the château's heyday, he imagined that the room was used by servants for the hidden tasks that maintained their masters' opulent lifestyle. Although it was less comfortable than the atrium he'd become accustomed to, it still had a certain archaic charm. Particularly with the modern air-conditioning set to maximum and the fireplace roaring.

He took a sip of water and then turned his attention to the flames. Normally, this late hour was his time to think. The silence and stillness always helped him consolidate what he knew and, more important, what he didn't know. It gave him a moment to analyze his position on the chessboard and to consider threats, both new and old. Most of all, it was a time to put aside the details in favor of a longer view.

Tonight, that view remained hazy. All roads seemed to lead into darkness. Oblivion. The dim glimmers of opportunity that he was such a prodigy at discerning had disappeared.

The modern world was becoming less rational with every passing year. In a way, it was a bizarre side effect of humanity's success. The advance of technology had transformed problems that seemed insurmountable only a few years ago into minor inconveniences. Food in the industrialized world was plentiful and of high quality, as were housing, medical care, energy, transportation, and virtually anything else a person could want. Even the poorest Frenchman enjoyed a quality of life that would have been unimaginable to the kings of the past.

The problem was that *everything* wasn't something his species was meant to have. The human condition was about striving and identity—instincts that didn't just disappear when identity became meaningless and there was nothing left to strive for.

What an irony that he had become the hero of humanity's continuing story. While world leaders and the media stoked rage and division, he'd taken a more constructive path. He just wanted to help his fellow man mask that quiet desperation. To wash away the pain, loneliness, and uncertainty.

Of course, his motivations weren't entirely benevolent. He'd involved himself in businesses like arms dealing in the past, but it had never been his focus. Drugs, sex, gambling, and the like were so much more profitable and productive. It was yet another irony that politics and religion were considered virtues, while the things he provided were labeled as vices. He didn't start wars or fan the flames of hatred. He'd never involved himself in genocide, threatened nuclear Armageddon, or destroyed a rainforest. All he did was sell candy-coated nihilistic hedonism. A much-derided vocation that might just be humanity's only hope.

There was a quiet knock at the door and Losa heard Julian's footsteps approaching from behind. When he came into view, his head and shoulders were hanging in a way that was easily identifiable after all their years together. Not bad news. Disastrous news.

"Yes?"

"We had to pay a great deal, but I finally managed to get a photo of the man the Syrians captured in Aleppo."

Losa held out a hand and his lieutenant gave him an iPad. The man depicted on it bore only a passing resemblance to Mitch Rapp.

"Omar Salim," Julian said. "The phone Rapp called us on was found in his flat during the raid. It was in a bag he'd been carrying that day, but he swears he doesn't know where it came from. The Syrian interrogators believe he's telling the truth."

Losa nodded slowly, continuing to examine the terrified eyes staring at him from the tablet.

"Apparently Mr. Rapp doesn't consider us trustworthy."

"For good reason," Julian said, not bothering to hide his concern.

But was that concern justified? It was something Losa had carefully considered when betraying the American. Historically, Mitch Rapp wasn't a man prone to expending energy on petty revenge. It was a philosophy Losa himself shared. Killing needed to serve a tangible purpose. Neutralizing threats, setting examples, eliminating competitors. But emotional satisfaction? That was for psychopaths and amateurs—two things Mitch Rapp was not.

"What now?" Julian asked, further unnerved by Losa's silence. "He must suspect that we were the ones who gave the Syrians information about that phone. What will he do? We can't even make contact because that was the only number we had for him."

Losa put down his drink and sank a bit deeper into his chair. "My assumption is that he considers his debt paid. Now he'll contact Kennedy or perhaps Claudia Gould to help him escape Syria. If he hasn't alrea—"

"And then?"

"And then we find ourselves in the same situation that we were in before. We've gained nothing."

"Except making an enemy of a man who tends not to tolerate them."

Losa shook his head. "I don't think so."

"I disagree, Damian. I think this is just another example of this situation slipping from our control."

"Not just this situation, my friend. Our adage has always been grow or die. But what happens when you succeed? Eventually, you create an empire that becomes too far-reaching to rule. If history's taught us anything, it's that."

"You're not making me feel better."

Losa laughed. "No, I suppose not. Let's spread some money around Syria and the countries bordering it. See if we can reacquire our new friend."

"And if we do?"

"I don't know," Losa admitted. "We'll cross that bridge when we get to it. In the meantime, we should continue with our plan to move. Were you able to determine whether the Prague property is available?"

"Yes, but it's only partially furnished."

"Then it'll be just like when we started, Julian. Remember the warehouse in Medellín?"

"Not fondly."

"No, but we've never used that flat and our involvement in its ownership would be virtually impossible for even Irene Kennedy to uncover. Until we can be sure of Mr. Rapp's intentions, I can't think of a better place."

"But will it be enough?"

Losa shrugged. "We'll soon find out."

CHAPTER 26

THE dilapidated motorbike wasn't the fastest or most comfortable mode of transportation, but it was the best Rapp had been able to do with what was left of his cash. Fortunately, he'd convinced the seller to throw in a leather jacket that was his only protection against the cold. It was nearly three in the morning and temperatures had dropped into the fifties.

The road was empty at that time of morning, as was the moonlit landscape that surrounded it. A few scattered buildings were visible on either side, but none gave any indication of being occupied. Most likely they'd been abandoned when their owners realized they were living on a battlefront that could erupt at any moment.

A glimpse of artificial light ahead prompted him to push the motorbike a little harder. A few minutes later, the massive wire fence splitting the Golan Heights became visible along with a number of Syrian military vehicles. The crossing normally closed at six p.m., but could be opened for emergencies. Those were normally medical in nature but, in this case, it was something a bit unusual.

There was little question that the Syrian government was pulling out all the stops to find him and would have their border patrol on high alert. On the other hand, money tended to talk in this part of the world.

According to Irene Kennedy, the soldiers coming into view near the gate were fully on board, and he had no reason to doubt her. There were very few people in the world he trusted, but she was one of them. With nothing certain in the business he'd chosen, she was about as close as you could get.

Rapp slowed to a crawl as a border guard stepped into the road and held up a hand. The spotlights were blinding, but all indications so far were positive. Only three Syrians were visible, and the huge wire gate had been partially opened. Just beyond, Rapp could see a UN peacekeeper waiting patiently next to a white SUV.

He cut off the motor and stepped from the bike before reaching slowly into the leather bag he was carrying. No one seemed particularly concerned. The guard towers hovering over him appeared to be unmanned and the soldiers on either side of the road were displaying willful disinterest. The one in front of him must have drawn the short straw and seemed anxious to complete his task and collect his US dollars.

He went through the motions of opening the passport Rapp handed him, but didn't even bother to turn to the photo page. Instead, he handed it back and called out toward the gate. Rapp started walking in that direction and a few moments later was safely in the demilitarized zone.

The UN representative proved to be even less interested in him than the Syrians were. He pointed to the passenger side of the SUV and Rapp climbed in for the short drive to the Israeli border.

As expected, security there was quite a bit tighter. The towers were manned, no fewer than eight soldiers were visible, and the massive gate was open just enough for a man his size to squeeze through. Rapp stepped from the SUV and crossed over without incident, handing Matthieu Fournier's passport to an Israeli colonel on the other side. She flipped through it much more carefully, glancing up to make sure Rapp's face matched the photo as the gate was closed behind him. For some reason, the metal clang of it didn't feel as satisfying as it should. The woman seemed nervous when she returned his documents, eyes darting around the area in a way that initially seemed random, but then took on a concerning pattern.

"Welcome to Israel," she said and then pointed to a civilian vehicle waiting some twenty yards away. The distance didn't make a lot of sense based on where he'd come through, making the voice in the back of his mind grow in volume. When the woman hung ten feet back instead of walking alongside him, the voice started to shout.

By the time camo-clad men burst from a guard building to the right, Rapp was all but resigned to it. Balaclavas hid most of their faces and their movements were smooth, fast, and precise. Within two seconds, they were in a position to cut him to pieces with the pull of a few triggers. Unless their comrades in the towers got him first.

The impressive performance suggested that they were Sayeret Matkal—Israeli spec ops that he'd fought alongside a number of times.

Not today, though. One of the men screamed at him to get on the ground and Rapp complied, kneeling before lowering himself face-first to the asphalt.

He would have liked to believe that it was a mistake, but the Israelis tended not to make a lot of them. It was possible that Ben Friedman was still holding a grudge about the hole in his leg, but that seemed a little petty in the context of their long history. Rapp and Kennedy had stood by that son of a bitch too many times to remember.

His hands were secured with flex-cuffs and a bag was yanked

over his head before he was lifted to his feet. An engine started up in front of him and he was stuffed into what he assumed was the vehicle he'd seen earlier. There was a slight chirp of wheels as it accelerated, but other than that, nothing. He had no idea where it would take him, but it probably wasn't going to be the bar at the Royal Beach Hotel.

CHAPTER 27

RAPP managed to work the bag off his head, but the flex-cuffs had been replaced with steel ones that weren't going anywhere. Fluorescent lights revealed a room measuring around twenty by twenty feet, with haphazardly whitewashed walls and a rough-hewn floor. The cell he was locked inside looked similarly temporary, basically a diver cage from one of those Shark Week documentaries. The takeaway was that he was cooling his heels in one of the many Israeli military encampments scattered along the border.

The question was, why?

For the hundredth time he looked up at the camera near the ceiling and, for the hundredth time, he found no answers. It wouldn't be long, though. Irene Kennedy would be monitoring the situation and that meant she'd soon start asking questions. The Mossad had no choice but to deliver him back to the US or face her wrath. Whether that delivery would be via El Al's first-class cabin or a coffin in the cargo hold remained to be seen.

Another hour passed before the only door accessing the room opened. The man who entered was in his early seventies, with a shaved head, deeply tanned skin, and a bull-like build that gave him a mob enforcer vibe. His untucked shirt hid the top of a pair of crisp blue slacks and, if memory served, the .38 revolver in the small of his back. More notably, he was favoring the leg that Rapp had shot him in, but it came off more as theater than injury.

"Hello, Ben."

The Mossad director patted his long-healed bullet wound. "Hurts me more every year."

"I should have aimed higher."

"Perhaps," he said, taking a seat in a folding chair near the wall.

"What am I doing here, Ben?"

"I'm sorry to say that you're waiting to be turned over to the Russians in Syria."

Rapp's eyebrows rose involuntarily.

"You're surprised. I suppose that's understandable."

An understatement. Friedman wasn't just burning him, he was burning Irene Kennedy. She had countless ways to retaliate. Omitting critical intelligence that Israel counted on. Opposing the transfer of weapons technology. Dragging some of Friedman's uglier skeletons from the closet. Or, if she was having a particularly bad day, sending Scott Coleman's team to show him the error of his ways.

Rapp just stared, causing the man to shift uncomfortably.

"Of course, I owe you an explanation, Mitch. After everything we've been through together, at least that, no? And to be fair, an explanation is in my best interest."

Again, Rapp didn't respond.

"Irene called and asked me to help you get across the Syrian border and into Israel. Of course I agreed. Why wouldn't I help an old friend?"

"Good question."

"Yes. Good question. But one with a complicated answer. A short time ago, my counterpart in Moscow told us that he was looking for a Canadian working for the Losa Cartel. The Russians believe that he's involved in financing insurgents through the narcotics trade. They went on to say that if this man were to try to cross into Israel, they would be grateful if I'd hand him over. It's my understanding that they've made similar deals with Jordan, Iraq, and Lebanon. I imagine Turkey as well."

"Matthieu Fournier," Rapp said.

Friedman leaned forward, propping his thick forearms on his thighs. "Imagine my surprise when Mitch Rapp came across my border using a Canadian passport in that very name."

"So, you work for the Kremlin now?"

"As you know, our relationship with Russia is complex. But what they're offering is quite attractive."

"Attractive enough to take sides against the United States in favor of a pariah state with a failing economy and a third-rate military? That seems shortsighted. Even for you."

"They're going to coerce the Syrians into signing a treaty conceding Israel's right to administer our part of the Golan Heights for the next half century."

"Bullshit."

"Clearly this is a top priority for them. *You're* a top priority for them. Why, Mitch? Are they really after a Canadian lawyer? Or are they after you?"

"A Canadian lawyer."

"Interesting. Tell me why."

When Rapp didn't respond, Friedman pulled a flask from his back pocket and unscrewed the cap. "I'd offer you a drink, but I suspect that if I got that close, you'd find a way to kill me."

"I'd damn well try."

He took a pull and wiped his mouth with the back of a hand glistening with sweat. "I want you to know that I strongly objected to this course of action. Unfortunately, my arguments didn't impress our prime minister. For him, the political prize is too valuable. I, on the other hand, am not stupid enough to discount the possibility that you'll escape. In fact, I think it's more likely than not."

"And?"

"And if you do, I want you to remember that it wasn't me who did this. It was him."

Friedman took another swig from the flask, followed by another swipe of his mouth. "It's the way of the world, isn't it, Mitch? We bleed and the politicians make speeches. Our prime minister will go over Irene's head to your president and they'll do some backroom deal that benefits them both. In the event you die, Irene will undoubtedly find ways to make my life miserable for a few years, but nothing more. She understands her place. We both do."

The vehicle was bucking over a rutted surface, but with the hood back on, Rapp could discern little more. The overwhelming stench of sweat, and no fewer than six male voices speaking Hebrew. Those things, combined with the fact that his hands were still cuffed behind his back, suggested that his near-term prospects were fairly grim. Nothing to do now but sit back and see what developed.

When they finally stopped, Rapp was pulled from the vehicle and marched for what he estimated was fifty yards. The cuffs stayed on, but the hood was yanked off from behind. About ten feet in front of him, Ben Friedman sucked nervously on a cigarette. To his left, the barrier that separated Syria and Israel glowed in the moonlight.

"A few years ago, we discovered that terrorists had dug a tunnel beneath this section. It was an above-average piece of engineering, so after we killed them, we kept it for use in our own operations. You'll be sent through and met by Russian agents on the other side. There's no indication that they know your real identity and correcting their intelligence isn't my job. They wanted a Canadian cartel lawyer and that's what I'm delivering."

He took a another drag from his cigarette, the embers momentarily illuminating his face. "I've instructed my men to remove your handcuffs before they take you across. There's no reason for the Russians to see you as a threat, and we'll play to that perception. Good luck, Mitch. I mean that sincerely."

"Fuck you, Ben. And I mean that sincerely, too."

CHAPTER 28

THE Mil Mi-24 attack helicopter was staying low, taking what appeared to be a route designed to avoid populated areas and potential rocket attacks. The aircraft had been heavily modified, now leaning more toward luxury than combat. Rapp was strapped into a surprisingly comfortable leather seat similar to the ones occupied by his guards. Wood paneling and an ornately painted Russian flag added to the feel of an armored executive transport.

The men with him were on low alert, with some asleep and others staring into space. That suggested that despite what had happened to their comrades, they didn't see him as a threat. The problem was that at this moment, they were right. The fact that his hands were once again cuffed was potentially surmountable, but even if he managed to free himself and take out the armed men guarding him, the Mi-24 had no direct access to the cockpit from the back.

Through the window, he spotted a distant artificial light source that was in the process of being swallowed by dawn. They banked toward it and a few minutes later were circling a secure compound plopped in the middle of the empty desert. Rapp examined it intently, doing his best to commit every detail to memory.

The eastern section of the structure was little more than a two-story concrete cube with minimal windows and a courtyard at the center. The south side contained a set of glass doors and an opening that looked like it led to underground parking. The latter was protected only by a drop-down tollbooth-type arm that was in the open position.

The western wing was more modern in design and clearly much newer. It rose an additional story, with long, unbroken windows on three sides of the top floor. There was even a rooftop deck with a canopy for shade, two sectional sofas, and potted palm trees. Someone—almost certainly the person who'd buffed out the chopper—was living large out there.

The fence that encircled the compound was chain-link and topped liberally with razor wire. In total, there were five towers: four at the corners and one looming over a guardhouse that covered the only entrance to the grounds. The barrier protecting it was surprisingly unintimidating—a slightly beefier version of the one on the garage supplemented by retractable tire spikes. At this time of morning, the entrance appeared to be unmanned and a set of rolling chain-link gates had been closed across it. Mostly likely they were only open when visitors were expected. Overall, the impression was of a reworked commercial property, as opposed to a purpose-built prison or military facility.

Its main security feature was the flat, open terrain that surrounded it. Anyone trying to attack or escape would be visible for miles.

The pilot slowed to a hover and then dropped onto a helipad just inside the northwestern fence line. The mercenaries immediately opened the door and jumped to the ground, pulling him out after them. Dust swirled in the rotor wash as they jogged toward the building and entered a steel door at the back. They passed through a stairwell and exited into a passage that led to a large, disused lobby with an elevator on the western side.

They entered and it rose for a few seconds before opening onto an outer office nearly the size of Irene Kennedy's at Langley. The difference was that this one was significantly more elegant and completely devoid of personnel. It gave the impression of something that had been built less for utility than for show.

Rapp and his three remaining guards entered an office at the back and stopped in the middle. The man sitting behind the desk that dominated the room was in his mid-forties, with a medium build and a pallor that suggested a religious avoidance of the rooftop deck. His uniform was that of a Russian general, with emblems and medals suggesting a long and distinguished career.

All complete bullshit.

While Rapp was hardly expert on the Russians, he knew enough to recognize Aleksandr Semenov. The man was well known to have never spent a day in the military, instead coming up through the intelligence ranks to lead his country's asymmetrical warfare program.

After giving the world a good, long look at Russia's shit military and losing their ability to hold Europe hostage with energy exports, all the once-powerful country had left were nukes and backstabbing. The former tended not to be a particularly convenient weapon to deploy, but they'd turned the latter into a formidable force on the world stage. Hacking, interference in foreign elections, support of fascist movements worldwide, bribery, assassination. If it was sleazy, pointless, and destructive, Russia—or more specifically, Aleksandr Semenov—was at the cutting edge.

It was impressive in a sick kind of way but, according to some CIA analysts, maybe a little too impressive. Semenov had disappeared from everyone's radar a few years back and the conventional wisdom was that he'd either been quietly executed or locked away in some remote prison. The theory was that Boris Utkin had been forced to deal with him while he still had the power to do so.

Another swing and a miss by the Agency's eggheads. Semenov was not only alive, he looked to be the picture of health.

The Russian looked up from the file he was reading and spoke in excellent English. "Matthieu. It's good to finally meet you."

Thankfully, there was no recognition in his eyes. His method of warfare wasn't one that often crossed into Rapp's sphere of influence. But you could never be sure. He was an admittedly brilliant man whose reach was apparently longer than Western intelligence agencies suspected.

He pointed and barked something at one of the mercs. A moment later, Rapp was free of the cuffs and his escort had retreated to the outer office.

"My compliments to Damian Losa and his organization. Tracking you to that farmhouse and getting you out alive was quite impressive. Even more so was getting you across the border into Israel. Apparently, we haven't done as much damage to his Syrian network as we thought."

Rapp had been maintaining an expression of stunned terror since he'd been handed over by the Mossad. Now he added a hint of confusion.

"But why? Why have you kidnapped me? I'm here as a negotiator. Beyond that, I have no value at all. Mr. Losa won't concede anything to get me back. Lawyers aren't hard to find if you have money."

"I wouldn't want to be seen openly negotiating with a criminal organization, would I?"

An unintentionally ironic statement. The Russian government was nothing but a massive crime family. A little like the movie *The Godfather*, but with characters that were stupider, drunker, and armed with nukes. Probably better not to say that out loud, though.

"Also," he continued, "I doubt your Damian Losa would agree to my terms."

"You shouldn't make that assumption. What are your terms? At the very least, that'd give us a place to start."

"Why don't you tell me about your client, Matthieu?"

"I know very little. Nothing really. I want to be clear that I'm not a criminal, sir. I'm an attorney representing the business interests of a client."

"Your *only* client," Semenov said, tapping the file he'd been reading. "You have no others, isn't that correct? You have no employees and work out of your penthouse flat in Toronto. My people searched it and found very little. No papers, no computer. No indication that you have any close family or friendships that go deeper than acquaintance."

"I don't use paper, and when I travel, I put my computer in a safe-deposit box. On the subject of personal relationships, I have very little time for them."

"Or the vulnerabilities they create," Semenov said.

"You've elevated my importance beyond its reality, sir. Again, I'm just here to discuss how all parties can work together to succeed in their goals."

"Where?"

"Excuse me?"

"Where is Damian Losa?"

"I communicate with him either by phone or email. Not in person."

Semenov's lips curled into something hinting at a smile. "Okay. Then why don't you tell me what Losa is prepared to offer me?"

It was clear that he didn't care. He was on a fishing expedition and the sudden changes in subject were designed to keep his opponent off balance.

"Mr. Losa is a businessman who's been involved in a number of partnerships over the years. If you look into it, you'll find that his conduct in them was exemplary, and all were extremely successful."

"What is he offering?" Semenov repeated.

"He's analyzed the captagon formulation that I assume you're responsible for—"

"And?"

"And he's concluded that it is indeed a very appealing and addictive drug. He also concedes that he can't manufacture it at a cost that would make it profitable. What he *can* do is provide you with a European distribution network that's much more reliable than the one you've put in place. With all due respect, your first attempt at a sizable shipment ended in disaster. Not only was it captured, but now it's associated with terrorism. That all could have been avoided had Mr. Losa been involved."

"I'm not convinced he wasn't."

"I don't understand."

"How can I be sure that he wasn't the one who informed the Italian authorities?"

"I'd be happy to ask him that question, but it's not the kind of information that I typically have access to."

"I wonder."

"What do you mean?"

"Every indication suggests that you play a key role in his organization. And if that's the case, you know a great deal about it. Convenient, because I want to know everything about him and his worldwide business dealings."

"You're mistaken. And even if I were better informed, betraying Mr. Losa is a death sentence."

"As will be refusing my request."

"Then I find myself in a difficult position."

Semenov reached into a desk drawer and retrieved a baggie full of white pills. "Samples of our latest formulation. Much more advanced than even the ones sent to Italy. My people have added a physical withdrawal component more intense than what opium addicts experience. Combined with the powerful psychological addiction, it's broken even the most dedicated resisters. After just a month of continuous administration, there's nothing users won't do to get their fix. Denounce Allah. Whore themselves. Kill. Perhaps you'd like to try it?"

"You don't make it sound very appealing."

"Are you sure? I imagine my people would be very interested in adding a Canadian lawyer to their research. Thus far, our subjects have been somewhat racially and culturally homogeneous."

"What is it you want, sir? Information on my employer? You've made that clear. But to what end?"

"What I want is simple. I want everything. Ownership of Losa's network in Europe, but more important, his operations in Latin America and the United States."

"Ownership? That's an interesting word choice."

"It's the one I intended."

"I see."

"Really? What is it you see, Matthieu?"

"We originally assumed that the captagon was coming out of what's left of the Syrian pharmaceutical industry. That they'd somehow found a way to manufacture it cheaply and wanted to use the profits to support the government."

"But you no longer believe that's the case?"

Rapp shook his head. "No. I believe that this is a purely Russian operation, and you can't produce your captagon formulation any cheaper than Mr. Losa could. This isn't about profit. It's about waging war against the West."

"An astute analysis. Losa chooses his associates well."

Rapp didn't respond. This situation had just gone well beyond Damian Losa and the debt he owed the man. For years, the West had struggled to adapt to Semenov's evolving strategies, and now he was about to open a new front that no one had even considered.

There was a time when Rapp wouldn't have taken a threat like this particularly seriously. But that had been a rare example of naïveté on his part. His love of country had blinded him to its weaknesses. He'd believe that the US model would eventually spread across the planet and last indefinitely. Why wouldn't the rest of the world want to emulate what had made America the most successful country of the modern era? And even if that didn't happen, certainly the American people wouldn't want to emulate what had made Russia a useless shit-hole.

Now he wasn't so sure. Semenov was a visionary who understood humanity's weaknesses and had a gift for exploiting them. If he could create sufficient chaos, could he divide the West? Could he break up the European Union and replace America's democracy with an authoritarian who promised stability and order?

Two decades ago, the entire idea would have been a joke. But he wasn't laughing anymore.

As confinement cells went, the one Rapp found himself locked in wasn't the worst of his career. Or even the worst of the last twenty-four hours. The space was basically a ten-foot concrete cube. There was a cot, a toilet, and a sink arranged against three walls, while the fourth was dominated by a steel door. A vomit stain on the floor was still fresh enough to give the hot, heavy air an acrid edge.

He glanced at a clipboard resting on the mattress next to him and the pages it contained. Rapp flipped through them again out of boredom, scanning the questions about Damian Losa's organization, but contributing nothing more than a few drops of sweat.

He was starting to regret not having killed Semenov during their meeting. There had been a number of fancy pens lined up on his blotter and less than ten feet between them. A quick sprint, a jab at the jugular, and that would have been the end of the threat he posed.

But also the end of Mitch Rapp. The mercs had still been in the outer office, armed and vigilant. Even if he'd been able to dispatch them with the same improvised weapon, what then? Find his way to the parking area and drive away? He had no knowledge of the interior layout of the facility, no sense of the level of security, and no idea if there were any drivable vehicles in the garage. Or even if it really was a garage.

And then there was the open desert beyond. He had only a vague idea where he was, zero familiarity with the road system, and would be hunted. Probably by chopper.

He stood and began pacing through the confined space, counting eighty-three crossings before Aleksandr Semenov's voice crackled to life over a hidden speaker.

"Have you started on my questions yet?"

"If I do, will you let me go?"

"No. But I'll move you to a more comfortable cell and give you some freedom to move around the compound. It will take time for us to check the accuracy of what you've given us."

"And after that?"

"A quick, painless death. Better than the fate you'd suffer at Damian Losa's hands, no?"

Normally, Rapp would have strung the man along, but in this case, he didn't know enough about organized crime in general or Losa's outfit in particular to even create plausible lies.

"I don't know anything you'd be interested in. I imagine that's why Mr. Losa chose me for this assignment."

"I'd have to be very stupid to believe that."

"It's the truth."

"We'll see, won't we?"

Rapp returned to the cot and let out a long, quiet breath. He'd been interrogated many times in the past and had developed an extraordinarily high tolerance to sleep deprivation and pain. He'd become almost accustomed to electrical shocks, simulated drownings, and even the occasional torch. An endless cycle of addiction and withdrawal, though, wasn't something he'd ever faced. And he wanted to keep it that way.

"So, I suppose I'll get an opportunity to sample your product after all."

The tinny sound of Semenov's laughter echoed around the cell. "That was nothing more than an idle threat, Matthieu. I have my areas of expertise, but extracting accurate information isn't one of them. No, you'll be sent to Moscow, where men with years of experience and training will take over. Now, are you certain that you wouldn't prefer to fill out my questionnaire and avoid spending the rest of your short life suffering like no man or animal should?"

Rapp suddenly felt a glimmer of hope. If they moved him, he might have an opportunity to escape. Certainly, his chances were better outside the fence line than they were inside.

"I've said what I have to say. There's nothing more."

CHAPTER 29

THE sliding hatch at the bottom of the door opened and a tray containing breakfast appeared. Eggs Benedict topped with fresh chives, fried potatoes, and a steaming cup of coffee. The scent of it overpowered the lingering vomit smell, but Rapp remained on the cot. With the number of pharmaceuticals produced in this facility, he wasn't anxious to eat or drink anything. Eventually, he wouldn't have any choice, but his hope was that he'd be long gone before it got to that. Better hungry and thirsty than tripping.

As expected, he'd slept like a rock. He always did when there were no decisions to be made or strategies in need of examination. At this point, his best course of action was to be rested enough to take advantage of whatever opportunity presented itself.

Hopefully that would be escape and not death, but those were the only two futures he could see. Ending up at a heavily secured FSB interrogation site flat out wasn't an option. The first thing they would do is strip him and reveal a road map of scars that would be hard to explain away. When they realized they didn't have a simple Canadian attorney, they'd set to discovering his real identity. And when they inevitably did, they'd spend the next decade exacting revenge on him for his many transgressions against Mother Russia.

At this point, all important questions were unanswerable. Would they consider it necessary to bind or drug him for the trip? Standard protocol would suggest yes, but the character he was playing didn't project much of a physical threat. Further, while Russians tended to be violent, they also tended to be poorly trained and arrogant. A bad combination for them, but a potential godsend for him.

If they took him out on the same chopper he'd arrived in, he'd have little choice but to try to disarm the guards and start shooting. The hope would be to create a controlled crash, but that would depend more on luck than skill.

If they took him out by ground, there would be more options, but still a lot of variables. Terrain, number of guards, type of vehicle, chase cars.

In light of that, he closed his eyes again.

The next time Rapp heard scraping metal, it wasn't the food slot. He didn't stand when the door opened and two Russians in plainclothes entered. Both were in their late twenties and looked to be a cut above the average Russian soldier. Probably members of Spetsnaz, the country's elite special forces. They positioned themselves strategically, staring icily at him as Aleksandr Semenov entered. The Russian general looked down at the clipboard now residing on the floor and shook his head sadly.

"If your roles were reversed, would Damian Losa suffer for you, Matthieu? Would he spend his last weeks and months chained naked in a cell waiting for his next session of questioning?"

Rapp didn't answer. There was nothing to say that would do anything but prolong his time there.

Semenov gave the soldiers a short nod. A moment later, they had scooped Rapp beneath the arms and were dragging him from the cell. He didn't resist, but purposely fumbled getting his feet beneath him to further enhance his aura of weakness.

They descended a set of stairs to the ground floor and instead of exiting, turned down yet another flight to the left. Rapp suppressed a smile. Not the chopper. They were almost certainly headed to the underground parking area he'd noted on the way in. His chances of survival had just doubled. Only from ten to twenty percent, but at least the needle was moving in the right direction.

They exited into a single-story parking garage supported by crumbling concrete pillars with exposed rebar. There was a long crack in the ceiling and a steel girder had been put in place to support an area where it was bowing badly. Two Tigr military transports were visible at the far end, but they looked like they hadn't been used in some time. Instead, he was directed toward three men milling around a group of vehicles that included two motorbikes, a decades-old SUV, and an even more ancient sedan. All were properly dusty and beat-up, chosen less for tactical capability than stealth.

The additional men looked roughly similar to the ones on either side of Rapp. The oldest was in his early thirties, all were in street clothes typical of Syria, and all had good tans and dark hair—possibly enhanced by dyes and makeup. None looked quite as fit or watchful as the two who had escorted him there, suggesting they might have been selected less for their skill than their ability to blend in.

His luck was holding. Russian soldiers tended to be second-rate at best. They'd lost a lot of their more experienced people in the war, and even then, the word *experienced* had a different meaning than it did in the US. Russia's mandatory military service was generally accepted as one of the worst jobs on the planet. Runaway corruption, a culture of uncontrolled hazing, and a persistent shortage of competent noncommissioned officers made it a brief, miserable stop for most people.

These guys looked to be a cut above that standard and would have benefited from their time in Syria, but still would be inferior to their NATO counterparts. Further, this assignment was very different from general combat, and they were unlikely to have relevant training.

That assessment was supported by the fact that he was shoved into the passenger seat of the SUV unbound. One of the soldiers got into the back, while another slid behind the wheel. The driver had a bulge beneath his shirt only a foot or so from Rapp's left hand. Almost certainly a standard-issue GSh-18. The man in the seat behind had the same, plus an AK-9 that had already been waiting for him there.

They exited the garage via a ramp that passed beneath a raised wooden barrier that looked stuck in that position. The sedan led, with the two bikes bringing up the rear. The gate in the perimeter fence was open and they rolled through, passing over the retractable tire spikes that had been visible from the chopper. Rapp put on his seat belt as they joined a dirt road that tracked southeast, but the other two didn't bother. The one in back lit a cigarette and no one protested when Rapp rolled his window down. He turned his attention to the side mirror and watched the facility recede in it. Not out of the woods yet, but at least he had some room to maneuver.

After two and a half hours of driving, not much had changed. They were headed west, staying to secondary dirt roads as much as possible. The rocky desert had given way to a somewhat more verdant landscape that supported primitive agriculture and low scrub. In the distance, rocky hills topped with forest suggested they were closing in on the Mediterranean.

Moscow had two military bases in Syria, both on the coast. The first was the air base in Hmeimim and the second, not far to the south, was the naval port of Tartus. There was no way to know which one—if either—was their destination based solely on their direction of travel, but the conversation between the two soldiers had been a bit more enlightening.

Rapp's Russian was nearly nonexistent, but he did have some tactical vocabulary—compass points, names of weapons, verbs like *run, retreat,* and *stay.* Also a few words relating to military branches and their general activities. So far, he hadn't heard anything about airstrips, planes, or the air force. What he *had* caught were "ship" and "sea."

That's where his luck had finally run into a ditch. Taking over a plane was one thing—they had limited crews and he was a moderately competent pilot. Ships were a completely different animal. Large crews, steel-walled cabins, and lots of water in every direction. He was still a decent swimmer from his triathlon days, but not good enough to make it to Greece.

That meant he had to make his exit before they reached their destination. The more difficult terrain ahead would favor him and reduce the advantage created by the Russians' superior number. How much remained to be seen.

CHAPTER 30

THE terrain had become more rugged, with the dirt road now winding its way up the east side of a forested mountain. The sun was pounding through the windshield and no amount of fiddling by the driver could get the air conditioner working. Russians weren't known for being at their best in the heat and based on the look of the two men in the vehicle with Rapp, that stereotype existed for a reason.

The lead car slowed to navigate a particularly rough section, allowing them to close a bit. In contrast, the two bikes maintained a fifty-yard gap in order to reduce the amount of dust the riders were eating. They tended to approach only in sections so steep that asphalt had been laid down.

Rapp examined the left side of the road, taking in the lack of a barrier and how it fell away at the edge. A sheer drop of about three feet ended in a steep, rocky slope that extended a good hundred yards before reaching the tree line.

Based on what he'd seen so far, the perfect spot for an escape wasn't going to materialize. Once they hit the top of the pass, they'd start a fast descent into the coastal area. After that, there was a modern highway leading to the Tartus naval base. He had to make his move soon.

Another fifteen minutes passed before they entered an S-turn steep enough to have been paved. The car ahead slowed enough to allow them to catch up and the bikes closed on the SUV's rear bumper.

The road narrowed to a single lane, forcing the lead car to slow further as it entered a blind corner. The driver blasted his horn in case there was a vehicle coming the other way, and for Rapp the entire scene seemed to slow. A better opportunity was unlikely to present itself.

He twisted left in his seat, ostensibly to stretch, as he'd already done often enough to desensitize the men in the car to the gesture. This time, though, his hand wrapped around the hand brake and yanked it up. The rear wheels locked, causing the SUV to fishtail wildly and putting the driver's face into the steering wheel. One of the bikes went directly into the back of them, with the rider's helmet hitting hard enough to crack the rear window. The other managed to swing wide, but then went down when the right side of his handlebars contacted the road cut.

Rapp released his seat belt and lunged for the driver's-side door handle. A moment later, they were both tumbling from the vehicle toward the asphalt. As planned, the Russian hit first and Rapp landed on top, cushioning the impact. What he couldn't control was the momentum carrying them to the unprotected edge. The Russian wasn't as dazed as Rapp had hoped and proved capable of a struggle as they rolled.

When they went over, Rapp caught a brief glimpse behind him, noting that both the SUV and the sedan were stopped, with the latter's door already thrown open. The remaining man in the SUV was a bit slower to react, having collided with the back of the passenger seat when the emergency brake engaged.

Rapp stayed locked to the Russian as they picked up speed, rolling and skidding down the steep gradient. His opponent threw punches to the degree he could, but the unexpected turn of events was disorienting him. Rapp, on the other hand, had spent hours mentally rehearsing this phase of his escape.

He knew that the men above would be hesitant to shoot, not only because of the danger to their comrade, but also to their prisoner. They'd been ordered to transport Rapp, not kill him. Instead, they'd chase, but at a somewhat more cautious pace.

Rapp ignored them and the body blows he was taking, instead focusing on the rocks they were careening through. Most weren't much more than glorified gravel, but occasionally something the size of a softball would appear. He tried to snatch one up as he rolled on top of the man, but missed and went under again. Two more revolutions took him to another, this one satisfyingly jagged. He got hold of it and swung, managing to open a large gash above the Russian's right eye, but nothing more. The man missed a desperate grab for Rapp's arm and paid the price when he absorbed a more solid blow to the top of his skull. Not enough to render him unconscious, but sufficient to set up a cleaner shot that landed in the center of his forehead.

His strength evaporated and Rapp released him to rag-doll down the slope, while he concentrated on arresting his momentum.

Detached from his opponent, it took only a few seconds to get his feet under him and continue his journey in a gravity-assisted sprint. About twenty yards ahead, the Russian had come to an abrupt stop at the tree line. Despite his injuries, he was already on his knees and groping for the pistol on his hip.

He'd almost closed his fingers around the butt when Rapp came alongside and brought the rock down one last time. The man collapsed onto his face and Rapp retrieved the GSh-18, glancing upslope to check the progress of his pursuers. There were only two, still fifty yards away and neither holding a weapon. More concerning was that one of the bikers had managed to stand and was staggering toward the edge of the road with gun in hand. His injuries and the fact that he was still wearing his helmet caused him to pull his first shot left. The whip of it penetrating the trees sounded like it was at least thirty feet away.

"Nyet!" one of the men picking his way down the mountainside shouted, stopping and turning toward his comrade.

Rapp took the opportunity to drop to the ground and steady the weapon he'd taken. The less-than-graceful trip down and the blows he'd absorbed had made him a little unsteady, but with the added support he managed to get off a credible shot.

The man on the left jerked and fell, managing to get a hand out to break his fall despite the impact of the bullet. It was impossible to know how badly he was hit, but it was certainly enough to neutralize the threat he posed. As an ancillary benefit, Rapp's aim had been impressive enough to cause his other pursuer to dive awkwardly to the ground.

Rapp briefly considered trying to fight his way back to the vehicles, but it was a long way and there was at least one man up there capable of firing a gun. Further, the car and SUV could be easily tracked, while the bikes were likely too damaged to be of much use. Better to take advantage of his speed and retreat.

To that end, he bolted for the woods, dodging nimbly through them like he did at least three times per week in the mountains surrounding his home in Virginia. The lack of a trail was a drawback, but the trees were less dense than he was used to, allowing him to maintain a respectable pace.

The distance between him and the Russians opened quickly, but that minor victory didn't outweigh the fact that he had no money, no water, and no identification. With that reality in mind, when he happened upon a defined trail, he turned onto it. The Russians were despised in this part of Syria and the fact that they were chasing him would provide a little credibility. Maybe enough to convince someone to help him.

Fifteen minutes of consistent effort put him at the edge of a small village. The little flat terrain that existed had been planted, while simple stone houses clung to a south-facing mountainside. Tucked in among truck-sized boulders, the homes looked abandoned, but almost certainly weren't. Hastily discarded farm implements were strewn across the fields along with the footprints of fleeing women.

Rapp took a path straight past the houses, unsure if he was going to make friends or take fire. In the end, he made it through without accomplishing either. Corralled livestock confirmed his suspicion that the village was a going concern, but apparently one that wanted nothing to do with him.

Understandable.

The trail led back into the forest and continued west. The coast couldn't be too far away, and it would have towns where he could get lost and steal a few necessities—most urgently a phone to contact Irene Kennedy.

Occasional movement in the trees suggested he was being watched, but there wasn't anything to be done about it. Getting captured was probably his best-case scenario at this point. While his dress shoes were still surprisingly comfortable, he wasn't anxious to try to run to the Mediterranean in them.

The ambush happened in a clearing about two miles past the village. Armed men appeared on his left and right, while a few more held back, barely visible through the foliage. Ahead, a man with an AK-47 stepped into view. Rapp slowed and finally stopped, hands raised. These men looked like just the kind of friends he needed.

Night had fallen and Rapp was still walking through the forest with five armed men behind him and four in front. At this point, it was clear that they were just going in circles, trying to disorient him. The effort was a waste of time due to the stars visible through the canopy and the fact that the terrain was rugged enough to provide unmistakable landmarks. On the other hand, their wandering might be a good sign. No point in hiding things from someone you planned to summarily execute.

The settlement they finally came to was less a village than an encampment. Small stone huts ran along the base of a heavily forested ridge that would make them invisible from the air. Though it was a cool night, no fires had been built and no electric light was evident despite various solar panels and old car batteries stacked beneath tarps. A few women and children were scattered about, but most of the inhabitants were men in their prime fighting years. Undoubtedly outlaws of some kind—political, criminal, terrorist. Maybe all of the above. It didn't really matter. He wasn't in a position to be picky.

Rapp was taken to one of the more primitive dwellings and presented to the old man sitting in front of it. Or at least he appeared to be old. The beard, much longer than customary in Syria, was gray and he wore traditional Arab garb. The darkness was deep, but when he looked up, the starlight made his eyes seem a bit glassy.

"My men said you killed Russians and then escaped," he said in Arabic. "They say they've never seen anyone who could move so fast through the forest."

"Being chased by Spetsnaz is very motivating."

The old man's head cocked slightly, undoubtedly noting Rapp's Iraqi accent.

"Who are you? What is the Russians' business with you?"

Those were dangerous questions to answer. There were too many factions in Syria to count and most of them hated each other. This man could be ISIS, Hamas, al-Qaeda, or a hundred other organizations no one outside of Syria had ever heard of. An Iraqi might have raped this man's daughter at some point during the war or, just as likely, fought alongside him.

"My name is Mohammed Hassan," Rapp said, picking a name that was the Iraqi equivalent of John Smith. "I only arrived in Syria a few weeks ago, but not to fight. I work for a European narcotics cartel, and we believed the Syrian government was trying to move in on our business. I was sent here to gather information."

"And were you successful?"

"Yes. I discovered it isn't the Syrians at all. It's the Russians. They're trafficking a new kind of captagon."

"Now that you know this? What will you do?"

"Pass the information on to my superiors."

"To what end?"

"So that we can outcompete them. Or kill them."

The old man laughed. "And how would you do that? The Russians control everything here. Not the old women in Damascus."

"I don't know. I just deal in information."

"A simple detective," the man said, not bothering to hide his suspicion.

"That's correct. Do you know anything about this? About the Russians' involvement in captagon?"

The old man leaned against the stone wall behind him, eyes locked on Rapp.

"I know a great deal," he said finally.

"Yes?" Rapp prompted, keeping his tone respectful, but making his interest clear.

The still-unnamed Syrian nodded. "We used to be involved in the drug trade. Not in Europe. Nothing so grand. Mostly Jordan. Damascus and the Syrian military still control the regional trade, but they have little involvement in the European market. All that is run from a facility not far from here. Perhaps three hours in a car."

The hatred in his voice intensified whenever he spoke of the

Russians. Men like him had seen the Syrian civil war as an internal conflict that they had a solid chance of winning. Right up until the Kremlin had decided to get involved.

"It used to be a hospital used by the country's elite," he continued. "It was abandoned during the war and didn't suffer damage because it was of no strategic importance. The Russians took control of it about three years ago, adding security and a new wing. Many people who were captured fighting against the regime have been taken from prisons and refugee camps and transported there. No one ever sees them again."

"Maybe I can help you," Rapp said. "Either by weakening the Russians or bringing you into one of our operations. Do you have a way to communicate with the outside? Access to the Internet or a satellite pho—"

"No, what I just told you isn't true," the man mused, seemingly oblivious to what Rapp had just said. "One man did escape. But I don't know if he's still alive."

"He is," someone behind Rapp said. "I've seen him. He lives alone on the other side of the mountain."

"I'm told that he spent over a year in that building with the Russians," the old man said. "That he has many stories about what happened there. Fantastic stories to be sure, but I wonder if some aren't true."

"He's insane," the same voice from behind offered. "He avoids contact with people. They say he screams and throws rocks at anyone who gets too close."

Rapp started to ask about their communications capability again, but then thought better of it. He desperately wanted to find the closest border and throw himself over it, but that wasn't just some random Russian asshole manufacturing captagon. It was Aleksandr fucking Semenov. The genius behind Russia's remaining offensive capability and a good bet to be their next president. While Rapp wasn't anxious to hump over a mountain to have some crazy hermit throw rocks at him, was he missing a major opportunity here? If the guy had spent a year there, what did he know about the operation and Semenov's plans?

Unfortunately, the answer was obvious. Too much for Rapp to ignore.

CHAPTER 31

GENERAL Aleksandr Semenov muttered under his breath as he strode through the dust he so despised. The sun had receded behind the facility's main building, providing a two-meter strip of shade that seemed to do nothing to counteract the oppressive heat. The three mercenaries accompanying him followed at a prudent distance, moving silently.

Something had gone wrong. The soldiers he'd sent to Tartus had been attacked and Fournier was gone. Beyond that, he knew nothing. The security of communications in Syria was highly questionable due to antiquated technology and monitoring by both Damascus and Western intelligence agencies. Sharing any more detail than was absolutely necessary could turn into a windfall for his many enemies.

A plume of dust appeared on the horizon, and he stopped to watch it elongate. Another fifteen minutes would pass before the vehicle arrived, but that didn't prevent him from glancing repeatedly at the gold

Rolex strapped to his wrist. Despite the timepiece's impeccable reputation, the hands seemed to slow to a near halt.

If the Canadian was indeed dead or missing, Semenov knew that
he could find himself in a very difficult position. It was he who had
convinced Moscow to trade the Golan Heights for Fournier and prom-
ises about Losa's European and American networks had been made. In
his semi-banishment, bold action was the only path available to him.
Unfortunately, it was a treacherous one. The distance between Syria
and Moscow tended to mute his achievements and amplify his failures
to the degree that nothing but an unbroken series of successes was ac-
ceptable. Anything less would give his rivals a weapon to use against
him.

When the SUV passed through the gate, his guards moved to more
strategic positions, but otherwise remained in the background. Semenov examined the vehicle as it pulled to a stop in front of him, but,
except for the man behind the wheel, it appeared to be empty.

The driver threw open the door and stepped out, giving a quick salute over the hood before rushing to the back. He opened the hatch and
carefully extracted a man who moaned in agony during the process. It
was clear that Captain Sergei Lenkov wanted help but, finding none on
offer, he managed to get his comrade's arm over his shoulders and hold
him upright.

The second man's face was spattered with dried blood and one of
his legs was twisted at a grotesque angle. That wasn't the full extent of
it, though. His pallor and fluttering eyes suggested injuries that went
significantly deeper.

"Report," Semenov said.

"Sir, Mikhail is badly injured. We need to get him—"

Semenov pointed to the sidearm carried by one of the mercenaries
and then at the injured soldier. A moment later, his bloodstained face
had been shattered by a bullet. Stunned, Lenkov tried for a moment
to support the dead man's weight, but then let the body slide to the
ground.

"Report," Semenov repeated.

"It . . ." he stammered. "It was another ambush. No less than . . . No less than twenty men, sir."

"Where's the Canadian?"

"Gone. The insurgents who attacked us took him."

"So, he's still alive?"

"The last I saw of him, yes, sir."

Semenov fell silent, watching the young man become increasingly nervous beneath the weight of his gaze. After a few seconds, it became too much and he started talking again.

"I was in the lead car and started taking fire from the trees on a narrow stretch of mountain road. I had no choice but to slam on the brakes and the driver of the SUV did the same. The motorcycles crashed into the back of it and Mikhail was injured by the impact. The other rider was killed. The Canadian jumped out and ran toward the forest, while I and the men from the SUV chased. But the insurgents had men down there, too. Dmitri was shot and Oleg was beaten to death after falling down the slope."

"But you're completely unharmed," Semenov pointed out.

"Once the insurgents had the Canadian, they disappeared into the trees. Getting him back would have been impossible and any attempt might have endangered him—something you specifically warned us against. Like I said, there were at least twenty men."

"In total or in the trees?"

The young officer's eyes narrowed briefly. "It was impossible to—"

Semenov pointed to the dead man at his feet. "What about him? Why did they let him live?"

"He was unconscious," Lenkov said after another telling pause. "They probably thought he was dead. But even if they didn't, there was no reason to prolong the battle. They appeared to just want the Canadian."

Semenov nodded silently. Soldiers were famously incompetent liars. Military leadership was always trying to foist these men off on the intelligence services, but it was almost always a disaster. In the modern world, they were useful as cannon fodder, but little else. Often they couldn't even manage to die properly.

"So, then they let you drive away. These twenty—perhaps more—men just let you walk back to the road, put your injured comrade back in the SUV, and drive here. Unconcerned that you might call for air support. Or that you had additional personnel nearby. Maybe the Syrian insurgency has suddenly developed a fondness for Russian soldiers?"

"Sir, I don't—"

"Shut up," Semenov said, and then turned to the mercenaries. "Interrogate him and find out what really happened. Also, send men to examine this supposed ambush site. See if there's anything useful to be learned from it."

"And the Canadian, sir?"

Semenov didn't immediately respond, instead stepping back into the shade. His manpower at the facility was limited and he'd just lost five men in addition to the three who had died trying to retrieve Fournier after he'd been captured in Saraqib.

Calling on the Syrians for assistance was impossible. Damascus was infuriated by the loss of the Golan Heights and revealing the Canadian's escape would undoubtedly filter to Moscow.

For one of the first times in his life, Aleksandr Semenov found himself unable to proceed by the sheer force of his will and brilliance. He'd never learned to do battle with men who were his equal because, in his experience, they didn't exist. In Damian Losa, was it possible that he'd finally stumbled upon an opponent capable of challenging him?

CHAPTER 32

WEST OF AL-KAWM
SYRIA

ON the back of the motorcycle, the morning air was cool and devoid of the ubiquitous dust due to a rain shower the night before. It wouldn't last, though. Afternoon temperatures were expected to climb into the low hundreds, but by that time Rapp planned to be kicked back in the shade of his adopted village.

He'd been accepted by the people there with surprising speed. His killing of multiple Russians combined with their desperation made him an unofficial member of the family. It was something that most Westerners would never know about the Arabs. In many ways they could be the warmest people in the world. The problem was that the line between sitting around a campfire telling jokes and getting decapitated around that same fire could be pretty thin.

The dirt road steepened and Rapp's fifteen-year-old guide pushed the old bike a little harder, trying to maintain its momentum despite the weight of its two passengers. The tire tread was in even worse shape than the motor and they finally bogged down in a section of loose gravel bordered by trees. The kid at the throttle seemed like the type who would spend an hour trying to free it to avoid a five-minute walk, so Rapp swung a leg over the back and dismounted.

"How much farther, Akhil?" he shouted over the shriek of the gunning engine.

"Not much." He shut down the bike with a deep frown. "Maybe a kilometer?"

"Why don't we just cover the rest on foot?"

Despite his youth, he didn't seem particularly excited about the prospect, but finally came around to the inevitability of it. After stashing the bike in the woods, they started up the path at a more casual pace than Rapp would have liked. Better not to push. While his relationship with the locals had gotten off to a good start, it was still precarious.

"He's lived up here for almost a year now," the kid explained. "He moved into a building that has been abandoned for as long as anyone can remember. But he's done very well despite . . ." His voice trailed off for a moment. "His problems."

"Speaking of that. When we get close, I want you to hang back and let me take the lead."

Akhil, apparently unimpressed with the suggestion, ran forward kicking a rock as though it were a soccer ball.

"Why?"

"Because people tell me that the man we're going to see can be dangerous."

"To you!" he exclaimed, deftly flicking the rock in the air and juggling it on his knees. "But he's my uncle. My father's brother. He likes me very much."

"Your uncle?"

"Of course! But they don't want him with us anymore. People say he's evil. That he died and came back. But that's stupid."

"Is it?"

"The elders believe these things from the old days. My uncle went through a great ordeal and was harmed by it. He was held by the Russians for a very long time. They did terrible things. And then they tried to kill him, but he survived. How can anyone expect that he would not have problems after this? Maybe brain damage. Or maybe just emotional issues, yes? These are very common. Someday I want to be a doctor and help people like him. Like all the people who have been harmed by the war both in their bodies and minds. Do you think that's possible? That I could become a person with an education? A doctor?"

"I wouldn't bet against you," Rapp said honestly.

The boy unleashed a broad grin. "My mother says the same. But many of the men in my village can't see farther than its edges. It's why they sent me here. I'm the one who takes care of my uncle."

"Takes care of him?"

"He's an engineer, did you know that? Before the war and the Russians. He went to university like I will one day. But then he fought against the government and was put in prison. Then the Russians took him. But he escaped with his life and now he lives here. But it's hard alone, so I bring him things he needs sometimes. Food. Clothes. Medicine when it can be found. Sometimes a little money, but I don't think he has anywhere to spend it. I think he might feed it to his goats, but I haven't told anybody. Nobody but you!"

The hike devolved into a forty-five-minute bushwhack, with a conversation so depressing that Rapp's responses became mere grunts. He'd spent a lot of time with war zone kids over the years and they tended to fall into two categories. The first were the ones who had fallen into the same pit of rage that he himself had toppled into in his youth. Their reaction to the horrors they'd seen was to pick a side and cling to it until death. They never so much as considered the possibility of peace—or even understood the concept beyond the definition printed in a dictionary they'd never looked at. What they wanted was the power to inflict the same suffering on their enemies that they themselves had endured.

And then there were the ones like Akhil. They clung with all the same intensity, but to hope. No matter how bad it got, they never lost their innocence. Their ability to laugh. Their passion for making plans for a future that would probably never exist for them. They were the ones Rapp had fought for his entire career. And they were the ones that made him wonder if he'd done anything more than prolong their suffering.

Out of the corner of his eye, Rapp saw movement and immediately grabbed the kid and yanked him back. The rock was aimed a bit high, sailing over them and clattering through the group of boulders.

"Nephew! Run! Escape!"

The man was invisible in the trees, but Rapp was able to pinpoint his rough location by the emergence of another rock.

"No!" the boy shouted, stepping in front of Rapp and throwing his arms out protectively. "This is Mohammed! He's a friend! He just wants to talk to you."

"He's Russian! A spy! He came to take me back!"

"No, Uncle. He's from Iraq. The Russians took him. But he escaped. Like you did."

"They killed him? Allah brought him back from the dead?"

Akhil shot Rapp an apologetic glance that suggested this was a typical discourse.

"No," Rapp called out. "They were transporting me and I jumped from the vehicle. Allah didn't bring me back from the dead. But He guided me through the forest to your nephew."

"Is this true?"

"It's true, Uncle. He just wants to talk. Please come out. And don't throw any more stones."

The man appeared a moment later, completely naked, with a foot-long beard, and sun-damaged skin blotched with dried mud. His cautious approach was preceded by a powerful stench.

His name was Kadir, but he didn't introduce himself and he didn't seem to want to get too close. Instead he turned north, waving for them to follow. Akhil took the lead, while Rapp hung back, trying to stay well upwind.

Eventually they arrived at a stacked stone house with a roof ingeniously constructed of tarps and tree branches. Kadir took a seat at a firepit and indicated for them to sit on the other side. He was perched on a small log, but Rapp and Akhil had to settle onto the bare ground. For obvious reasons, the man wasn't set up for visitors.

"I went to prison for helping my people fight for their freedom," he said. "I built and repaired weapons. Shored up damaged buildings. Fixed power and water infrastructure . . ." He seemed to lose his train of thought and fell silent.

"Because you're an engineer," Rapp prompted.

"Yes. An engineer. I worked at a university. I was a man of respect. I had a family. A wife. Two daughters. They're dead now."

His eyes took in everything but his two guests. In a war like Syria's a man like him would have quickly done and seen too much. But his behavior didn't suggest PTSD.

"They took you to the facility," Rapp said, trying to get him back on track.

"Facility?" Kadir finally met his eye.

"The Russians took you out of prison and to the old hospital in the desert."

He nodded. "Were you there?"

"I was," Rapp said. "I escaped."

The man's gaze shifted again. "I didn't."

"But you came back from the dead. Isn't that true? Allah saved you."

"But why? My family is gone. My life. I have nothing."

"Allah always has a purpose," Rapp said. "We're just His instruments."

"Yes!" he shouted, jumping to his feet suddenly enough to startle even Akhil. "Come! I'll show you."

Rapp motioned for the boy to stay and followed the man into the structure he'd made his home. It was strewn with broken furniture, rusted cans, and small projects that seemed to have been abandoned before they could become identifiable.

Kadir reached into an old trunk and came up with an improvised explosive device that looked sufficient to blow them into the goat corral. Rapp took a cautious step back as the man shook it violently. "They did this to me! And I'm going to make them pay. I'm going to destroy them. That's my purpose. That's what Allah has tasked me with."

"Maybe you should put that down, Kadir. It—"

"They took everything!" he shouted. "My life. My family. And then they stole from me who I am. Who I was. They made me dependent on their drugs. I knew what they were doing. I saw their experiments. But I couldn't stop. I couldn't fight them. There was nothing I wouldn't do for their pills. I knew what they were doing, though. I knew. The others didn't. But I could see it. I could feel it."

"That they were trying to addict you?"

"At first, yes. But that was easy. I'm a scientist. I understand. Once we stopped resisting, why keep us there? I discovered it. I discovered why. They were destroying our minds. Some of us died. Some of us were murdered. Some of us went insane."

"I don't understand," Rapp said, keeping his eye on the IED that the man had forgotten he was holding.

"I used to be an engineer. I had a family. But at the end, I couldn't think. I couldn't control myself. Look at me! Look at how I live! When they were done with me, they took me into the desert. They took us all there. They made us kneel and cut our throats. Like animals. But Allah brought me back. I was in the sand. With the others. But I got out. Here. You can see."

Rapp tensed when the man dropped the explosive and pointed to a thick scar on his neck.

"I went back to the village where I was born. My home. I still had people there. Like Akhil. But I wasn't who I was before. Do you understand?" Tears began flowing down his face, creating trails through the sweat-caked dust. "I harmed a child. A child! Because she was crying. I had two daughters. I never lifted a hand to them. Never. But the crying . . . The sound . . ." He fell silent for a moment, lost in the memory. "They said I couldn't live there anymore. That I had to leave. And they were right."

Rapp nodded in the semidarkness, trying to make sense of what he'd just heard. According to Akhil, the man had escaped Semenov's facility a year ago. Was it possible that the captagon could still be affecting him? Could the wound to his neck have starved his brain for oxygen?

"So, you haven't taken any of their drugs since you escaped?"

"No."

"You're sure. You didn't get out with any?"

"No," he said, his expression suddenly turning hopeful. "Why? Did you? Do you have some?"

"I'm sorry. I don't."

Kadir's expression darkened again. "I saw it. Because I'm a scientist. They took the drugs from us and made us beg. We resisted, but eventually, almost all knelt. They made us do horrible things to get them. Fight. Kill. Renounce God. Many thought it was just cruelty, but there was a method. I could see it. Then, finally, no matter what we did, they wouldn't give us more. They told us they would if we did what they wanted. But it wasn't to fight or turn our backs on Allah anymore. It was mental tests. Intelligence. Behavioral. Agility. Brain scans. Some people just disappeared. No one knew where they went, but I did. They were studying their brains. Dissecting them like lab animals. I know it. I'm a scientist."

"Why? What were they looking for?"

"Don't you see? They wanted to know if what they'd done to us was permanent. If we would ever be the same again after they stopped giving us their drugs."

"But you weren't," Rapp said. "You weren't the same."

"No. None of us. And when the Russians were sure of that, they replaced us. They brought in new people from the prisons and camps. New test subjects. Then they took us to the desert and buried us there." He stared at Rapp, the despair in him suddenly replaced by fury. "Is that why you're here? To take me back? To study me?"

Rapp wasn't expecting the naked man to suddenly charge, but it wasn't much of a problem. As Kadir had said multiple times, he was a scientist, not a warrior. His attack was easily sidestepped, which in turn caused him to trip and land face-first on the warped planks that made up his floor. Before he could harm himself, Rapp pinned him with a knee to the back.

"I escaped, too, Kadir. Remember? I'm a friend of Akhil's. I want the same thing you do. To make the Russians pay for what they've done. To all of us."

The man struggled for a few moments, but then just went slack. When he did, Rapp eased the pressure a bit. "Allah brought you back to destroy His enemies. Isn't that right?"

The Syrian didn't move, his body feeling almost dead beneath Rapp's knee. Finally, he spoke, but this time his voice contained an eerie calm.

"I dream sometimes, Mohammed. I dream about what I was. What it felt like. But it only lasts for a few seconds. Then I wake up and remember that I have nothing."

Rapp helped the man back to his feet. "Then tell me what you know about the facility, Kadir. Interior layout, procedures, manpower. You were there for a long time and you're an engineer, right? Tell me how that place works."

Akhil ran ahead to retrieve his bike, while Rapp took a more leisurely route back. The brand-new satphone he dug from his pocket had been a gift from the elder of his newly adopted village. The fact that they had a small stash of them suggested they were still involved in the fight against the government. And the fact that they were willing to part with one suggested that the fight wasn't going so well. Again, desperation bred hope. But in this case maybe not so poorly placed.

Rapp turned it on, glancing occasionally at the sky as it started up. While the Russians had been forced to reduce their presence in Syria, they almost certainly still had a drone or two capable of homing in on phone signals. At this point, though, the situation had devolved badly enough that there weren't a lot of options. Reluctantly, he dialed and put the phone to his ear.

"Is that you?" Kennedy said, picking up on the second ring.

"Yeah."

"I'm happy to hear your voice."

"I'll bet. That exit plan wasn't your finest moment."

"Ben betrayed us and now he won't take my calls. Apparently, the prime minister has promised to make amends, but I haven't been included in those discussions. I'm not easy to surprise, but this has done it. I can't imagine what would make a move like this worth the blowback."

"They're getting the Golan Heights."

"Excuse me?"

"Syria's going to sign over administration of it for the next fifty years."

"I find that hard to believe. How solid is your information?"

"Take it to the bank. I'm guessing it'll be announced in the next few weeks."

"No offense, but you don't seem that important. I assume you're about to tell me what I'm missing?"

"Yeah. The Russians are one hundred percent behind the new captagon formulation. I was taken to the facility where they're developing it. Care to guess who's running the operation?"

"I have no idea."

"Semenov."

There was a lengthy silence over the phone. "Are you sure? How do you know?"

"He and I had a long conversation about his work and his plans to distribute it in the West."

"But you're safe now."

"For the time being."

"And this is why he's interested in Losa?"

"Yeah."

"But if Semenov's involved, this has to be about more than just making money."

"It is. The drug he's selling is heavily engineered. It's not just incredibly addictive, it seems to cause permanent psychoses in its users. This is an outright attack on the Europeans and eventually on us. Money's irrelevant. He's selling it at a loss."

"I'd hoped the man was dead. As much as I hate to admit it, he's a visionary. The cost of defending against his programs and repairing the damage when we fail is astronomical. If there's anyone more dangerous in the world right now, I can't think of who. He's not just constantly reinventing asymmetrical warfare; he's actively waging it."

"Agreed," Rapp said. "In the beginning, I didn't take him all that seriously. A scrawny Russian asshole who thought he could end democracy with a few mean-spirited Facebook posts. I was wrong to underestimate him."

"As was I."

"So, what do we do about it?"

"Your tone suggests that you've already answered that question," Kennedy said.

"I say we go after him. He's vulnerable here."

"There's no way. The president inherited his position when Anthony Cook stepped down. He has no mandate and courting a confrontation with Moscow isn't in his plan."

"Screw him and screw Moscow. The Russians have no economic power, no military power, and they're not going to use their nukes because they've got young mistresses and dachas that they don't want to see incinerated. The threat is Semenov. And if he gets his hands on the Kremlin, that threat gets multiplied by ten."

"I don't disagree, but I answer to the president."

"Yeah? Well, I don't. I work for a drug cartel."

"I'm not sure that's going to provide as much political cover as you think."

"Then screw that, too. Look, I agree there are risks, but think about the rewards for a minute."

"I'm not arguing that they wouldn't be substantial."

"The way I see it, getting people out of Syria is hard. But getting them in is easy. Send me my guys. After that, wash your hands of the whole thing. It'll be purely a cartel operation."

"If you're identified, that isn't how the Kremlin's going to portray it."

"Then I won't get identified," Rapp said, glancing at the sky again. Still nothing, but that didn't mean much anymore. "We both know that this is a once-in-a-lifetime opportunity. At least let my team assess it from the ground. If it doesn't look good, we'll abort. But if it does, we've got a chance of putting a knife in the Russians that they'll never be able to pull out."

She sighed quietly. "Let me see what I can do."

CHAPTER 33

A T two in the morning, Prague was at peace. Through the massive arched window, Damian Losa could see the Charles Bridge and the Gothic cathedral beyond. The headlights of occasional cars flashed into existence and then went dark again, leaving nothing in their wake.

The penthouse flat smelled of plaster and paint, and there were still a few wires hanging from the ceiling where chandeliers were to be installed. The web of offshore companies that owned the property, combined with its newness, would make it difficult to trace. Difficult, but not impossible. Nothing was impossible for the enemies he was accumulating.

In Saraqib, the battle that had been sparked by the Syrians' capture of Mitch Rapp was still raging. Further, it seemed to be spreading to other major cities, creating the possibility that the civil war would be reignited. Hardly Losa's fault, but his involvement would be noted by the world's intelligence agencies. Organizations whose blessing he needed to operate.

Mitch Rapp was still missing and was almost certainly aware that he had been betrayed. How would he react to that? A reasonable man would simply see his debt as paid and retreat. A less reasonable man would seek revenge. Which category did he fall into?

A couple of weeks ago, Losa had bet on the former, but now he wasn't sure. There was no evidence that Rapp had returned to his life in America or even left Syria. Of course, he could have been captured or killed, but those weren't possibilities that Losa was willing to wager his life on. People who underestimated Rapp eventually became his victims.

Finally, there were the Russians, who seemed less interested in a partnership than stripping Losa of everything he'd built. And with their paramilitary and intelligence capability, the chances of them succeeding in those ambitions were uncomfortably high.

"The connection's gone through, Damian."

Julian had several laptops set up on a grand piano centered in the cavernous room. The candelabra among them and the ancient stone wall behind made the scene a bit surreal. As if his old friend were a time traveler making one last attempt to get home.

Julian connected a set of speakers to one of the computers and a dull ring emanated. A moment later, a hushed, accented voice came on.

"Yes? Go ahead."

Behzad Nafisi was third in line at Iran's Ministry of Intelligence, a man clever enough to understand that patriotism was nothing more than an illusion created to uphold the power structure. And so, while he maintained a certain allegiance to his country, his primary loyalty was to his Swiss bank account.

"Do you have information for me?" Losa said simply.

"Very useful information, I think."

Julian's eyebrows rose at the potential stroke of good luck, but Losa was more cautious. The Iranians had close relations with both Syria and the Russians, but their intelligence was often tainted by politics and religion.

"I don't recall," Nafisi continued. "Did we agree on price?"

"How is your daughter enjoying her first year at King's College?" Losa responded. "What is it she's studying again? Economics?"

Nafisi would be moderately difficult to get to because of his personal security detail. His daughter, on the other hand, lived a life like any other university student. Blissfully unaware of how precarious it could be.

"Yes, of course we did," the Iranian said quickly. "My apologies. My life has been rather hectic. Things sometimes slip my mind."

"I understand perfectly."

"The man you're interested in passed from Syria to Israel through the Quneitra gate four days ago."

"And after that?"

"Our sources within Israel aren't as good, I'm afraid."

Unquestionably true. If Nafisi had more, he'd be trying to sell it. "As always, I appreciate your help, Behzad. I'll make the bank transfer we agreed upon immediately."

Losa ran a finger across his throat and Julian disconnected the call.

"Contact our people in the Mossad. See if they know anything."

"Right away, Damian."

"Still no activity at Rapp's house in Virginia?"

"Nothing. Accessing the subdivision isn't practical, but we have people watching from outside. No sign of him or Claudia Gould."

She and her daughter had vanished just after her return to the US from Paris. A disappearing act so complete that it suggested the involvement of Irene Kennedy.

"And his South Africa house?"

"Also nothing. But I doubt he'd go back there. It's currently under renovation."

"So, he could be anywhere," Losa said, turning back toward the window. He didn't approach, though. While the glass was reputed to be bullet resistant, that no longer offered much comfort.

CHAPTER 34

RAPP eased back on the throttle as he approached a building with a façade that resembled a waterfall. Rubble had drifted far enough across the street that he had to jump the bike up onto what was once a sidewalk in order to get by.

Irene Kennedy had chosen the city of Idlib for its reputation as a rebel stronghold, but that label was a bit optimistic. At dusk, very few signs of electricity were visible, and many of its inhabitants looked like worn-out shells. The influx of refugees fleeing the government had overwhelmed the area's resources, leaving hunger, exposure, and disease to eat away at the populace. Undoubtedly, that was Damascus's plan—a de facto siege that would eventually allow them to reclaim the region with little more than token resistance.

Kennedy still had people on the payroll there, but all were an example of the strange bedfellows that the CIA tended to attract. The area was controlled by a patchwork of factions, the most powerful of which was Hayat Tahrir al-Sham. About the only thing positive to say about the al-Qaeda–allied group was that they were desperate enough to be bought. Or at least rented short term.

The directions Kennedy had provided were a little sketchy in a city where structural collapses and bombings constantly redrew the road network, but he finally found the building he was looking for glowing in the twilight.

"This is it," he said, getting off and handing his Richard Mille watch to the Syrian who had been clinging to him from behind. He examined it as if he were some kind of expert on timepiece authenticity, but finally nodded and stuffed it in his breast pocket.

"May God be with you," he said, sliding forward and taking hold of the bars. "Don't make us regret not killing you."

Rapp watched him make an awkward one-eighty and a few moments later he was alone in a city that was reported to still have two hundred thousand inhabitants.

The neighborhood was as advertised—industrial and now all but abandoned due to the heavy damage it had taken during the war. The one exception was the structure in front of him. Comprising two stories and surrounded by properties that were once twice that height, it had been shielded to some extent from the shelling. Not exactly a high-tech fortress, but beggars couldn't be choosers.

Until the owners had been accused of sedition and tortured to death by the government, it had been the home of an engine repair shop. The stink of the incident still clung to the property, and despite its condition, no one had conjured the courage to squat in it. Whether that was due to the fear of vengeful ghosts or the possibility of guilt by association was hard to say.

The front door was still solid, and a new lock had been installed. Rapp found the key beneath a deteriorated Pepsi can he'd been briefed about and entered. A powerful flashlight had been left by the entrance and he turned it on, washing the beam over the interior.

The repair equipment was low-tech, but all still in place. The fact that it looked like a war zone seemed to be less about the Syrian conflict and more about the previous owner's lack of organization. Tools were mixed with auto and engine parts, most of which were strewn across the floor or stacked on makeshift shelves. Even the stairs leading to a clapboard loft that served as the property's living quarters had been partially repurposed to store boxes in various stages of decomposition.

Beneath a pile of rusted fenders, Rapp found a motorbike that looked like it hadn't run in decades, but was reportedly in perfect working condition. Apparently, all he had to do was inflate the tires and gas it up.

Rapp was about to check out the living quarters, when he heard a powerful knock on the door. Not a fist. Some kind of club or rifle butt. It wasn't entirely unexpected. Even in this neighborhood, neither the recent activity in the building nor his sudden arrival would have gone unnoticed. The question was, what kind of reception would he receive? A few old ladies with a platter of homemade barazek? Doubtful. But that didn't necessarily point to disaster. The Syrians were trying to survive and that meant people selling things, seeking work, and offering up local expertise. Hell, maybe it was just someone happy about the possibility of the local repair shop reopening and looking to get something fixed.

When he opened the door, the old ladies with pistachio-dusted snacks were nowhere to be found. Instead, he was faced with two men wearing Jihadists "R" Us scarves wound around their faces. The one in front had an AK-47 slung over his back, while the second held a similar weapon at the ready. They both looked alert, but the one bringing up the rear seemed almost paranoid—glancing behind him every few seconds. The overall impression was that he saw Rapp as less of a threat than the locals. Possibly other tough guys competing for whatever scraps were left in the neighborhood.

"What can I do for you?" Rapp said, keeping his tone light. "I'm not open for business ye—"

The man in front pushed past, while the other took a more direct route, using the side of his rifle to drive Rapp back. The American didn't resist, stumbling back as the young man entered and slammed the door behind him.

The angrier one was tall—rising a good three inches above Rapp's six feet, and formlessly bulky beneath his jellabiya. The dark eyes that were the only visible part of his face didn't suggest much in the way of intelligence, but hinted at an impressive capacity for violence. The smooth skin at their corners suggested that he was young enough to have never known anything but war, making concepts like compassion, mercy, and trust completely foreign. In contrast to the boy who had recently guided Rapp through the mountains, this one woke up every morning angry about having been born.

Rapp allowed himself to be manhandled to the center of the building, where the other man was waiting. His eyes were older, leaning more toward fatigue than his companion's nihilistic rage. A man who could be reasoned with to the degree that reason had any meaning in Idlib.

"What are you doing here?" he said.

Rapp opened his mouth to speak, but before any sound came out, he was struck from behind by the younger man's rifle. Not hard, but enough to cause him to stumble forward a few steps.

"My . . . My plan is to reopen the garage."

"You've picked a very dangerous place to start a business, my friend. Where are you from?"

"Iraq."

He nodded sagely. "We can help. For fifty thousand Syrian pounds per month, we can keep you safe and promote your new enterprise."

This was actually even better than a reception by the local baking club—a straight-up protection racket. If they could provide him with some local knowledge and keep the other hyenas at bay, they'd be well worth the twenty dollars they were asking.

"I'd be grateful."

"We'll take the first payment up front."

"I don't have it," Rapp said honestly.

If Kennedy had done her job—and she always did—his money and gear were upstairs in a steel locker. Not something he wanted to open in front of them.

"Liar!" the young man behind him screamed and then slammed the rifle into his back again. Rapp didn't bother making a show of stumbling this time, starting to feel his anger grow. If these two pricks could just exercise a little impulse control, everything had a chance of working out.

"I swear I can have your first payment by tomorrow," Rapp pleaded. "My belongings haven't arrived yet. All I have is the clothes on my back. If you want, take some tools as collateral. They're worth something. Bring them back tomorrow and I'll give you your money."

The one in charge looked around, but from what Rapp could see of his expression, he wasn't impressed. Finally, his gaze fell on the rickety steps to the east.

"What's up there?"

"Nothing much more than a mattress."

"Really?" he responded. "Then you won't mind us having a look."

"Of course not," Rapp said, making sure his voice didn't betray the fact that everyone's luck had just run out.

The staircase was bolted to the wall with rusty hardware and missing its guardrail. The structure flexed dangerously as they rose, suggesting that one full-grown man at a time would have been wiser. Having said that, *safety first* wasn't exactly Syria's national motto.

Rapp followed the older man, avoiding a broken tread and looking over at the steel, stone, and concrete debris on the ground below. Just the right combination of gravity and jagged castoffs existed two steps from the landing—a selection of rebar and angle iron that was stored vertically in a series of racks. Climbing higher would give a falling object more momentum, but also create the potential for a more comfortable landing on a large, horizontal compressor tank.

Rapp slowed when he heard the kid behind him clear the broken step. A moment later he felt another blow to his back, giving him a solid idea of his opponent's position. Instead of tripping forward as was undoubtedly expected, he spun, sweeping an arm into the young man's shoulder. The impact caused him to stagger left, putting a foot to the side to regain his balance, but finding nothing but air. He released the AK and windmilled his arms in a way that recalled the cartoons Rapp had watched as a child, searching for something to grab but finding nothing.

When the fall was inevitable, Rapp faced forward again, grabbing the weapon slung on the other man's back. It was even easier to send him plummeting to the floor, but with a somewhat less catastrophic result. He bounced off the compressor before landing on his back on the concrete floor. Rapp ran down the stairs, noting that the older man was still conscious, but unable to get up or free the weapon pinned behind him.

The younger man had suffered a significantly worse fate. As planned, he remained where he landed—impaled on a piece of angle iron that had penetrated his hip and exited mid-stomach. His lower body was deathly still, while his hands pawed uselessly at the steel bar, suggesting damage to his spine. Blood poured from his mouth as his head turned toward Rapp, but the fury was undiminished in his eyes. At his age, and in the same position, Rapp imagined his own expression wouldn't have been much different.

"Naahil!"

The voice behind Rapp was desperate, but didn't manage much in the way of volume.

The man on the floor had managed to roll on his side, but seemed to have forgotten the rifle on his back. Instead, his eyes locked on his dying companion for a moment before moving to Rapp.

"Please! My son . . ."

"I'm going to take care of it," Rapp replied calmly. "But you need to answer some questions first. Is there anyone else with you? Anyone outside?"

"No," he said, struggling to breathe. It was almost certain that he'd broken a few ribs and maybe even collapsed a lung.

"What about your organization? How many are there?"

He shook his head. "No organization. This neighborhood is dead. Just . . . Just us."

Rapp saw agony in the man's eyes, but no deceit.

"Please . . . Help him. Please."

What he was asking was clear. Idlib wasn't a town of ambulances, emergency surgeries, and wheelchair ramps. The strong survived and everyone else died.

Rapp picked up a length of pipe, swinging it full force into the boy's forehead and then dropping it to the ground. "You see? It's okay. He's with God now."

Rapp finished the weld and then lifted his helmet to examine his handiwork. It looked like the work of an eighth grader flunking shop class, but it would do the job. With a healthy amount of grinding and a can of Syria's answer to Rust-Oleum, no one would ever look at it twice.

The chance of him getting two corpses out of the building and safely stashed out of sight had been right around zero. The only vehicle available was the motorbike, and some kind of half-assed *Weekend at Bernie's* ride into the desert would attract attention even in war-torn Idlib. The other option—stacking them up in an unused corner of the building—would have been even worse. After a few days, the stench would become overwhelming.

Cutting a hole in the compressor tank was the best solution he could come up with. Getting both of them inside had been a messy meat puzzle, but he'd finally managed. Hopefully, the seal would be airtight, but with the pressure buildup as the bodies decomposed, he wasn't sure. Maybe he'd pick up some epoxy along with that Rust-Oleum.

The tiny enclosure on the second level wasn't much to look at. There was a mattress on the floor and a bathroom with water filtered through a system that would keep him from falling prey to the cholera outbreak making its rounds. A set of metal lockers lined one wall and he used his key to open them. Inside, he found the treasure trove Kennedy's contacts had left for him. A laptop, a satellite link, and a Russian GSh-18 pistol that would have to suffice in a country more or less devoid of Glock products. In the category of creature comforts, there was a sleeping bag, various changes of clothes, and basic toiletries. He grabbed a toothbrush and used it gratefully while inventorying his food supply, cash, and collection of passports.

All as promised. Not a long-term solution, but enough to either deal with Aleksandr Semenov or to decide it was impossible and escape the country.

He powered up the laptop and waited for the proprietary operating system to request a password. Once entered, he was able to access a file folder containing various satellite photos of Semenov's facility as well as drawings that denoted its scale. Using the trackpad, he added what he knew from his time there and what he'd been told by Kadir.

While he wasn't exactly the most reliable man Rapp had ever debriefed, his memory of personnel and layout seemed credible. The biggest blank was the facility's modern section, which Kadir had never seen, and Rapp had only spent a few minutes in. Semenov's quarters were almost certainly on the top floor with his office—that's where the massive windows and access to the rooftop deck were. Other than that, the layout was hazy. Kennedy would almost certainly be capable of getting plans from her informants in Moscow, but had deemed it too risky. Any sudden interest in this remote outpost was bound to attract attention.

A second file folder contained more overhead photos, but these were focused less on the building and more on activity. The geeks at Langley had managed to identify individuals by their physical characteristics and use that to corroborate Kadir's estimates: between fifty and sixty workers, with no fewer than twenty-five armed. Inmates could be occasionally seen in an interior courtyard and the Agency also agreed with Kadir's estimate of twenty.

The chopper Rapp had flown in on was almost always on-premise and it appeared to be the only aircraft that ever came in or out. Based on the luxury retrofit he'd noted, it was almost certainly reserved for travel by Semenov. No airstrip existed to allow planes to land. All shipments—human or otherwise—came in by truck.

Langley's analysts had taken their best shot at piecing together a timetable for those shipments and had done a workmanlike job. Food and other supplies arrived regularly from Damascus and various port towns, but with the random schedules and vehicles common in countries ravaged by war. Much more interesting were the inflows and outflows of test subjects. While also not on anything that could be described as a precise schedule, the procedures and timing seemed much more rigid.

There were no pictures of the test subject trucks leaving the facility, likely because they were timed to avoid US spy satellites. He knew how things worked from Kadir, though. The Russians piled all the people they were done with into the back of a transport, before taking them to the desert for disposal. The truck then came into satellite view near the town of al-Taibah, continued to the Sednaya prison, and then visited a refugee camp northeast of Damascus. After that, it took a consistent route back to Semenov's facility. Once again, its arrival was timed to avoid US surveillance.

Rapp scooted back on the mattress, leaning against the concrete wall behind. There was a hell of a lot of open territory around Semenov's compound and it was certain that the men in the towers would be keeping a close watch over it. Also possible were electronic sensors. Maybe even land mines.

The luxury accommodation, big windows, and tricked-out helicopter suggested that Semenov was comfortable there. And why not? His facility was in the middle of nowhere, well secured by Syrian standards, and within easy reach of aircraft from Russia's base in Hmeimim. Undoubtedly, he figured he could do whatever he wanted there without fear of reprisal.

And until now, he'd been right.

CHAPTER 35

ALEKSANDR Semenov took a sip of his vodka and then went back to studying the reports in front of him. For the first time in memory, they had no scientific component. No trials, no failures, theories, or novel chemical compounds. The new captagon formulation gave every indication of being in its final iteration. After years of effort, its addictiveness, long-term damage, and cost had been fully optimized. In a few weeks, they'd bring in another group of test subjects to make absolutely sure there were no issues, but neither he nor the research team anticipated anything but unequivocal success.

Unfortunately, that success would generate an entirely new set of problems: scaling production, expanding his distribution network, and pushing into new Western European countries. Systems with high levels of complexity were normally his forte but, strangely, he was struggling to concentrate on the pages in front of him.

Or maybe it wasn't so strange.

Semenov laid the folder next to him on the sofa and gazed toward the massive windows in front of him. Through them, spotlights high-lighted the fence line and contrasted the darkness beyond. The object of his interest, though, was somewhat closer.

Tonight, Alea was wearing a red satin dress that was a bit less de-mure than the one she'd worn during their first encounter. She was sitting in a chair near the glass with her thighs—visible to ten centime-ters above the knee—clamped tightly together.

Her skin glistened with a thin film of sweat that matched the sheen of the satin almost exactly. This time she was further along in her cap-tagon withdrawal. Not enough to make her outwardly ill, but enough to give her a preview of the suffering that would soon begin without his intervention. In his experience, timing was everything. The evening he had planned was to be significantly more adventurous than their last and he'd need a bit more pliability.

She stared past him with dark, youthful eyes. The anticipation was as horrifying to her as it was delicious to him. Unable to scream, cry, or commiserate with her fellow inmates, she could do nothing but imag-ine what the next few hours would entail. He focused for a moment on where the hem of her dress met her skin and then reached for the folder again.

In truth, the kinds of mundane operational details it contained were better handled by others. He was a creator. A visionary. His work was done and there was no reason for him to continue on in Syria. But what did that mean? Would the president allow him to return? Could he afford for Semenov to reenter the Kremlin triumphant? And if not, was he still clinging to enough power to prevent it?

A contrite knock on the door caused Alea to look hopefully in its direction. As always, Semenov had provided instruction that he wasn't to be disturbed that evening unless it was urgent. The anger he'd nor-mally feel at the intrusion was overpowered by curiosity. Could it be the information he'd been waiting for?

"Come!"

The man who stepped through was a former Wagner Group

commander with above-average intelligence for a man in his profession. His fatigues were badly bloodstained, with some of it still wet enough to gleam crimson under the overhead lights. The girl's eyes widened in horror and Semenov reveled in it for a moment before turning his attention to the man now standing at attention in front of him.

"What?"

"Lenkov finally broke. He held out longer than I would have thought."

Indeed. It had been three days since the young soldier allowed Matthieu Fournier to escape. Three days of extraordinary physical suffering, while Semenov's was more intellectual. He'd been forced to spend the last seventy-two hours speculating without data—an activity he abhorred.

The most plausible explanation for what had happened was that he'd been betrayed by his own forces. The Canadian's first escape was easy to explain away by the involvement of the Syrians. They were infinitely corruptible, and it wasn't completely implausible that Damian Losa had the resources to orchestrate the farmhouse ambush. This was different, though.

In order to carry out an ambush on the road between there and Tartus, the attacking force would have to possess extremely accurate intelligence. Information that could have only come from inside his organization. The best explanation was that Captain Lenkov and any number of other men at the facility were taking orders from Moscow. That Kremlin leaders were trying to sabotage his efforts in an attempt to weaken him politically. Or perhaps that assessment was overly optimistic. Was it possible that the men Semenov counted on for his physical well-being could come to endanger it? Would Boris Utkin dare to take such a bold course of action? It was a credible enough threat that Semenov had significantly reduced the number of men he came into direct contact with and had avoided leaving his quarters since Fournier's disappearance.

"And?"

"There was no ambush."

Semenov felt the sweat break across his back. "Then Lenkov orchestrated Fournier's escape?"

"No. It's not what we thought at all. The Canadian escaped himself."

"What? Nonsense. He's still lying to you."

"I don't think so. The discrepancies between his original account and what we found on the road now all fit. Fournier engaged the emergency brake from the passenger side and both motorcycles hit the back of the vehicle. Then he pushed the driver out through the door and went over the slope with him. He killed that man with a rock and shot another. After that, he ran for the trees. Lenkov was the only man in a condition to chase, but he couldn't keep up. When he returned to the vehicles, one of the motorcyclists was still alive and he brought him back here to report and get him medical attention."

"Then everything he initially told us was a fabrication?"

The man nodded. "Devised on his drive back. For obvious reasons, he didn't want to admit that a lone man overpowered him and the others."

Semenov's eyes narrowed as he tried to process what he'd heard. Over the course of less than a minute, his entire strategic situation had changed. But what did that mean, exactly?

"What do you want me to do with Lenkov, sir?"

"Put him in the program."

"I'm not sure there's enough left—"

"Put him in the program!" Semenov shouted.

The man saluted and beat a retreat to the door. Once closed, Semenov stood and began pacing under the watchful eye of the increasingly distressed girl.

He should have felt relieved that Moscow wasn't behind recent events, but the sensation was surprisingly muted. Despite a thorough investigation by the FSB, Matthieu Fournier wasn't who he said he was.

Losa had managed to get an operator inside this facility and within inches of him. He remembered how close he'd gotten to the man—a killer who had calmly played the frightened attorney while he waited for an opening. It seemed likely that the only reason he had survived was that Fournier had no hope of escape after carrying out the assassination.

Where was he now? Had he escaped Syria? Or was he still out there with substantial knowledge of the compound's layout, security measures, and personnel? Was it conceivable that he could organize an attack? There was an endless supply of battle-hardened locals willing to do anything for money. And Fournier had already taken out an astounding number of Semenov's men. Eight highly trained soldiers, the loss of whom had significantly degraded his security force.

Semenov was in a badly weakened position that he was incapable of improving. A call to Moscow for reinforcements was out of the question. Any display of weakness or incompetence would do nothing but fuel the forces plotting against him. A quiet request for reinforcements from Damascus was equally impossible. The Syrian president was embroiled in trying to control the violence spreading from Saraqib and infuriated by the loss of the Golan Heights.

Semenov looked toward the windows again but saw the same thing as before. The dull glow of the guard towers. The flash of the wire fence. The dark, empty desert beyond. Was it real? Or just what he was supposed to see? Were there forces out there organizing against him? Not only Losa, but the Kremlin itself?

He was too lost in thought to notice the girl's approach. She startled him when she reached out, causing him to take a step back. Her fingers were damp with sweat when they grazed his cheek, but he felt none of the lust or power that she and the girls before her had so reliably provided. Instead, he felt only impotent rage. For her. For the old men in Moscow. For the country that he'd spent the last two years of his life toiling in.

Semenov swung a hand into her face, but instead of the customary slap, he balled a fist. She spun and dropped to the floor, bleeding badly from a gash on her cheek. He grabbed her by the hair when she tried to crawl away, dragging her toward the bar. She struggled weakly as he opened a drawer and poured out a bag of captagon pills.

"Is this what you want?" he screamed, forcing her head back and shoving a handful of the white tablets into her mouth. Tears ran down her face and she began to choke, but he didn't relent, instead keeping his palm clamped over her mouth and using it to slam the back of her head repeatedly into the floor.

CHAPTER 36

A KNOCK sounded on the door, rising above the scrape of the truck bumper Rapp was dragging across the concrete. He'd already had a few visitors, most of whom were just curious and a couple who were looking for minor engine repairs.

This one was different. Three powerful strikes in rapid succession. Two a bit slower. Finally, a long pause that ended with more of a slap. The concept of the secret knock had been around long enough to be adopted by fraternities, immortalized in B spy movies, and described on papyrus. But for good reason. They never failed.

He dropped the bumper on a growing pile of debris in the corner and crossed the space to open the door. Like the men now entombed in the compressor tank, this one was wearing a scarf wrapped around his head, hiding everything but a pair of piercing blue eyes. Unusual in the region, but hardly unheard-of.

"I was on my boat, asshole. Floating around the Med with a fishing pole in one hand and a beer in the other."

Scott Coleman stepped inside, and Rapp closed the door behind him.

"But, hey, no worries. This place is nice, too."

"At least it was a short trip."

"Don't try to smooth things over," he said, removing the light pack and AK-47 he was carrying. "I'm planning on holding a grudge."

"I'd offer you a drink to ease your suffering but, you know, Muslim country."

"Outstanding."

"Where do we stand?" Rapp asked.

"My guys are either already in-country or will be by tomorrow morning. We've got another thirteen Arabs coming in from around the region. Might be another day or two before all their boots are on the ground."

"Reliable?"

"Absolutely. All men I've worked with in the past. And they'll blend in."

Rapp nodded. Coleman and his men were the best in the business, but between their Caucasian features and questionable language skills, they had a way of attracting attention.

"So, no problems getting in?"

"Piece of cake. Not too hard to get into a country that everyone with half a brain is trying to get out of. The gear is tougher. We're smuggling it in via existing channels—established criminal gangs from Turkey, Lebanon, and Iraq. Not the sharpest tools in the shed, but they'll get the job done."

"Claudia?"

"She's not involved. Irene has her and Anna on ice somewhere. She didn't give me a location because, you know, we're in Syria being targeted by the local government, the Russians, and the Losa Cartel. But she told me to tell you not to worry about them. They're safe."

Not an assurance Rapp would have accepted easily from anyone else, but if Kennedy was confident, that was good enough.

"So, what's the job, Mitch? Seems like a big team."

Rapp took him upstairs and showed him the information on Semenov's facility.

"What do you want to do? Level it?"

"Not exactly. I'm interested in getting hold of the guy running the place."

Coleman let out a long breath. "Destruction's easy, but snatching someone from a compound like that is a heavy lift. Can we just wait for him to leave and grab him when he's somewhere less secure?"

"I doubt he leaves very often. And when he does it's in a Russian gunship."

"What about just killing him instead?"

"That's better than nothing, but I want him alive."

"When you say 'want,' is that just a vague preference or more of a deep desire?"

"The second one."

Coleman dropped onto the mattress, propping the laptop up on his knees and staring at the screen. "How many people are in there?"

"Call it seventy-five. Twenty-five shooters at the most. Maybe as few as seventeen if they're not replacing their casualties. The rest are either noncombatant personnel or prisoners."

"So worst-case scenario, eight guys on duty if you figure three shifts a day. Thirteen on twelve-hour shifts. Or as few as six or nine if your low estimate is right. Are they any good?"

"A mix of mercs, Spetsnaz, and regular army."

"So, yes. Do you know where their barracks are located?"

"We don't have any interior details that aren't on the diagram. And those are based on my memory and the memory of a man who was imprisoned there for a while."

Rapp decided to omit the fact that the informant in question was brain damaged.

"So, you've actually been inside? How hardened is the interior?"

"A lot of concrete and secure doors, but most of it was built as a hospital. Not a military installation."

"What about the civilians?"

"Don't care."

"So, we can just shoot at anything that moves?"

It wasn't ideal, but it was the reality. Beyond the guards, they were talking about scientists doing experiments on their fellow human beings and a bunch of hopelessly drug-addicted insurgents. Even the women from the refugee camps likely wouldn't be completely innocent. Not many people in Syria were and he wasn't going to endanger his men trying to sort the good from the bad.

"If everyone in that building dies except our target, I'm not going to lose sleep over it."

"Is there anything you lose sleep over?"

"Not much."

"Okay. Well, I admit that makes things easier. Do we know where our guy is?"

"Skip to the next page."

The former SEAL did, taking a moment to scan it. "Let me guess. The top floor with all the windows."

"Yeah."

"It'll keep him out of harm's way, but also make him harder to get to. Doable, though. My main problem isn't the compound, it's what's around it. Nothing. They'll see us coming twenty miles out. Are there any supply vehicles we could catch a ride on?"

"One in particular," Rapp responded. "A Russian Ural. The schedule's a little loose, but we know where it originates. They bring in prisoners from near Damascus."

"Might work," Coleman conceded. "A Ural's big enough to fit all our people and gear if we squeeze."

He set the laptop aside and ran his fingers through close-cropped blond hair. "Getting hold of the truck is workable. We've done this kind of thing before and there are going to be plenty of lonely places on the road that won't support high speeds. What bothers me is what happens when we get there. Depending on which estimate you rely on

we're outnumbered by experienced operators with a home field advantage. We also have the problem of them getting out a call for help. We
could have Russian choppers on top of us in less than an hour. Finally,
we've got a target who can't be harmed and who I assume is someone
their security forces are going to be specifically looking out for, right?
You didn't bring us here to grab the janitor."

"No, not the janitor," Rapp confirmed.

"And there's the issue of getting him out of there and out of Syria.
What am I not seeing here, Mitch? Even if we manage to pull it off,
we'll be lucky to not lose half our men."

Rapp pulled up a chair he'd salvaged and sat. "What you're not seeing is the underground garage."

"I don't think parking is our biggest hurdle here."

He ignored his friend's jibe. "It's a big space with serious structural
problems. Our target is in the newer, better-built section."

"I'm not following you."

"We let our guys out at the gate. Then someone drives the truck
into the garage and blows a few hundred pounds of incendiaries and
Semtex. Even if we don't bring the building down, we go a long way
toward neutralizing their advantage."

"It's an interesting idea, and you said they're supposed to be bringing in prisoners, right? That means a bunch of shooters are going to be
in that garage waiting for them to get there. The problem is that I don't
see any version of your plan where the driver of the truck survives."

Rapp leaned the chair back on two legs, causing it to creak dangerously. "Let me worry about that. You just worry about the rest."

CHAPTER 37

NEAR CAZENOVIA
NEW YORK
USA

CLAUDIA turned down the grill and used a wire brush to clean off what looked like years of grime. The outdoor kitchen was a feature she loved, but this one had a bit to be desired. The day was stunning, though, with temperatures in the high seventies, blue skies, and a significant reduction in the bugs that had plagued them earlier in the week. Anna had been insisting that they put the grill to work and tonight was the night. An American feast that Mitch would have loved—steak, baked beans, potatoes, and corn on the cob. Her quintessentially French mother would have been horrified. Anna and their security detail, on the other hand, would be delighted.

She hung the brush back on its hook and looked up at the glass prow of the house looming over her. Its style and condition suggested that it had been built in the eighties, but the layout and attached bunkhouse had turned out to be ideal. Even more attractive was the two hundred acres of rolling grass crisscrossed with white fences. She shaded her eyes to examine distant tree-topped hills and then turned her attention to a somewhat less distant figure astride a horse.

Anna was having the time of her life. She went from stall to stall, corral to corral, seeking out her next steed, talking breathlessly with the staff who cared for them, and hanging on every word uttered by her riding instructor. Dinner table conversation rarely strayed from horse-related subjects, and she'd barely even mentioned the absence of Mitch or her friends. Of course, that was coming, but Claudia calculated she had another week before her daughter's equestrian bubble burst. By then, the hope was that Mitch would be done with Syria and they could all go home.

He was supposed to have returned a week ago, after Damian Losa's betrayal, but there had been some kind of delay. Irene Kennedy had assured her that he was fine, but that the first attempt at extraction had failed. Was it the truth? Or just one of the many lies that slid so gracefully from the tongue of the longtime CIA director? Much more credible was the idea that he'd found something that interested him there. And based on Kennedy's sudden involvement, it was something that went well beyond Damian Losa.

So here she and her daughter were, imprisoned in a castle designed to keep them beyond Losa's extremely long reach. But also locked out of what was happening—completely in the dark and unable to use her own considerable skills to help. It was a torment that had been made significantly worse when Scott Coleman and the rest of SEAL Demolition and Salvage's operators had disappeared. Over the past few years running the company's logistics, she'd come to think of them very much as her men. Her responsibility. If anything went wrong, there would be nothing she could do about it. And while Irene Kennedy was the best in the world at what she did, ceding control was painful and terrifying.

"How is everything?"

"Fantastic," one of the men seated at the picnic table said. The other three nodded enthusiastically, but with mouths too full to otherwise respond. Her protection detail ate in shifts, with half of the team always deployed. Two men were currently roving the perimeter with dogs, one was inside monitoring the state-of-the-art surveillance system, and another was with Anna. Claudia could see her piloting a horse around a corral chosen for its lack of jumps or obstacles. What they didn't need to deal with was a trip to the emergency room.

Her daughter was outside of shouting distance, so Claudia started across the expansive lawn to convince her to take a break. She'd barely made it halfway to the fence line when her phone began to ring. Hoping it was an update from Kennedy—or even Mitch himself—she snatched it from her pocket. It turned out to be neither. Instead, the initials DL pulsed on the otherwise blank screen.

She stared down at it, initially unwilling to answer, but knowing she had no choice. Finally, she tossed her hair aside and eased the phone to her ear as though it might explode. Unlikely, because it had been provided by the Agency and was configured to make it look like she was at home in Virginia. But you never knew.

"Hello, Mr. Losa."

"Please call me Damian," he said smoothly. "How are you, Claudia?"

"I'm well. And you?"

"The same. But I'm afraid I haven't heard from Mitch in some time. My understanding is that he left Syria. Is he with you? And if so, may I speak with him?"

"He's not with me. I thought he was still in Syria working for you."

It was a game of cat and mouse to see who would reveal more. Unfortunately, Damian Losa was typically the cat in such exchanges. In all exchanges, really.

"I tried to get him out, but he seemed to change his mind at the last minute."

"Did you give him a reason to change his mind?"

Losa was unusual for a criminal in that he tended to be fairly straightforward in his dealings. He wanted everyone to be clear on why he was killing them, their family, and everyone they'd ever met.

"I sent him there to negotiate, but he kept avoiding the job."

"Maybe he thought you were looking less for a negotiator than for a canary for your coal mine."

"You're alive because of the information I provided him. He agreed to my terms and one of them was that I get to define the job."

"Having lived with Mitch for some time, I can tell you that he creates his own definitions."

Losa fell silent and Claudia fixated on her daughter. In theory, they were safe, but it was hard to have an adversarial conversation with Damian Losa without wondering if someone was lining up a set of crosshairs.

"This call appears to be connecting from your home in Virginia," he said finally. "But you're not there."

"No."

"Because of me?"

"Yes."

"Would it help if I said that I regret my actions with regard to Mitch's extraction?"

"Because those actions didn't give you the result you wanted?"

He laughed in an easy way that was either genuine or extremely well practiced. "Partially, Claudia. Partially. But my main concern now is that he might believe we've become adversaries and could be looking for revenge. What I did was a business decision. In retrospect, the wrong one. But a battle between us would be expensive for all parties involved."

"I doubt that's on his mind."

"Then maybe he should come into plain sight and demonstrate his goodwill."

"He could be dead."

"I admit that would take a weight off my mind, but I doubt I'm that lucky. Particularly in light of the fact that I suddenly can't locate Scott Coleman or any of his men."

"I wouldn't know anything about that," she said, aware that her lies were becoming increasingly transparent as the conversation went on.

"I don't want a war, Claudia. But if one comes, we both know I have the resources to fight it."

"If I hear from him, I'll pass on your message."

"That's all I can ask. Thank you, Claudia."

The line went dead, and she let out a long breath before continuing on. When she finally entered the corral, Anna looked a bit disappointed. Dinner was just the first step in a series of events that included bath, pajamas, story time, and finally bed.

Her instructor helped the girl dismount and she trudged reluctantly toward her mother. When she got close, Claudia crouched and held out her arms. "Why don't you give me a really humongous hug?"

"How come?"

"Because I need it."

CHAPTER 38

R APP kicked the bike's starter and it fired right up. Feathering the throttle, he maneuvered it around the building, testing the steering and brakes as he wove through the remaining debris. Satisfied that everything was fully functional, he shut it down.

"Sounds better than it looks," Coleman observed as he descended the stairs.

"I think it'll get me where I need to go."

"Which is?"

Rapp didn't give an answer and the former SEAL didn't really expect one. He was making a joke about the oppressive need-to-know nature of this particular operation. Irene Kennedy had involved herself, but with the understanding that secrecy was paramount. This was as far off the books as it could get without falling off the edge of the earth.

Ironically, they'd set the operation up very much like the terrorist cells they'd spent their lives fighting. Mostly two-man teams with no knowledge of each other or the mission they'd signed on to. Communications were carried out via encrypted texts and chat rooms, and limited to narrow instructions regarding times, places, and equipment. The Arab members of their team were handling most of the preparation due to their ability to blend in, while Coleman's American contingent were carrying out tasks that would allow them to stay out of sight. Where exactly they were doing all this, Rapp had no idea. It was information he neither needed nor wanted. He didn't plan on getting captured, but if he did, the more compartmentalized his knowledge, the better. In fact, he'd have preferred to also be in the dark about the final objective, but that cat was out of the bag. The Agency had experimented with erasing those kinds of specific memories a half century ago, accomplishing nothing but to create a highly classified disaster. Too bad. It would have been a useful trick.

"How long until I should start to worry about you?" Coleman asked. "You can tell me that much, right?"

"I'll send you a text asking for Joe's location. Give me five hours."

"And if I don't hear from you by then?"

"Then you're not going to. Pack up and get everyone out of here."

"Understood."

He kicked the bike back to life and started toward the bay door. Coleman opened it and Rapp gave one last command as he passed through.

"Don't use the compressor."

Rapp had stashed the bike in the same trees as the week before and was now walking a similar path. This time without his young guide and protector, Akhil.

The afternoon sun was fully overhead, but the altitude and intermittent shade were keeping temperatures reasonable. Even more important than protection from the sun, though, was the protection the forest would provide from flying rocks.

By the time he reached the clearing where Kadir lived, he suspected he was being watched. That suspicion turned to certainty when a stone suddenly arced from an irrigation ditch to the north and cut through the branches in front of him.

"I'm not going back!" came a muffled shout followed by another rock. This one went wider, clacking off a partially collapsed stone wall before falling into the dust.

"Kadir! It's me, Mohammed! I was here with your nephew. Do you remember? The Russians took me, too. But I escaped!"

The man rose, wearing clothes this time, but also brandishing a hoe lashed together from a tree branch and a sharp rock. Otherwise, he was just as wild-eyed and filthy as when they'd first met.

"Why are you here? Did they send you?"

"No one sent me. I came to talk."

A switch seemed to flip in the man's damaged mind. He dropped the makeshift weapon and turned toward his house. "We should have tea."

Rapp accepted an invitation to sit on the ground and watched Kadir build a fire. Best to let the man process this visit on his own terms, and the act of making tea seemed to be centering him a bit.

"Thank you," Rapp said, accepting the steaming cup as Kadir sat on an upturned log that was out of the smoke's path.

"What do you want to say to me? No one comes here. No one wants anything from me. Not anymore."

"When we talked last, you said you wanted to kill the Russians who imprisoned you in that facility. The ones who addicted you."

Kadir leapt to his feet. "I have something for you to see!"

He wrenched open the door to his home and disappeared into the gloom, reappearing a moment later with the IED he'd shown Rapp the last time.

"I built this," the Syrian said proudly, holding it a little closer to the fire than was advisable. "I need more explosives, but they're expensive. The fighting's started again now. I may be able to find some unexploded ordnance. It's heavier and more difficult, but I can make it work. I used to be an engineer. I worked at a university. Then I can take it back to that place. I can kill them."

Rapp nodded approvingly.

"Do you know where the facility is?"

Kadir dropped onto his log again, hugging the bomb. "They took me there in the back of a truck. Me and the others. They took us out the same way. I don't know where exactly. But I can find it. God will guide me."

"Maybe Allah is already guiding you, Kadir. Because I know exactly where it is."

His eye widened. "You do? You can tell me how to get there?"

Rapp ignored the question for the time being. "Have you seen the exterior?"

"No. There were no windows where I was and they only let us outside in an interior courtyard. They made us fight there. They made us fight to get the drug." His eyes moistened. "And I did."

"There's heavy security," Rapp said. "A fence topped with razor wire, guard towers, and no way to hide your approach. They'll see you coming for kilometers. You wouldn't even make it to the gate."

"Allah will protect me. He sent you to me, yes? He'll make me invisible."

"Maybe. But if He does, how much damage can you do with that explosive? Kill a guard? Two? And they aren't the people who did this to you. They're not the ones responsible."

"Maybe it will only be a guard," Kadir responded defensively. "That's for Allah to decide. But He doesn't want me to live like this. Alone. Remembering late at night who I once was. An engineer. A man of respect."

Rapp took a sip of his tea. It tasted like it came out of one of the goats in the corral behind him. "Did you see inside the garage?"

"Yes. They brought us in and took us out there."

Rapp pulled up a rendering of the facility on his phone and handed it to the man.

"The garage is beneath the shorter of the two buildings. What if I got you in there with a truck full of C4?"

The wild look in Kadir's eyes transformed as that switch flipped again. This time to the mathematical side of his brain. The engineer he talked about was still in there.

"It was in bad condition. I remember. The ceiling was sagging, and they supported it with a single steel beam. Many of the original columns were crumbling. The cracks in the ceiling looked deep. Structural."

"That's what I remember, too."

"How much C4?"

"Call it a hundred kilos."

"Real? Good quality?"

"The very best. So, what do you think? Could you bring the building down?"

The Syrian stared at the phone's screen, deep in concentration. "That temporary support beam isn't designed for lateral forces. I could use the truck as a battering ram and knock it out of position before detonating. Would it collapse the entire section? Possibly. The rebar I saw was inadequate and I would wager that some of the structure has none at all. The corruption in the Syrian construction industry is legendary."

"And the other wing?"

"It looks much more modern, and I doubt it relies on the other building for support. I don't think a detonation in the garage would have much effect on that part other than the glass sections."

"Do you remember how many guards there were in the garage when you arrived?"

"Many," Kadir said. "Perhaps eight. There were a lot of us in the transport truck. As many as twenty in all. A few women and a few weaklings like me, but most were hard men. They needed many guns to control them."

Rapp nodded. It was exactly what he wanted to hear. As many as half the shooters in the facility could be taken out by the initial blast, with another five or so killed in the first few minutes of the assault. That left between five and ten, depending on whether Semenov had been able to replace the men Rapp had killed. Worst-case scenario it was the high number and all of them were safely barracked in the modern section. They'd still have a home field advantage, but lose their numerical one.

"What do you think, Kadir? Do you want to be the man behind the wheel of that truck?"

The Syrian stiffened. After a few seconds frozen like that, he walked over to Rapp, bent at the waist, and embraced him. When he spoke again, the words constricted in his throat. "I knew Allah had a greater plan for me. That my suffering was just a test of my devotion. Now I understand. Thank you."

CHAPTER 39

THE streets of Ma'arrat Misrin were indistinguishable from virtually every other city Rapp had visited over the past three weeks—rubble, blooms of twisted rebar, and people trying to scrape out a future for themselves and their children. There was one improvement, though. The phone taped to Rapp's handlebars had a CIA navigation app created by overlaying Google Maps with current satellite information on blocked streets, collapsed buildings, and military outposts. It wasn't perfect, but with a few creative detours and the deceptively capable bike, Rapp and his passenger were making progress.

"I was here before. As a boy," Kadir shouted over the whine of the motor. He had his arms clamped around Rapp's waist and was leaning in close to his ear. "It was different, then. The government . . ."

Rapp tuned him out. The man hadn't stopped talking for over two hours—rambling through subjects as diverse as the history of concrete, soccer, the war, and classic cars. He seemed ecstatic about the prospect of a spectacular death and had come to believe that Rapp might be something more than human. A herald sent directly from God, but on a greasy motorbike instead of a flaming chariot.

No point in arguing.

The coordinates that Coleman had sent took them to a largely un-inhabited area at the far edge of town. The benefit was that it had been spared from heavy bombing and was remote enough that a few new inhabitants wouldn't attract much attention. On the downside, electricity was supplied by a single frayed cable draped from building to building. Water, it seemed, was courtesy of a glorified rubber hose that traced a similar path.

The warehouse they arrived at took up nearly an entire block with embedded bay doors on three sides and a normal entrance on the fourth. The walls were constructed exclusively of corrugated metal with rust taking hold everywhere that lacked a protective film of graffiti. Anti-government slogans were still legible in places, but now the artwork leaned toward idealized images of Syria's president. The government was probably spending more on portraiture than feeding the population. But it wasn't a bad investment. Propaganda had been a constant throughout history for one reason and one reason only: it worked.

Rapp parked next to the southeast bay and hammered a fist into the steel, following a predetermined rhythm. The sound of distant shelling caused Kadir to shift his monologue from Thai cuisine back to the war, but he fell silent when the door began to rise. Perhaps less because of the movement than the two-hundred-and-fifty-pound tower of muscle on the other side.

The Syrian immediately ducked behind Rapp, shoving him forward and attempting to escape. He only made it a couple of steps before Rapp grabbed him by the collar and dragged him past the former Delta operator and into the warehouse.

"He's a friend," Rapp said as Maslick retrieved the bike and closed the bay door again.

"Joe, Kadir. Kadir, Joe."

"Good to meet you, Kadir."

The Syrian backed away to what he saw as a safe distance. "You're an American. I know the accent. I watch American television. Do you like *Friends*? It's very funny. And Rachel is very beautiful."

Rapp raised his eyebrows in surprise. He hadn't actually considered the fact that the man spoke English. The filth, smell, and unhinged chatter made it easy to ignore his educational background.

"Yeah," Maslick responded hesitantly. "Good show."

Kadir approached and held out a hand, which Maslick enveloped in his own.

"It is very good to meet you, Joe! You are a very big man. The Americans eat well. But you have no cuisine of your own. Do you like Thai food?"

"Sure. I guess."

"I do, too. Maybe I can make some before I die. The ingredients are hard to get, though. Because Syrians like their own food and because of the war. No Thai people live here. We had a restaurant in Damascus. But that was before the war. It was said that they served beer there, too, but only in the back room. Where the government officials ate. It would not be for . . ." The Syrian's voice faded, and his gaze wandered to the back of the building. "What is that?"

"A Russian transport," Maslick said. "A Ural-4320."

Kadir began to back away. "It's how they took me there. How they took all of us. They put us in the back. And they killed us in the desert. I'm the only one who came back." He turned to Rapp. "You tricked me! You're one of them! You won't put me in there! I won't let you!"

He lunged in Rapp's direction, but Maslick grabbed him by the back of the neck. Despite a fair amount of flailing, he had no hope of freeing himself.

"Kadir!" Rapp shouted, grabbing the struggling man by the shoulders. "We talked about this. You're not going to be in the back. You're going to be driving. It's how we're going to get through the gate. This is why Allah brought you back, remember? To destroy His enemies."

He calmed, sagging for a moment, and then suddenly straightening with pride. Maslick loosened his grip and the Syrian started toward the truck, stripping off the clothing Rapp had given him.

"Interesting guy," Maslick said as Kadir picked up a chunk of concrete and began attacking the vehicle with it. "Should I stop him?"

Rapp shook his head. "We're not actually going to be using that truck. It's just for training."

"And him? What's his story?"

"He's going to give us an assist."

"Doing what?"

"The thing we're here to do."

"So that's how it's going to be, huh?"

"For this one, yeah."

"I don't mean to be skeptical, boss, but he doesn't look all that reliable."

"Sorry to hear you say that because he's the lead on the op. A completely unique skill set."

"Really?"

Kadir exhausted himself and was now bent forward, gasping for air with his hands on his knees.

"Yup," Rapp confirmed. "Don't let anything happen to him. And if you run into a problem, make sure he's not captured. He knows too much."

"So, when you say make sure he's not captured . . ."

"I mean under no circumstances is he to be captured."

"Got it."

The Syrian's head was only inches from the truck's front tire, and he began sniffing loudly. "Penetrating oil. You're using penetrating oil."

"Uh, yeah," Maslick responded. "I'm seeing what works in case we get in trouble with the lug nuts during the operation. They tell me we have to take off wheels."

"Do you have a long bar? For leverage on your wrench?"

Maslick's brow furrowed.

"He used to be an engineer," Rapp said quietly. "You're going to hear a lot about that over the next few weeks."

The big man shrugged. "A breaker bar. Yeah. There's one hanging on the wall."

"What about fire?" Kadir pantomimed holding a propane torch.

"Got one of those, too."

He nodded approvingly and opened the hood. When he leaned in to examine the motor, his underwear slid most of the way down his ass.

"He's got some mental problems," Rapp commented.

"You don't say?"

"This is a Kamaz-740 engine," Kadir said. "The Russians make very bad machines, but this is one of their best. Not sophisticated, but reliable. Where are the explosives?"

"Explosives?" Maslick said.

Rapp ignored him and responded in Arabic. "In another location, Kadir. Don't worry, it's all top-of-the-line. But we're not to talk about these things, remember?"

Maslick motioned Rapp toward a shadowed corner of the building. "Are you going to tell me anything at all about what I'm doing here, boss?"

"The less you know the better."

"But this isn't an Agency op, right? That's what Scott said. It's private."

"Completely private. Irene has nothing to do with it," Rapp said, heading back toward his bike. "Enjoy your new roommate."

CHAPTER 40

THE sky was typically clear and awash with stars. This far from civilization there was no artificial light, allowing the smear of the Milky Way to be silhouetted against distant mountains. Rapp hung an arm out the pickup's window, directing the cool night air into the cab. He was less than ten miles from his destination and hadn't seen another vehicle in forty-five minutes. Exactly as he'd hoped.

Secrecy was a key component to success, but also a depressing reality if he failed. A few years ago, the idea of his body rotting in an anonymous Middle Eastern ditch wasn't something that much bothered him. In fact, it seemed like the inevitable conclusion to the life he'd led.

Claudia and Anna changed that. They had serious enemies—a fact that had recently come into sharp focus. If he died, who would protect them from the people who wanted to do them harm? Suicide missions in service of God and country had felt vaguely romantic when he'd started in the business, but now they felt like a betrayal of a woman and a girl who needed him.

Threats like bioweapons and assaults on America's power grid were easy calls—they would devastate everything in their path, including Claudia and Anna. The threat that Aleksandr Semenov posed was different. His strategies relied on an endless supply of willing victims. Politicians thirsty for a level of power that only dictatorship could provide. Media companies who sold fear and hate for advertising dollars. A populace eager to take dangerous narcotics and accept any lie that confirmed their tribal biases. Did he really want to give his life for people so willing to trade their freedom for an opportunity to unleash their rage and hate? He'd spent decades in the Middle East drowning in both, and now that the same attitudes were exploding across his own country, he wasn't sure it was his problem.

So what the hell was he doing? He could have found a way to slip across the border into Iraq or Turkey. Instead, he'd called Irene and convinced her to back this operation. Why? Was it just habit? Did he live his life like he was strapped to the front of a rocket because he had to? Or because he liked it?

All things to be considered at a later date. Always a later date.

The road surface steepened as he circumnavigated a rocky outcropping. Instead of following it, Rapp eased the truck to the right, kicking up a cloud of dust as he left the pavement and parked out of sight of it.

After turning off the ignition, he stepped out and searched the darkness for anything out of the ordinary. Having spent the last two nights working his ass off in that exact spot, he'd developed an intimate enough understanding of the environment to notice anything amiss.

Satisfied that everything was as he'd left it the morning before, he strode toward a couple of softball-sized rocks and kicked them away. That allowed him to drag back a sandy canvas tarp and reveal a hole the size and shape of a shallow grave. After that, he walked the pattern he'd created, uncovering other holes of varying sizes, depths, and shapes. Each dug by him using nothing more than a shovel and a pick.

Once done, his phone suggested that he still had fifteen more minutes of solitude. He used the time to empty the truck's bed of various footlockers, cardboard boxes, and even a plastic tub that looked like the one Claudia used to store her sweaters. In Syria, you took what you could get.

The footlockers were heavy enough that he had to drag them, leaving a trail he would have to deal with before leaving. He dropped them and the rest of the gear into appropriately sized holes, then re-covered them with the canvas. A few artistically placed stones and shovels full of sandy soil made them melt back into the landscape.

The hum of a motorbike began to separate itself from the sound of wind and he grabbed a night-vision scope from the truck's glove box. Climbing the ten or so yards to the top of the rocky hill, he dropped to his stomach and scanned the road to the north. It was only a few seconds before he spotted a bike with a single rider, traveling fast with no headlight.

Right on time.

Charlie Wicker was the best sniper Rapp had ever worked with. He was a man of few words who preferred to spend his time in a remote corner of his native Wyoming, but when active he was one of the deadliest men in the world. No complaints, no mistakes, no questions. The perfect operative.

Tonight, though, they wouldn't actually connect. Wick would stop some five hundred yards away and find a strategic vantage point to set up his gear. After that, he'd disappear back the way he'd come.

By the time he returned to his truck, headlights were approaching from the south. The power and height of them looked to be right, but still Rapp stayed hidden until the Russian transport left the asphalt and came to a stop next to his pickup. Joe Maslick killed the motor and jumped out, squinting into the sudden darkness.

"Mitch?"

"Right here. Any problems? Did you get everything?"

"Smooth as silk. It was all where you said it would be and no one loading me up seemed bothered."

Rapp nodded in the darkness. Having Maslick driving around in a Russian army uniform was less than ideal, but the risks were manageable. The Syrian smugglers he'd been dealing with wouldn't be anxious to fuck with a two-hundred-and-fifty-pound man wearing Spetsnaz insignia. And to the degree that communication was necessary, it could be done in broken English. The fact that Maslick's Russian accent had a bit of a *Saturday Night Live* vibe to it would be lost on the average Arabic speaker.

They opened the back of the truck in order to unload a set of tires that were a hell of a lot heavier than they looked. Once on the ground, they rolled them into holes dug to match their size. After that, Rapp concentrated on the more delicate gear, while the big man lugged the heavy stuff.

"How are things going with Kadir?" Rapp asked, dumping a couple of garbage bags into a hole.

"That guy's about ten sandwiches short of a picnic," the former Delta operator replied. "But he's kind of growing on me, you know?"

They were on their way back to the truck, when Charlie Wicker's motorbike engine started up in the distance. Maslick froze. "What's that?"

"Nothing," Rapp said, glancing at his phone. The sniper had been even faster than he'd anticipated.

"Right. Nothing."

"Just one more load, Mas. Then you can get out of here. I'll cover everything up."

"And then what?"

"We wait. But be ready. When things start up again, they'll start fast."

CHAPTER 41

"I GOTTA get out of here," Rapp said. "I'm going nuts."

"*You're* going nuts?" Bruno McGraw countered. "I haven't set foot outside this shithole for almost three weeks and *you're* going nuts?"

"What are you complaining about? You charge by the day and no one's shooting at you."

McGraw grumbled something unintelligible before continuing to pace in front of the third-floor flat's only window.

The entire space was no more than three hundred square feet, but with a functioning hot plate, electricity that was on more than off, and water that was reassuringly transparent when poured into one of the two available glasses. A virtual palace by this neighborhood's standards. Once again, Irene Kennedy had come through.

"We have to eat," Rapp pointed out.

That caloric reality, combined with the dwelling's lack of a refrigerator, gave him an excuse to get out into the city every couple of days.

McGraw wasn't so lucky. He was a top-notch shooter, but also about as American as someone could get—voice, gait, mannerisms. You could dress the guy up like Lawrence of Arabia and he'd still be the personification of a Bruce Springsteen song. Not a man who could easily move around a city that hadn't seen much in the way of tourism in more than a decade.

"Get that fish thing you got last time, Mitch. The spicy one."

"Samaka Harra."

"Gesundheit. Oh, and we're running out of water purification tablets."

"I'll do what I can, but we'll probably be better off with bleach. A lot of counterfeits out there."

"Whatever. But remember, you're pulling a double shift tonight. That's the deal. The price of you getting to go out in the world."

"Hang in there, Bruno. It won't be much longer."

"You say that every day."

Of all Scott Coleman's men, McGraw was the most susceptible to the crushing boredom that was inevitable in battle. While Charlie Wicker's idea of a good time was letting snow pile up on him while he waited for an elk to wander by, McGraw was Manhattan born and bred. He loved action whenever and wherever he could get it. Combat, sports, fast cars, Las Vegas binges. Give him something to do and he went full blast. Give him nothing to do and he went slowly insane.

Unfortunately, a low-tech stakeout was the only viable option. They didn't have interrupted satellite coverage of the area and couldn't roam the Syrian skies with a surveillance drone. The prison where Semenov got many of the guinea pigs for his experiments was about fifteen miles southwest of the city and the most practical path there was right down the street they were living on.

The last few weeks had been an exercise in staring out the window twenty-four seven, searching for the Russian transport that would eventually come to collect a fresh crop of victims. *Eventually* being the operative word. Based on the intelligence Kennedy had gathered, the intervals were a bit random and likely based on the shifting needs of the Russians' experiments. When the day finally arrived, the fuse would be lit, and McGraw could recoup his sanity.

Rapp passed through the flat's door and then descended a treacherous set of stairs to the street. His comrade's increasing discomfort notwithstanding, the situation seemed to be more or less under control. Their equipment was safely buried on the only road leading to the facility. His men were scattered strategically throughout the region, ready to move at a moment's notice. Tensions were still high in the country, but none of the flare-ups were occurring anywhere near where they would be operating. Even Kadir appeared to be holding it together in anticipation of a glorious, Allah-approved death.

The cracks would eventually start to appear, though. Even he could feel the weight of time. Risks increased, edges were dulled, chances for careless mistakes expanded. McGraw was right. Sooner was better than later.

The city hadn't seen much damage during the war and what rubble existed had been cleared from the road long ago. Traffic was light, with cars and motorbikes mingling with pedestrians in a dance that the people of the Middle East had more or less perfected.

Rapp would have preferred not to return to the same place day after day, but the central market was unavoidable if you wanted to eat. And if you wanted to keep Bruno McGraw from bouncing off the walls, it was necessary to frequent the same stand.

"Samaka Harra?" a woman in her late seventies shouted as he approached.

"You know me too well," Rapp said sincerely.

"How can I forget you?" she responded, dropping a couple of fish in a plastic bag that looked a bit less used than the others on her counter. "You're both my saddest and most prosperous customer."

The next part of the conversation was unavoidable in light of the fact that those two qualities made him the most eligible bachelor in town.

"You come to my stall. You buy food. You go home and sit alone eating it. This is why you need a wife."

"I don't know. I kind of enjoy my life as a bachelor."

"Shopping and cooking? This is the work of women. Let me show you a good life." She pulled out her phone and held up a photo of a woman wearing utterly formless clothing that included a scarf that left only the space between her chin and eyebrows visible. "This is Nakeya. A beautiful, wonderful woman. She's twenty-six years old. The perfect age for you. Her husband was killed in the war and her son died six months ago of an infection. She's alone in the world like you. Perhaps I could make an introduction?"

It was the sixth woman she'd suggested in their brief acquaintance, but he couldn't blame her. What she saw in him was a well-educated Iraqi with no attachments. From her point of view, it was a terrible waste. Through no fault of their own, these women were in situations that bordered on complete hopelessness. He had the ability to save one of them and get a good, loyal wife in return. What possible downside could there be for either party?

"The problem is that I only have eyes for you, Omaira."

She averted her gaze in feigned shock. "You are impossible."

He accepted the food and paid without bothering to haggle. "Let me think about it."

"Don't think too long!" she called after him. "You'll lose out!"

Rapp weaved back through the crowd, watching for anyone paying him too much attention or who looked like a government operative. Not that he'd necessarily recognize the latter. No one wanted what had happened in Saraqib to spread any farther, so Damascus was keeping an uncharacteristically low profile.

He'd almost made it back to the main road when he heard a sudden cacophony of blaring horns followed by a deep, rattling rumble. He pushed his way to the sidewalk in time to see a modified Ural-4320 transport speed past. Based on the expressions of the people with him on the street, they had some sense of what the truck meant. Details would be hazy, of course, but they'd know that the people it gathered from the local prison never returned.

Rapp crossed the street, moving as quickly as possible without drawing attention. He barely made it a block before the phone in his pocket began to vibrate.

McGraw's text was vague and translated into Arabic with Google, making it a little hard to decipher.

We're a go. Thank God.

Rapp stopped in the doorway of an abandoned building and typed a password that he then sent out to all the men involved in the operation. With it, they'd be able to access an encrypted file folder that would provide details on their specific roles and objectives.

Based on what the Agency had been able to glean from analyzing historical satellite photos, the loading of prisoners would take about forty minutes. After that, the truck would take roughly another four hours to reach the ambush point.

T minus two hundred and eighty minutes and counting.

CHAPTER 42

RAPP turned the motorcycle off the asphalt, immediately bogging down in the silt that his pickup had handled with no problem. He killed the headlight and got off, using a combination of throttle and muscle to get the bike out of sight behind the rocky berm.

As expected, two men had beat him there—Arab operators Coleman had worked with in Egypt. They barely acknowledged his arrival, instead focusing on exposing the pits he'd dug. Rapp grabbed one of the canvas sheets they'd tossed aside and used it to cover his bike. The addition of a few rocks and some loose dirt made it disappear satisfyingly into the terrain.

He joined their efforts and by the time another motorcycle arrived, all the gear was uncovered. Rapp grabbed another loose tarp and tossed it to Scott Coleman, who dumped his bike on its side and covered it in a similar fashion.

"I have confirmation that everybody's safe and on their way," the former SEAL said. "ETA of the last man is sixteen minutes."

"And the Russian truck?"

"Last report said forty-nine minutes. I'll get a couple more updates before it reaches us."

"All right. Let's get to work."

They joined the Arabs, retrieving equipment and arranging it in neat tiers based on the numbers and letters on the labels. They left the tires alone until Joe Maslick and Kadir arrived on a bike that looked barely adequate to hold them.

The big man jumped down into a hole and single-handedly wrestled one of them out, passing it off to someone who then rolled it to the other side of the road. Kadir tried to follow them, but Rapp grabbed him by the arm.

"Are you still with me?"

"Of course."

Based on Maslick's periodic reports, Kadir was reasonably solid when he had a simple, well-defined task to focus on. But what lay ahead wasn't simple and might demand last-minute improvisation.

"You can still do this?"

"I've practiced it a hundred times. A thousand. With Joe."

"This isn't practice, Kadir. It's the real thing."

"You're asking me if I can kill the infidels who destroyed my country, killed my family, and made me the way I am? Can I serve God and go to Him? Why wouldn't I want this?"

What he was saying rang true. Rapp wondered if it wasn't his own reticence that was the problem. He'd lost men before and he blamed himself for every one of them. He was in charge and that's where the buck stopped. But this wasn't some unforeseen variable, bad luck, or intelligence glitch. Kadir's death wasn't a bug, it was a feature. For the first time in his career, Rapp had created a plan that turned entirely on the death of one of his team.

The Syrian seemed to read his mind and clapped him on the shoulder. "I can see it in you, my good friend. You are one who fights. Who survives. But you can hold on too tightly to this world. Sometimes death is better."

By the time all their men were accounted for, the gear had been secured and Coleman was passing out communications equipment. Rapp put on his throat mike and earpiece, toggling it to transmit.

"Test. Count off with the numbers you were given."

He got the full count loud and clear, including from Charlie Wicker, who was dug in around half a kilometer to the north. Coleman came on a moment later, updating the ETA of their target. Twenty-two minutes.

"All right, suit up," Rapp said as Maslick and McGraw walked past carrying a large windshield.

The remaining men approached a line of duffels, retrieving the fatigues and body armor assigned to them, and stripping off the civilian clothes they'd arrived in. Rapp kept Kadir with him, helping him empty his duffel before opening his own. In a few minutes, everyone was clad in the desert camo favored by Russian troops in Syria. Kadir looked a little uncomfortable, tugging compulsively at the uniform for understandable reasons.

Like Rapp, he was clean-shaven, but the effect seemed to have backfired a bit. Instead of making him look more regular army, it just served to expose dark skin permanently damaged by his life as a mountain hermit. Nothing to be done about it now, though. The time to have figured out how to buy light foundation in war-torn Syria was long past.

"How do I look?" he asked.

"Perfect," Rapp responded, starting for another line of gear that his team was already digging into. The Russian firearms wouldn't be familiar to all of them, but they were fast learners and in Syria you had to work with what you could get. AK-74s and a few RPG-7s, mostly. His suppressed Volquartsen .22 was the most exotic thing on the menu.

"Nine minutes," Coleman said over his earpiece. "Repeat. Nine minutes. Questions? Problems?"

Everyone indicated that they were good to go, so Rapp handed Kadir off while the now-empty pits were covered.

"Do exactly what Joe tells you, Kadir. I'll see you soon."

Rapp jogged toward the road, cautious on the uneven terrain, but then picking up speed when he hit the pavement. After less than two minutes, he cut into the desert, once again easing his pace as he used the starlight to navigate rocks and sand. A quiet metallic clack sounded to the northeast, and he headed for it. Charlie Wicker's ghostly hand appeared briefly from the desert floor and then vanished again beneath the canvas he was hiding under.

At five foot six and barely one hundred and forty pounds, he wouldn't have been all that helpful dragging gear around, but out here he was very much in his element. Rapp slipped under the tarp next to him, taking a position behind a bipod-mounted McMillan .338 Lapua Magnum. Checking one of Wick's rifles would be a waste of time, so instead he scanned the target area through the Nightforce scope.

A moment later, Coleman's voice came over their earpieces. "Four minutes, eighteen seconds. Problems? Questions?"

There were none.

Showtime.

CHAPTER 43

"**I** HAVE eyes on the truck," Scott Coleman said over the comm. There was a brief pause before he came on again. "I'm confirming that this is the target. Repeat, this is the target. Approximately one minute, twenty seconds out. No other vehicles in sight."

"Wind's unchanged," Wick said. "Three miles an hour directly in our face."

Rapp slowed his breathing and concentrated on the rhythm of his heartbeat. Based on their calculations, distance was four hundred and fifty-eight yards with a sixteen-foot loss of elevation. Not a giveaway shot, particularly since rifles weren't his specialty. Further, they had to penetrate the Ural's windshield, which, even with the armor-piercing rounds they were using, could be unpredictable.

"Thirty seconds," Coleman said.

Wick was the better sniper, so he was targeting the driver. Hitting the man in the passenger seat was less critical, but missing wouldn't be a good start to an operation with this many moving parts. Worse, he'd never live it down.

The sound of grinding gears reached them as the driver slowed to navigate a steep corner.

"I've got a shot," Wick said calmly.

The glare from the headlights made it impossible to see through the windshield, so Rapp had to make an educated guess. "I've got a shot."

They fired in unison, causing a flash that lit up the desert around them. The sound, muffled by a pair of Thor Thundertrap suppressors, lasted a little longer, but then faded back into the night.

Rapp cycled his rifle's bolt and watched through the scope as the truck began to weave. There was a long list of things that could go wrong at this moment. He could have missed the passenger, creating a situation where his men would have an unpredictable shooter to deal with. Wick could have failed to kill the driver, leaving him capable of making a run for it. The truck could flip. Mathematically, they had enough men, ropes, and bikes to right it again, but those kinds of calculations tended to fail in the field.

Lady luck was with them. The truck drifted right and slowed to an idle as Coleman and his men appeared from both sides of the road. No shots were fired and a moment later they were dragging two bodies toward the shallow pit that would be their final resting place.

Rapp came out from cover, running toward the road, while Wick stayed behind to break down their position. By the time he arrived at the truck, Coleman was conducting a chaotic symphony of activity. Flex-cuffed prisoners were being unloaded and hustled out of sight. Men were jacking up the truck and removing lug nuts at a speed that would have impressed an F1 pit crew. Tires on both sides of the road were being uncovered and rolled toward the vehicle for installation. Cleaning teams were sopping up blood from the interior while trying to stay out of Maslick's way as he removed the damaged windshield.

The former SEAL seemed to have everything well in hand, so Rapp went around the rocky outcropping to where the prisoners were now blindfolded and lying facedown in the dirt. A Jordanian mercenary was standing guard with an AK-74 in hand. The smart move would be to summarily execute them and then dump them in the holes he'd spent so much effort digging, but that was going too far. Even for him. While it was true that most had at one time been active with any number of terrorist outfits, what did that mean exactly? In Syria, the lines between good and evil, terrorist and freedom fighter, were blurry at best.

"Listen to me," Rapp said in Arabic. "If any one of you causes any trouble, tries to get free, or opens their mouth, *all* of you get executed. On the other hand, if you just stay still and quiet, you'll be released in a few hours. After that, what you do is up to you."

When Rapp arrived back at the road, four men were wrestling the last crate of explosives into the truck and Kadir was pounding the windshield in place with an open palm. Three of the new tires had been installed and Bruno McGraw was tightening the last lug nut on the fourth.

Eight minutes had passed since the Russians in the cab had been killed. By Rapp's calculations, his team was fifteen seconds ahead of schedule.

"Kadir," he said, walking around to the front of the truck. "Are you almost done?"

"Less than a minute. We used epoxy instead of the proper adhesive. It will dry quickly and there will be no noticeable odor."

It had been Maslick's idea to put the Syrian in charge of the installation and it appeared to be keeping him focused.

"Good work," Rapp said and then used a penlight to examine the interior of the cab. Military vehicles tended to have very few upholstered surfaces capable of absorbing bodily fluids and the Ural was no exception. Both seats were still wet in places, but those sections would be covered when they were occupied. Other than that, the epoxy oozing around the interior edges of the windshield was the only thing out of the ordinary.

He heard Coleman issue orders for anyone not otherwise occupied to get in the back of the truck. Rapp watched as the last few tools were buried and the men began to climb in. Coleman was last, and Rapp closed, but didn't lock, the steel doors behind him. When he went around to the cab again, Kadir was finished with the windshield and had taken his place behind the wheel. As promised, the odor given off by the epoxy was already dissipating.

"You ready?" Rapp said, pulling himself into the passenger seat.

The Syrian didn't respond. His lips were moving silently as he talked to himself or, more likely, his god. It didn't seem to be a distraction, though. He moved smoothly through the gears as they began to accelerate. Rapp reached through his open window and adjusted the side mirror, searching the starlit landscape behind them. The road in both directions was empty and there was no sign at all of what had just happened there. Other than the remaining blood on the seat soaking through his fatigues, everything was going as planned.

CHAPTER 44

THE truck hit a fairly innocuous pothole and Rapp once again felt his spine compress. In the back, his packed-in team would be taking even more of a beating, but there wasn't anything to be done. The military suspension and new tires were built neither for comfort nor for speed. Only durability.

Kadir still looked steady, despite his lips continuing to move manically in the dim light of the gauges. Who he was talking to and what he was saying wasn't particularly relevant at this point. All that mattered was that his demons seemed to have been temporarily overpowered by his commitment to the mission.

"There it is," Rapp said, pointing to a dead tree on the west edge of the road.

When Semenov's facility had served as a hospital, the turn had been paved. Not anymore. Based on satellite images, the first half mile had been torn out to camouflage the entrance and the tree had been erected to mark the turn.

Kadir downshifted and eased the truck onto what looked like open desert. The truck swayed and bounced, finally regaining asphalt behind a low rise that hid it from the main thoroughfare.

According to the Agency's cartographers, it would be another 4.8 miles of rolling terrain to the facility's gate. At their maximum practical speed, that translated to a ten-minute ETA.

"You still good?" Rapp asked his companion.

"I've been chosen to do God's work. Why wouldn't I be?"

Certain death had a strange way of calming the mind. Rapp had experienced the sensation a number of times before finding a way to cheat the Grim Reaper at the last minute. For Kadir it was different. He had no interest in wiggling out of this trap. Very much the opposite.

"And you, my friend?" Kadir said.

"What?"

"Are *you* still okay?"

Rapp noted a dull glow in the distance. There was no detail to it, but also no doubt about its source.

"Yeah."

As they closed, the facility came into sharper focus, largely matching his memory and the Agency's photos. The chain-link fence was supported by concrete pillars every twenty feet or so and topped with razor wire. Thirty-foot towers had been erected on each corner, with a fifth to the left of the only gate. All were assumed to be manned, as was the guardhouse next to the entrance.

From this angle, the two buildings seemed even more independent than he'd expected—physically touching, but of completely different designs and shapes. The older section betrayed its history with a boxy concrete construction, a central glass door, and small windows. The west wing was a story taller, with no windows at all until the top floor, which was constructed almost entirely of glass. Aleksandr Semenov was known for his love of luxury and Rapp was confident that his living quarters were on that floor along with his office suite. Predictably, the windows were dark. At this hour, Semenov would be asleep. Probably next to his latest underage rape victim.

When they got to within a couple hundred yards, Rapp checked to make sure the RPG-7 on the floorboard was out of sight and retrieved his .22 pistol. As they continued to close, he saw that the lights in the underground parking garage were on and that there was still no barrier beyond the wooden arm in the up position. Based on Kadir's experience, around eight armed men would be waiting there to take charge of the prisoners they believed were in the back of the truck.

Spotlights came to life when they got inside of one hundred and fifty yards, and the chain-link gate began to slide back. A barrier similar to the one on the garage remained down, but it was there less for security than to show drivers where to stop in order to hand over their papers. The real deterrent was a set of aggressive tire spikes that spanned the opening. Sufficient to shred the standard Ural tires, but not a problem for the solid rubber ones that had been compacting his vertebrae since they'd set out.

Otherwise, everything was quiet. The prisoner-swap procedure would have been carried out so many times that the Russians would just be going through the motions. Empty the truck of scared, flex-cuffed people weakened by their living conditions and battered by the trip. Hustle them off to their cells. Refill the truck with the test subjects they no longer had use for. Go back to bed. Nothing bred complacency like a long string of successful repetitive operations.

At least that was the hope.

Rapp retrieved a wireless detonator not much larger than a lipstick tube and installed a double-A battery. The light on the side came on red, then changed to blue when it connected to the explosives in the back.

"Do you understand what you're going to do?"

"Of course," Kadir said, rolling down his window.

"And you understand how the detonator works?"

"I've practiced this a thousand times with Joe. Ten thousand. A million. The button can only be pressed once. When it's released the truck will explode."

"And what about—"

"How many times have you simulated your role?" Kadir countered. "I know mine better than anyone."

According to Maslick, it was true. He'd worn a groove an inch deep in Kadir's damaged brain, forcing him to go over the mission hungry, thirsty, and sleep-deprived. Even wearing headphones blasting Justin Bieber while being jabbed with a stick. According to him, the Syrian could pull this off with a spike through his skull.

"Then may Allah be with you, my friend."

The Syrian grinned. "He *is* with us. I can feel Him."

He let the vehicle drift to a stop next to the guardhouse. The soldier who appeared looked a little bored as he walked toward Kadir's open window. Rapp had the .22 in his right hand and his left on the lever that toggled the truck's high beams. The Russian came even with the sill and opened his mouth to say something, but before he could speak, a round penetrated under his chin and passed into his brain. The sound of the shot was absorbed by the suppressor and the cab, and Rapp had turned on the beams simultaneously with pulling the trigger in an effort to obscure the muzzle flash.

Kadir caught the Russian and pulled him partially through the window, creating the illusion that he was leaning inside to look at something. Anyone watching from the tower wouldn't buy it for much more than a few seconds, so Rapp slipped out the passenger-side door and snatched up the RPG. He was blocked from view as he moved along the side of the truck, finally breaking into the open near the back. He tensed slightly, half expecting to take a round to his body armor, but it didn't materialize. Instead he got the grenade off and the top of the tower was converted into burning debris cartwheeling through the air.

The sound of the explosion was the signal that the operation had begun, and his men came pouring from the back of the truck, some carrying heavy gear, others with only light arms. When Scott Coleman hit the ground, he tossed Rapp a pack, filtered face mask, and rifle. Joe

Maslick and Bruno McGraw came out last, each carrying one side of an electromagnetic device that was jamming all communication frequencies except the one they were using. At this point, tactical comms between guards, as well as cell and satellite service, would be down.

As the men scattered to carry out their assigned tasks, Rapp slammed a fist into the side of the truck three times in rapid succession. It immediately launched forward, crashing through the flimsy gate and bouncing over the tire spikes before angling toward the garage entrance.

Coleman was crouched about twenty feet from the guardhouse, surrounded by burning debris and holding a more sophisticated version of the RPG-7 that had taken out the tower. He depressed the trigger and a moment later the projectile hit the older section of the facility, destroying a series of cables and conduits that carried both electricity and landline communications. The few lights burning at the complex went dark and about half the windows shattered, raining glass down the front.

The only illumination now came from the stars and Kadir's headlights as the truck descended the parking ramp. Rapp and Coleman both ran, trying to put some distance between them and the building. Neither turned when the sound of gunfire began reverberating from the garage, but when they heard the crash of the truck hitting the makeshift support column, they dove to the ground.

The explosion was earsplitting. Rapp rolled on his back in time to see a jet of flame erupt from the garage entrance and the sparkle of the remaining glass in both buildings cascading to the ground. The hospital section shook dangerously, expelling dust and smoke for a few seconds before the second level partially collapsed. The sound of cracking concrete rose over the echo of the detonation, but the roof mostly held.

The incendiary element included with the C4 started to do its work, generating flames that were increasingly bright through billowing smoke. The southeast tower was hit by an RPG, adding another pillar of fire to the already chaotic scene. A machine gun erupted from the southwest tower, creating a brief arc of tracer bullets before it, too, was decapitated by a rocket. The north towers were being targeted by two-man teams, but the distance and worsening visibility would make them more challenging.

"Not a bad start!" Coleman shouted through his face mask.

"Don't get overconfident," Rapp responded, but he doubted the former SEAL heard him.

Wicker, McGraw, and Maslick formed up on them as they started back toward the entrance. They covered Wick as he climbed into what was left of the tower, using a fire extinguisher to put out the remaining flames on the shattered platform. When he indicated he was in position, the four other men entered the compound, staying low as they made their way toward the new section. It was largely undamaged, but that might not last. The spread of the fire would be unpredictable. Coleman and McGraw broke off and headed east to try to access the chopper behind the building just as another explosion sounded. Rapp assumed it was one of the north towers and got confirmation over the comms a moment later.

"Northeast outpost neutralized."

Another explosion followed, and a similarly accented voice confirmed the destruction of the remaining guard tower. Unfortunately, that piece of good news was overshadowed by the fact that Rapp and Maslick were taking fire from an upper-floor window in the hospital section. With the smoke, they couldn't see the shooter, but it was clear that he could see them—probably through a thermal scope. Rapp shoved his comrade forward and then broke left to create confusion as they sprinted toward the burning building.

"Wick! Are you on this?"

"Doing what I can," came the immediate response.

They made it to what had once been a set of glass double doors without getting hit and slipped across the threshold. Inside, the dust and smoke were tinged red by multiple emergency lights.

They turned toward the modern wing, bypassing the elevator in favor of a stairwell. Bruno opened the door and Rapp moved inside, starting up the steps at a pace that bordered on reckless. He couldn't be sure what the windowless levels below Semenov's penthouse contained, but a personal security detail was a good bet. And unless they were extremely sound sleepers, they were about to become a problem.

Maslick dropped a tear gas grenade on the floor and threw another. It spewed hazy spirals as it passed over Rapp's head and hit the second-floor landing just as the door there flew open. Rapp used his AK-74 to take out the first man who came through, but missed the second in the increasingly dense smoke. With no better option, he fired at the concrete walls, hoping to get lucky with a ricochet as the Russian climbed toward Semenov's living quarters. Maslick concentrated his fire on the partially open door, hitting the steel plate with short bursts until someone inside slammed it closed.

The soldier above was coughing and choking audibly, but not so much that the scrape and clang of him opening a door and closing it again was obscured. Gunfire was intermittent outside as Rapp's team engaged what was left of the men in the hospital section. Those engagements would be limited, though. Their orders were to remain at as safe a distance as possible and to focus on preventing any Russians from leaving the building. Achieving the mission objective didn't require any more than that.

After they passed the second level, Maslick settled into a position that would allow him to take out anyone unwise enough to try to exit onto it. Rapp grabbed a flash-bang grenade from the side of his pack and tossed it onto the top-floor landing. It was almost certain that the fleeing guard had taken refuge in Semenov's apartment, but there was no point in taking chances. It clattered around for a moment and then detonated, with Rapp continuing his upward sprint right after.

There was a trail of blood on the steps—a shred of good news Rapp hadn't expected. Apparently, he'd gotten lucky with his Hail Mary volley up the stairwell. But not lucky enough. The man hadn't been killed and was likely now barricaded somewhere on the other side of that door. Almost certainly with his rifle trained on it.

A burst of gunfire sounded just below, suggesting that the Russians were trying to escape. Whether that was out of a sense of duty to Semenov or their fear of being trapped by fire was hard to say. Either way, as time went on, their motivation would only increase.

Rapp moved to the broken window on the south side of the landing and took in the scene below. The towers visible from that position—with the exception of the one Wick was perched in—were just starting to burn out. In contrast, the main building was in the process of being engulfed. A light desert breeze was pushing the smoke around a bit, making visibility intermittent. He could see flashes in the haze as his men fired at anyone trying to escape the growing inferno, but little else.

Not his problem. His mission was on the other side of the door to his right.

A support column about two feet wide separated the window he was leaning through from the much larger one that looked out from Semenov's quarters. It was in a similar condition, with most of the glass lying on the ground twenty-five feet below. Rapp eased out a little farther, putting himself in a position where he could see a section of Semenov's apartment.

The soldier who had run up the stairs was in the living area aiming his rifle over an overturned dining table. A sofa in the center of the room further protected his position from anyone coming through the door. How badly he was injured or whether he was still bleeding was impossible to discern. Unquestionably, he was still capable of pulling a trigger.

Semenov, on the other hand, was nowhere to be seen. There looked to be a kitchen to the northeast, but taking refuge there would put him downrange of his guard. More likely, he was behind the closed door directly to the man's left.

With no other viable course of action, Rapp dropped his rifle and pack, then pulled the Volquartsen .22 strapped to his thigh.

He toggled his throat mike as he stepped up onto the windowsill. "Mas. I need another two minutes."

He was initially answered by a burst of gunfire, but then the big man's voice came over his earpiece. "Not much more than that, though, okay? They're not going to hole up in there forever."

CHAPTER 45

ALEKSANDR Semenov bolted upright in bed, confused by the light flickering through the open door to his bedroom. Initially, he thought it was dawn breaking, but then he noted the low rumble. Still groggy, he rolled on his side to turn on a lamp. The illumination from it was comforting for only a moment before being swallowed by a blinding flash.

He raised a hand instinctively to protect his face as the lamp hesitated and then went out. A moment later, red emergency light bathed the room, combining with the glimmer of what he now understood to be fire. Fully awake, he slid from the mattress and snatched up a robe hanging nearby.

His cell phone was fully charged, and he used a shortcut to call the guardhouse, but failed to get a connection. A closer examination of the screen suggested he had neither cell signal nor Internet.

He started hesitantly toward the door, when the air around him seemed to compress. The entire building shuddered, shifting beneath his feet violently enough to knock him to the floor. Next to him, the massive west-facing window spider-webbed and then collapsed, sending glass shards falling into the desert below and hurtling toward him through the chemical-scented air. Again he covered his face, this time less in confusion than in terror. Adrenaline surged through him as the sound of machine-gun fire mingled with additional detonations.

The facility is under attack.

The realization caused his stomach to revolt, and he struggled not to vomit as he stumbled toward the living area. The main window looking south was gone, and through its empty frame he could see the south guard towers being consumed.

He stumbled back as smoke began to drift across the scene, trying to process what was happening. Moscow? Had Boris Utkin decided that getting rid of him was worth the political blowback? No. Not like this. It was too overt. Too reckless. The Syrians? Impossible. Even taking into account their fury over the loss of the Golan Heights, they were still entirely dependent on Russian support.

Damian Losa?

For some reason, the thought of the cartel leader had the effect of bringing Semenov's mind fully back online. Was it conceivable that this was the doing of a common criminal with delusions of grandeur? The Mexican's remaining manpower in Syria was virtually nonexistent—nothing more than a few defeated insurgents and out-of-work drug dealers. In contrast, Semenov had a cadre of highly trained soldiers, some of whom were barracked directly beneath him.

But how many? The Canadian had killed three of his men in the Syrian countryside and another five had died in the attempt to transport him to Tartus. He froze for a moment when he realized that Fournier could be out there. The seemingly demure attorney who had been responsible for the deaths of eight of his best men could be out there leading the assault. Who else would Losa send?

Semenov ran back into the bedroom, flinging open his closet and trying to calm himself as he dressed. The soldiers in this building weren't the only ones charged with defending him. There were the guards in the main part of the facility. And with the test subjects locked in their—

He froze again, this time hunched with only one leg in his pants.

The truck.

They were bringing in prisoners that night. Is that how Losa's men had gained access? Could they have hijacked the incoming vehicle? Is that where the main blast had come from? If he was using terrorists, it was conceivable that a jihadist could have gotten into the underground garage with an explosive. If so, they would have instantly incinerated half of his remaining men.

The smoke was getting dense enough to burn his eyes by the time he finished dressing and ran to an old-style telephone in the living area. It was hardwired to the facility's communication system and would have backup power. When he brought it to his ear, though, there was nothing but silence.

Machine-gun fire erupted in the stairwell and Semenov spun. When the door started to open, he panicked and slammed his body against the steel in an effort to close it again. The effort failed and instead he was pushed back with sufficient force to send him to the ground.

"No! Don't shoot!" he screamed before recognizing the soldier lurching across the threshold.

The man moved as if he were blind, and his right pants leg was soaked with blood. Still, he managed to secure the door behind him. Semenov began to choke and suspected that some kind of gas had been deployed in the stairwell. He wiped at his eyes as the armed man stumbled into the kitchen and turned on a faucet, splashing water over his face.

"You have to get me to my helicopter!" Semenov shouted as he struggled back to his feet. "Now! Where is the rest of your team? We have to move!"

The mercenary turned toward him, bright red eyes capable of focusing again. "They're trapped by the tear gas and at least two combatants in the stairwell. But they're not injured, and they have masks. It's going to take—"

His voice was drowned out by another blast, this one just outside. Dust billowed through the gaps around the steel door, but it held.

"Have you called for reinforcements? Our people in Hmeimim?"

"Comms are down," the man said, flipping an oak dining table on its side and dragging it toward the back wall. "By the time anyone even knows about this, it'll be over."

"You have to get me out of here!" Semenov repeated as the man took a position behind the table and aimed his rifle over it.

"Shut the fuck up."

"What did you say to me?"

The mercenary swung his weapon in Semenov's direction and sighted along it. "I said shut the fuck up."

CHAPTER 46

RAPP swung out over the twenty-five-foot drop, clinging to a crack in the support pillar and easing a foot onto the sill on the other side. There were still a few shards of embedded glass, making it impossible to get much more than the tip of his boot onto it. The smoke billowing around him became both denser and a bit paler, suggesting that Maslick had thrown another tear gas canister.

Rapp used the additional cover to lean left, bringing half of his face around the edge of the column and giving him a better view of the apartment on the other side. Blood was flowing beneath the edge of the table the man was barricaded behind and a puddle was forming. He remained vigilant, but with his attention centered entirely on the door. Blood loss had a strange way of sharpening one's focus at the cost of situational awareness. It was a phenomenon that Rapp himself had experienced.

The fingertips on his right hand were starting to split on the sharp edge he was clinging to, creating a countdown of sorts. The pain was irrelevant, but if he waited long enough for them to become slick with blood, he'd be headed to the ground the fast way. He tried to brace his gun hand against the column, but it was hopeless. The amount of muscular tension necessary to keep him from falling caused it to shake slightly. Combined with smoke, a slightly foggy face mask, and the fact that only a small portion of the man was visible behind the table, it made the shot impossible.

The Russian's gun wavered as he wiped at his eyes. The smoke and tear gas weren't particularly thick in the apartment, but were still bad enough to affect his vision. How much, though? Certainly not enough to prevent him from killing anyone coming through the door. But how fast could he adjust his attention to the window? How much blood had he lost?

None of those questions were going to be answered in the few seconds that Rapp had left before his grip gave way. So when a burst from Joe Maslick's AK briefly sharpened the Russian's focus on the door, Rapp tossed the .22 inside the apartment and used his newly freed hand to pull himself around the column.

A graceful landing wasn't feasible and instead he came down on his shoulder, rolling toward the pistol and snatching it up just as Maslick's gun went silent. At that same moment, any questions about the Russian's competence were answered. He spotted the incursion immediately, swinging his weapon smoothly and beginning to pulverize floor tile in an arc that was headed straight for his target.

Rapp ignored the approaching stream of bullets and used both hands to line up the Volquartsen. He squeezed the trigger and the Russian's head snapped back, but without the comforting spray of blood, bone, and brain matter that a 9mm round would have produced. Still, he tipped back and his rifle barrel rose, sending rounds harmlessly through the empty window frame and into the night.

By then, Rapp was already on his feet, fighting for traction in the broken glass as he ran toward the Russian. He hit the overturned table at full speed, flipping over it to find the man on his back, but still alive. The .22 round had struck him in the forehead, but lacked the energy to fully penetrate. Despite the impact and blood loss, he was trying to bring his weapon to bear again. Rapp put an end to that by pressing the barrel of the .22 under his chin and firing twice.

"Mas, I'm in!" he said into his throat mike. "Come up!"

Rapp ran across the room and opened the door, covering Maslick as he ran up the steps. The big man tossed a fragmentation grenade toward the second-floor landing and then scooped up Rapp's pack and rifle before throwing himself across the threshold. Rapp slammed the door and had just managed to slide the bolt into place when the grenade exploded.

"Tense," Maslick shouted through his face mask.

"Walk in the park," Rapp responded. "Watch the window. It's the easier access."

"Roger that," he said, taking up the Russian's position behind the overturned table.

Rapp grabbed his AK and pack before jogging back across the living area and gently testing the knob to the door at the back. Not surprisingly, it didn't budge. The stylish wood slab wouldn't survive more than a few kicks, but it was impossible to know what was on the other side. What Rapp didn't need was to get clipped by a lucky shot from some piece-of-shit faux general. So instead, he reeled through the ten or so Russian phrases he'd been working on for the past week. Selecting the most appropriate, he pulled up his mask and shouted through the door.

"General Semenov. Are you injured?"

Are you in there or *Are you inside* would have been better, but he didn't know how to say either.

The answer was mostly unintelligible, with Rapp catching only the Russian word for "helicopter."

The door was jerked open a moment later by a panicked Aleksandr Semenov, coughing from the fumes and holding a pistol loosely in his right hand. Rapp swung his rifle butt into the man's stomach, and he collapsed, losing his grip on the gun and vomiting on the elegant floor tiles.

Rapp kicked the weapon away and entered the bedroom, dumping the contents of his pack on the floor while Semenov continued to empty the contents of his stomach.

The small explosive charge Rapp had brought turned out to be unnecessary. The long, west-facing window was already devoid of glass. So instead, he selected a length of nylon rope, which he tied around the convulsing Russian's torso.

The next part was a little more complicated. Rapp found the black mark he'd made on the rope and placed that section just below the windowsill. Then he carried the free end to the four-poster bed that dominated the room. It felt as substantial as it looked, so he secured the rope to the frame and activated his throat mike.

"Mas. Time to go."

"Hang on. I've got one more grenade and I don't want to waste it."

Rapp walked back to Semenov, and the man squinted up at him.

With the smoke and full face mask, recognition came slowly. But it came.

"You!" he managed to choke out before Rapp grabbed the rope and began dragging him toward the window. Semenov flailed impotently, trying to get a grip on the line behind him and screeching from the pain being inflicted by the shards of glass strewn across the floor. Probably also from the anticipation of what was to come. It wouldn't be lost on him that a great deal of effort had been expended to capture and not kill him. He'd know better than most that the remainder of his life was likely to be short and excruciating. After all, he'd been on the other side of similar scenarios more times than anyone could count.

They arrived at the window just as a final grenade detonated in the stairwell. Maslick appeared in the doorway a moment later, watching skeptically as Rapp yanked the Russian to his feet.

"You sure you measured right?"

"Only one way to find out," Rapp said, throwing Semenov through the opening. The man's scream was surprisingly piercing, cutting through the sound of gunfire as he dropped. The rope caught him about three feet from the ground and Rapp heard the scrape of the bed as it was dragged across the tile floor. In the end, not having anything more solid to tie him off to had been a stroke of luck. The fact that both Semenov and the end of the rope were on the ground would make life a little easier.

"You're up," Rapp said.

Maslick grabbed the larger of two pairs of gloves lying on the floor and used them to slide down the rope. Rapp slung his weapon on his back and went to the bedroom door one last time to check if there was any sign of an imminent breach.

Nothing.

One of the many problems with the Russian regular army was that most of the soldiers were fully aware that they were little more than cannon fodder. The mercenaries were no better—men who were smart enough to know you couldn't spend your money if you were dead. With all the tear gas, gunfire, and explosions, it was possible that Semenov's protection detail had decided to seek their fortunes elsewhere.

Rapp grabbed the remaining pair of gloves and used them to half slide, half free-fall down the line. By the time he hit the ground, Maslick had freed Semenov and was running him toward the chopper pad to the northeast. It was another benefit of Semenov's softer-than-expected landing. They'd planned on him breaking at least a couple of ribs from getting caught by the rope—a reality that would have forced Maslick to carry him.

"We're on the ground with the target," Rapp said over his throat mike.

"You have cover north," responded an Arabic-accented voice.

Bruno McGraw, who was with Coleman securing Semenov's helicopter, came on just after.

"In position."

With Maslick focused on keeping the Russian moving, Rapp hung back, sweeping his rifle in search of anyone moving in on them. Their tactical situation wasn't great, but it could have been much worse. The only high ground was Semenov's apartment and the roof-top deck—neither of which was easily accessible at this point. Even less accessible were the widely spaced west-facing windows of the hospital section. All had at least partially collapsed, and most were filled with flame.

Even if any enemy combatants were looking down on them, all they'd see was two Russian soldiers trying to escort Semenov to his aircraft. Without comms, they'd be hesitant to shoot and might even be inclined to provide cover if one of their less cautious comrades got trigger-happy.

When they arrived at the chopper, the blades were starting to turn, and McGraw was on the ground searching for threats through a thermal scope. Maslick lifted Semenov completely off his feet and threw him into the aircraft before climbing in himself.

Instead of immediately following, Rapp crouched and activated his throat mike. "The target is in the helicopter. I repeat: the target is in the helicopter. Do we have any casualties?"

Rapp swore under his breath when an accented voice responded. "Gunshot wound to the stomach near the southwest tower."

"Can he be saved?" Rapp was forced to ask. This wasn't a military operation. It was a bad combination of pitch-black CIA and drug cartel. Dead men got left behind.

"If we get him medical attention."

"Understood. Any others? Everyone sound off."

His entire team did, confirming that they had only the one injury.

Rapp turned toward the chopper, where he could see Coleman flipping switches in the glass-domed cockpit. The former SEAL had spent much of the last month in a mock-up created from scavenged auto parts and papier-mâché. Combined with a laptop flight simulator, it had been as accurate a training environment as they could create. Hopefully, it would be enough.

"Scott," Rapp said over his throat mike. "Get Semenov out of here and fly south. We'll grab our injured man and head in the same direction. When we're a klick out and sure no one's following, you can circle back to get us."

"You sure? I could just hop this thing over and pick him up where he is."

It was tempting, but too risky. Rapp wanted Semenov out of there. "You have your orders, Scott."

"Roger that. Rendezvous one klick south on your signal."

Rapp switched to Arabic to make sure there were no misunderstandings with the men they were on their way to help. "We are two men, coming from the direction of the chopper pad. ETA less than two minutes. Do you copy?"

"Copy. Will provide cover."

The rotors started to pick up speed and Rapp slapped Bruno McGraw on the back. "You're with me! Let's go!"

They began running across the compound as Coleman took to the air. Flames from the facility provided plenty of light, but were a bit disorienting as they played off the smoke. Despite this, they found the men they were looking for. One was snipping through the chain-link fence with a set of bolt cutters, while the other was lying on his stomach with a bloody bandage tied around his midsection. He was hit badly, but still capable of sighting through his scope to cover their approach. Barely.

Rapp dropped down next to him, while McGraw went to the fence and began bending back a flap of chain link. When Rapp looked over at the injured man, he saw that he'd given all he had. Now that cover was no longer necessary, his eye had drifted from the glass and his bearded cheek was propped on the butt of his rifle.

Rapp rolled him aside and took over, using the thermal scope to cut through the smoke and scan for threats. The snap of links being severed behind him was comforting, but he'd have liked the rhythm to be a little faster. The sooner he could put Syria in the rearview mirror, the better.

He spotted two shapes that were a little too well defined to be artifacts of the smoke and adjusted his rifle to center them in his scope. A few seconds later, he'd confirmed that he was tracking two shooters moving in front of the building.

"I have two contacts crossing the new section from west to east. Are they members of our team?"

All responses suggested that they weren't.

"Wick, can you see these guys?"

"Not yet."

"Roger that. They're headed toward you and the gate area. Probably just looking for an exit. Don't engage them unless you have to. There's no reason to give away your position if they're just looking to run."

"Understood."

A moment later, Bruno appeared and began dragging the unconscious Arab toward the fence. "We've got a hole, Mitch."

"Okay," Rapp said, keeping his scope trained on the two men. "Get him out of here. I'll catch up."

"We're in position," Bruno McGraw said over the comm.

"On my way," came Scott Coleman's immediate reply.

They had traded off carrying the injured man in order to maximize their speed and it was currently Rapp's turn. His deteriorating knee felt like it had a hot dagger in it, but they were making good time over the open terrain. The glow of the burning facility was a half mile back and all their men were clear of it. They'd melt into the desert and wait for extraction by locals getting paid enough to do the job and keep their mouths shut. After, it would just be a matter of smuggling them out of the country and putting them on a flight home. That would take a little time, though. Based on his experience in Israel, it made sense to proceed with caution.

The chopper became audible to the south before creating a silhouette against the stars. Dust kicked up with the force of a sandblaster, but Rapp ran straight into it. He deposited the man inside as Bruno and his Arab comrade provided cover against threats that likely weren't there.

The aircraft was on the ground less than ten seconds before they were all loaded and arcing west.

"I have eyes on our people," Coleman said over their headsets.

Joe Maslick opened the aircraft's doors as they pulled into hover and descended to within fifteen feet of the Mediterranean. Rapp could see the lights of Cyprus in the distance and the scent of the sea became overwhelming as the rotors kicked up a salty mist. It was a beautiful night that Aleksandr Semenov wasn't enjoying. He seemed almost catatonic, barely resisting when Rapp unbuckled him from his seat and once again threw him into space. The dark water swallowed him for a few seconds before his life jacket forced him back to the surface.

With no better option, McGraw and Maslick dragged their injured comrade out with them, each holding one of his arms as they fell. Rapp watched as two frogmen took charge of their casualty and then he motioned to the last man in the chopper to jump. A few moments later, everyone but Semenov was swimming toward a cigarette boat rocking in the chop created by the Mi-24's rotors.

"I'm out," Rapp said into his headset before sweeping it from his head and jumping. When he was clear, Coleman began sideslipping away from the boat. At about one hundred yards, he backed off the power and put the helicopter into the water. He escaped the cockpit without any problems and started swimming toward the boat.

Rapp climbed into the craft and looked back, spotting Semenov bobbing about thirty feet off the starboard bow.

"Get in!" Rapp shouted.

"I won't!" the Russian shouted back.

Coleman swam by him, maintaining a solid clip considering the swells. Less than a minute later, he was on board, uninjured and wearing the same toothy grin he always did when he got to crash or blow something up.

"It's a long way to shore," Rapp yelled, pointing east. "But if you want to do it, Syria's that way."

He signaled to the pilot, who eased the throttle forward.

"Wait!" Semenov shouted, and the engines wound down again.

"Wait for what?"

It didn't take long for the Russian to reel through his nonexistent alternatives and begin swimming toward the boat.

CHAPTER 47

R APP crossed the house's living area with a satphone pressed to his ear. The sliding glass door at the back was open and he stepped out onto a flagstone terrace. The property maintained an ancient agrarian feel, but had been updated with the expected creature comforts. Even more important were the ancient root cellar just beyond the tree line and the fact that there were no neighbors within earshot. Nothing like a mile or so of wooded mountains to absorb screams.

"Charlie was the last," Irene Kennedy said over the encrypted line. "So everyone's out of the desert and safe. In a couple of days, they'll all be out of Syria and on their way home."

"A couple of days? I thought you said it would take a couple of weeks?"

"That was the initial thinking. We were going to smuggle them over various borders by various methods, but I've decided that a better option is to get them out through Israel."

"Because it worked out so well for me?"

"Ironically, yes. Now that Ben and the prime minister are aware that you survived, they're anxious to mend fences."

"Just so long as you make it clear that if any of my guys get so much as a scratch on their way out, I'm going to put my thumbs in their eye sockets."

"I don't think that'd be productive. Instead, how about I convey your undying gratitude?"

"Your call," he said, watching the distant streetlights of Agros flicker to life as the sun dipped behind the horizon. "How's Ahmed doing?"

"Just fine. The medical team we had on standby repaired the damage and they say he'll make a full recovery."

Rapp heard awkward footsteps approaching from behind and a moment later Scott Coleman hobbled by holding a bottle of local beer. Rapp muted the phone.

"Are you going to put the steaks on or what?"

"I'm injured, man."

While technically true, it hadn't happened during the operation. The night before, he'd had a few too many post-operation drinks and tripped over the hose Rapp was using to top off the pool.

"Get your ass over to the grill."

"I have to admit," Kennedy continued, unaware of the exchange, "that everything went more smoothly than I expected. But we're not out of the woods yet. The next phase of this is going to have to be handled carefully. There's going to be a lot of scrutiny from the SVR and every other intelligence agency in the world. Not to mention the media."

"I'm less worried about that than I am Damian Losa. He's not going to be happy about what we're planning."

"Agreed. It's a problem I've been working on since I first got the call from you. Give me a few more days and I think I'll be able to offer a solution."

• • •

Rapp penetrated the trees via a dirt footpath, finally descending a set of steps cut into the earth. The door he came to was constructed of thick hardwood, but had taken a beating from more than a century of local weather. Deep cracks ran vertically along the grain, and the iron hardware that kept it in place was half rusted through.

Rapp removed an incongruously modern padlock and passed into an oppressive room about eight feet square. Walls were constructed of haphazardly stacked stone that had turned black with mold. The floor was nothing but damp soil, scattered with a few farm-related relics and an impressive number of rodent carcasses. The ceiling was in about the same condition as the door, held up by rotting beams and slung with a wire connected to a single bare bulb.

Rapp had considered leaving it turned off, but as soul crushing as darkness could be, this place was even more depressing in the light. And now that the overwhelming smell of mildew had combined with the stench of urine and excrement, it was enough to make even Rapp's stomach roll over.

Aleksandr Semenov, the source of that new layer of stink, was looking far less fastidious than normal. Instead of a crisp uniform covered in unearned medals, he was sitting naked in his own filth. The dust caked to his pale skin was streaked with sweat and what may have been a few tears. A gash on his leg looked like it was getting infected and if left untreated would add the stench of rotting flesh to the current bouquet.

A CamelBak with water and nutrients hung from the rafter above him, with the hose dangling within reach of his mouth. It was half-empty, suggesting that the Russian wasn't willing to give up yet. He wanted to survive.

"Wake up, Alek."

His eyes fluttered to take in the man standing in front of him.

Rapp was freshly showered and shaved, wearing a pair of pressed khakis, a green polo shirt, and a new Rolex Submariner. Not his normal look, but to some extent he was still playing the Canadian lawyer.

As an added benefit, the careful grooming would deepen the contrast between their current circumstances.

"Who are you?" Semenov managed to get out. "Who are you really?"

"Damian Losa's negotiator," Rapp said. Not really the truth, but also not a lie. For now, this was nothing more than a business dispute between two criminal organizations—the one known as the Losa Cartel and the other known as the Russian government.

"A negotiator," Semenov repeated weakly.

"That's right. But Mr. Losa understands that parties can't always come to an agreement. That's why he has me."

"Let me talk to him."

"You had your chance for that."

"Do you have any idea who I am?" the Russian shouted at a volume that belied his condition. "I'm General Aleksandr Semenov! One of the most powerful men in Russia. One of the most powerful in the world! Do you really believe that the SVR won't discover who's behind this? You've declared war on the Russian Federation!"

Rapp didn't acknowledge the threat. "I have a script that you're going to read on camera. After that, we can talk about what your future looks like."

"What did you say? A script?"

Rapp unfolded a piece of paper and laid it on Semenov's bare thighs. The Russian scanned the lengthy handwritten message for a few seconds, finally looking up and meeting Rapp's eye.

"Never."

It was obvious that his resolve was nothing more than bravado. While breaking a battle-hardened jihadist could be a long, messy chore, breaking a man like Aleksandr Semenov would be more of a minor inconvenience. The man had enjoyed a life of privilege since the day he was born. He wasn't a patriot. He had no religious beliefs or family he was close to. Semenov was a man who cared only about himself and wielding power over others. Just the kind of prick who would be utterly incapable of enduring even a few moments of real suffering.

Rapp retrieved a cattle prod that was leaning against the wall and discharged it into the man's testicles. His earsplitting scream suggested that there was a good chance they could have this thing wrapped up before morning.

It had taken longer to clean Semenov up than it had to break him. But now he was perfectly presentable—carefully arranged hair, a fresh shave, and wearing a flawless reproduction of his uniform courtesy of Irene Kennedy. The smell was gone, too. Washed down the side of the mountain with the hose Coleman had drunkenly accused of attacking him.

Of course, he still looked haggard. The memory of the pain he'd so briefly endured remained etched across his face and the red rims of his eyes stood out even in the soft light. Rapp checked the tripod-mounted iPhone and made sure that it didn't frame anything that could provide a clue to the Russian's whereabouts.

"Okay," Rapp said when he was satisfied. "You ready?"

Semenov seemed to be on the verge of conjuring a little defiance, but then thought better of it. Instead he straightened and folded his hands in front of him.

"Give me a count to test your sound."

He did, and the mike attached to his collar functioned perfectly. With volume and light set, there was no reason not to get started. Rapp picked up a set of cue cards and took a position next to the camera.

"You're on, General."

The man stared at the first card for a moment, his magnificent brain straining to find some other option and coming up empty. The life of power, pleasure, and dominion he'd laid out for himself was gone. The only thing left to do now was focus on survival and minimizing his suffering.

"I am General Aleksandr Semenov, the director of the Russian

Federation's asymmetrical warfare program. I am responsible for developing protocols to interfere in the elections of foreign countries, supporting Islamic terrorist attacks in Europe, undermining democratic institutions, and carrying out cyberattacks. Both I and most of my programs are well known to Western intelligence agencies. What they don't know is that I've been working on a new program. I was using Syria's pharmaceutical production capability and Russian chemists to engineer a new, highly addictive form of a narcotic called captagon."

Rapp flipped to the second card. Semenov was actually pretty good at this. He'd probably spent the last decade practicing in the mirror for his inevitable entry into politics.

"More important, the use of it causes irreversible brain damage and psychoses. My plan was to distribute this drug throughout the West, overwhelming the medical and law enforcement capabilities of the US and Europe. Further, I planned to use a Muslim criminal network in the EU and a Latino network in the US in order to fan the flames of xenophobia and cause further divisions between political parties and allies. The eventual goal of Russia's combined asymmetrical capability is to break up both the EU and the United States."

Rapp flipped to the third card, starting to harbor hopes that they'd actually get this in the first take.

"The development of this new narcotic demanded hundreds of test subjects, all of whom we took from Syrian refugee camps and prisons. All of them either died as a result of the experiments that were performed on them or were executed when they were no longer useful. This brought us under the scrutiny of a number of Syrian insurgent groups whose family members and comrades had fallen victim to our program. Two days ago, one of them attacked my facility southwest of al-Qadr, Syria, destroying it, and capturing me."

Rapp moved to the last card.

"I deeply regret my involvement in this program and the suffering it caused. But I had no choice in the matter. I was under the orders of the Kremlin."

Rapp set the cards on a table and stopped filming. When the edited version was released anonymously on the Internet, it would be like a nuclear bomb going off in Moscow.

Even better, Semenov had already provided more than twenty pages of intel on methods, locations, bank accounts, and even his financing of the recent terrorist attack in Germany. The CIA's hackers were already using his uncanny memory for passwords to infiltrate sensitive Russian systems, introduce malware, and download classified documents. The opportunities for mischief were apparently endless.

Rapp couldn't help but smile. Russia was unique in that it was an almost entirely destructive force. The human race would be infinitely better off if the whole country just slid into the ocean. And with the unwitting help of Damian Losa, the skids had just been greased.

CHAPTER 48

THE only television in the Prague flat was in a small room at the back. Normally not an item that Losa had much use for, but now he found himself unable to look away.

Information kept dribbling into the public space at a pace so tantalizing that it was almost certainly planned. Reports of the destruction of a suspicious Syrian medical facility. Rumors that dangerous designer narcotics were being developed there. Accusations regarding the involvement of the Russian and Syrian governments, with the expected subsequent denials. All culminating in a video of Aleksandr Semenov describing his life's work in lurid detail.

And now, as if to add a touch of much-needed action to the narrative, a well-produced video of the assault on Semenov's facility. Technology truly was a marvel. The fact that the footage had likely been edited together from commercially available body cameras didn't detract from its professionalism. High-definition explosions, swirling smoke, combatants with concealed faces.

Everything he would expect from an operation conceived and executed by Mitch Rapp and Irene Kennedy.

Losa watched a truck speed across the compound and into an underground parking garage. The ensuing explosion was powerful enough to cause significant structural damage and would have vaporized the driver. It was an event so dramatic that the impact endured, even after watching it multiple times.

The action faded and was replaced by a roundtable with three participants—a news anchor, a former American special forces commander, and a retired German diplomat. The anchor started the discussion.

"The Russian foreign minister has made a number of statements insinuating that this operation would have been impossible for a group of insurgents to carry out. The implication is that this is just another attempt by the US to smear them as well as to kidnap and interrogate one of their top people. Colonel? Let's start with you."

The American scowled. "The Russians are nothing if not consistent. Every time they screw up or get caught with their hand in the cookie jar, they try to make it some kind of American conspiracy. The attack clearly started with a suicide bomber, which isn't exactly a common Western battle technique. And, frankly, from what we see on that video, the facility's defenses were typically shoddy. Once that truck exploded and they took out the guard towers, the fight was pretty much over. The real challenge would be getting Semenov out alive. Difficult, but certainly not impossible for a small, reasonably competent force."

"Also, we have the captagon tablets that managed to survive the fire in Salerno," the German interjected. "They suggest a level of sophistication that would be extremely difficult to conceive and manufacture. In light of what's happened, the chemical analysis of them has been revisited and it seems to confirm General Semenov's story. In fact, it appears that the previously unidentified compounds very closely resemble a schizophrenia drug developed by the Soviets."

"And the reports that Semenov was involved in financing the terrorist attack in Munich?" the news anchor said. "Credible?"

"Obviously an investigation needs to be carried out, but yes. I fear that it is credible. And if a direct link can be established, the ramifications—"

Losa used a remote to shut off the television and stood motionless in the ensuing semidarkness. Both Syria and Russia were scrambling to carry out whatever damage control they could. In Syria's case, the issue would blow over. They were a minor thorn in the world's side, and it was already known that they were heavily involved in the drug trade. Russia, though, was very different.

Historically, the West had met Russia's recklessness with a certain amount of restraint. The goal was to avoid direct confrontation and instead to just stand back and let the country slowly collapse under the weight of its own compulsions. Unfortunately, restraint wasn't a trait that the Russians shared with their Western counterparts.

What they did have a gift for, though, was revenge.

The Kremlin was certainly aware that he'd sent a negotiator to try to create a relationship with the creators of the new captagon formulation. And if that was true, it wouldn't be long before the SVR began to suspect he was the one responsible for all this.

From that moment forward, he wouldn't be at war with a rival cartel, the Italian mafia, or even the Syrian government. He would be at war with a country that was the world's premier nuclear power and almost supernaturally proficient at assassinating its enemies.

The question was what to do about it.

Losa exited into the living area and approached a wall of ballistic glass that looked out over the city lights.

Certainly, he could find some back channel to Russia's intelligence apparatus and provide information—even evidence—of Mitch Rapp's involvement. Once that was public, Irene Kennedy and her country would be put in an extremely difficult situation. Particularly if he was correct in his suspicion that Semenov's kidnapping was an unsanctioned operation.

Unlike the Russians, neither Kennedy nor Rapp was particularly prone to vengeance. They were problem solvers, and in the face of a political scandal like this one, it was possible that he'd be forgotten. But just as possible that he wouldn't be.

Rushed footsteps sounded on the marble floor behind him and he turned to see Julian hurrying toward him with an open laptop in his hand.

Mitch Rapp, he mouthed, tossing a wireless headset to Losa and then setting the computer on an expansive dining room table. Losa put on the headset but didn't speak until his lieutenant signaled for him to do so. The sophisticated software would seek to locate the caller's position but, in this case, it would be a waste of time. Or maybe not. While Rapp went to great lengths to hide Claudia Gould and her daughter, it was possible that he himself didn't take similar precautions. Seeking him out tended to be unwise.

"Hello?"

"The way I see it, I delivered on my promise," Rapp said without preamble. "Semenov and his facility are gone, and based on the pressure the Russians and Syrians are under, they're permanently out of the captagon business. You're back to dominating the European and American narcotics markets the way you always have."

"But how long until the Russians start to suspect that I was involved in Semenov's kidnapping? You've made me a target."

"I can't imagine that being a target is anything new to you."

"You say your debt to me is paid, but what you did wasn't in pursuit of my interests. It was in pursuit of your own. You kidnapped a Russian official and used me for cover."

"You set me up to be captured and interrogated."

Julian made circling motions with his right hand, indicating that he was getting somewhere. That Rapp should be kept on the line as long as possible.

"I sent you there to meet with them. You kept avoiding those meetings."

"You sent me there because I was expendable and couldn't reveal anything about you or your organization. And I don't take that personally. Business is business. But now you're thinking about contacting the Russians and telling them about my involvement. Maybe even releasing your side of the story to the media. You believe it'll start so much nuclear saber-rattling that you can just disappear into it."

"The Russians have a reputation for making examples of people who cross them."

"I'm sure you can stay one step ahead. In my experience, they're not the sharpest tools in the shed—particularly with Semenov out of the picture. Plus, you're ignoring the upside."

"Upside?"

"Your legend is a big part of what keeps you alive, and sticking your foot in the Russian Federation's ass isn't exactly going to hurt your image."

"Your arguments would be more persuasive if they weren't complete bullshit," Losa said, doing two things he religiously avoided—raising his voice and using profanity. Across the room, Julian's eyes widened, but not at his boss's unusual behavior. At what he saw on his computer screen. His hand shot out to the keyboard and the call disconnected.

"What? What is it?"

His lieutenant spun the laptop so that Losa could see the screen. "He's not calling from Virginia, Damian. He's calling from Prague."

When Damian Losa stepped through the door to his study, the staff had already lowered the shades and dimmed the lights so that his movements would be obscured from anyone with a sight line on the windows. All security shifts were now active, and they were bringing in more men from his operations around the globe. Various vehicles and aircraft, as well as a number of body doubles, were being coordinated to help him slip out of Europe to a property he'd acquired in Ecuador only a few days ago. Irene Kennedy was unquestionably brilliant, but she wasn't clairvoyant. If he could get out of there without being tracked, he'd be safe. Not forever, of course, but for long enough to contemplate his next move. And more important, to contemplate Mitch Rapp's.

What exactly were the man's intentions? Had he called to lull his target into a sense of false security while he approached from the shadows? Certainly, Losa's death would be convenient to him, the CIA, and America. As long as he was breathing, there was a chance he could leak the Agency's role in Aleksandr Semenov's disappearance.

He paused in the center of the room, looking at a bottle of Perrier on the sideboard and glancing behind him at the still-open door. Uncertain what else to do, he approached and carried out the ritual that had become so important to his mental state: the careful slicing of a lime, the placing of it in a crystal glass with a few cubes of ice, the pouring of the water. After an initial sip, he picked up the remaining item on the tray. A Glock 19.

This one had a silencer screwed to it, but there was nothing else remarkable about it. Other than the fact that Mitch Rapp had managed to put it there.

The message was clear. Their business together was done unless Losa decided otherwise.

He put the weapon back on the tray and walked calmly through the house as his staff rushed around him. Julian was in the living room, tearing down his electronics and trying to maintain some order amid the chaos that had taken hold.

"Send everyone home," Losa called to the man. "We're staying."

EPILOGUE

RAPP couldn't help feeling a little disoriented as he pulled up to his property. It had been less than two months since he last saw it, but it felt like two years. Further, Claudia hadn't opened the gate from inside when she'd seen his car coming. It had become a bit of a battle of wills between them—him insisting that those were the kinds of sloppy protocols that got people killed and her insisting that he was paranoid. Had her fear of Damian Losa won him the war?

Somehow, he doubted it.

Rapp pressed his thumb to the reader and waited for the barrier to slide open, glancing in the rearview mirror every few seconds out of habit. The neighborhood felt abandoned and would continue that way for another week or so. All of the men who had participated in the Syrian operation had been safely extracted and fully paid. Wick was already back in the middle-of-nowhere Wyoming, the only place he felt comfortable. Coleman had sailed from Cyprus to his place in

Greece, where he'd met Bruno McGraw and Joe Maslick for a couple of weeks of R&R. Ahmed was apparently up and walking around his Berlin hospital room against doctor's orders, demanding to be sent home to Jordan.

Losa had stayed put in Prague and was now under heavy CIA surveillance. Less because Rapp thought he would try to retaliate or run his mouth, and more in case the Russians came after him. Not that any of those scenarios seemed likely. The Kremlin had problems mounting so fast and from so many directions that a confrontation with Damian Losa was a headache they didn't need. In the end, Rapp had gotten the better of the Mexican, but his takeaway was that Losa wasn't a man to be fucked with.

As for Aleksandr Semenov, his situation had significantly improved. They'd transported him to a remote compound in Latvia, where the stick had transformed into a carrot. A talented chef, fawning staff, and a steady stream of high-dollar hookers had loosened him up even more than the cattle prod to the balls. Not only was he providing increasingly detailed information on Russia's asymmetrical warfare capabilities, but he was also gleefully critiquing and tweaking America's own. The man was a flat-out genius, but one with a pathological need to constantly prove he was the smartest guy in the room. CIA psychologists were carefully manipulating that trait and Kennedy was already comparing his potential to that of Wernher von Braun after World War II.

Not surprisingly, Russian intelligence was desperately trying to locate him, but would find nothing other than clues carefully designed to suggest that he'd been killed by the same insurgent group that kidnapped him.

Not a bad couple of months' work, as long as no one ever found out about it.

When he pulled through the gate, Anna was already sprinting across the courtyard. Claudia wasn't far behind, but keeping a more measured pace. Anna collided with him when he stepped from the car, leaping up and wrapping herself around his torso.

"We just got back, too!" she said breathlessly. "We were in New York. But in the country. It's not just one big city, you know. We had tons of land and tons of horses. My instructor was named Anna, too. And she said I was really good. I learned superfast and could even jump."

"You mean the horse jumped and you just sat on it."

"It's hard! I bet you couldn't do it."

"I dunno, Oompa Loompa. They say I'm a cowboy at heart."

"You don't even like horses," she grumbled as she dropped back to the ground. "Scott said we could have some, but you always say no."

He tossed her his keys. "Make yourself useful and go get my duffel out of the trunk."

She caught them and went around the back of the vehicle as Claudia walked up and kissed him. "Are we all right?"

She knew nothing about his involvement in the attack on the Syrian facility or the kidnapping of Aleksandr Semenov. Her concerns were centered on Damian Losa.

"Fine."

"So, he agrees that our debt is paid?"

Rapp nodded as a high-pitched squeal rose from Anna.

"Is this for me?"

"What?" Rapp said, wandering to the back of the car and looking down at a diminutive mountain bike lying on his bag. "How'd that get in there? I've never seen it before. But it looks too small for me, so I guess you can keep it."

"Take it out for me! Take it out! Take it out!"

"What, are your arms broken?"

She wet her lips before reaching in and giving the titanium tubing a yank. It came out so easily, she almost fell over backward.

"It's so light! It's like it doesn't weigh anything! Like a feather!"

He ignored Claudia's painful jab to his ribs. She thought he spoiled the girl, and she probably had a point. But he decided to ignore that, too.

"Didn't we agree that the bike would wait for her birthday?" she said as her daughter pedaled enthusiastically across the lawn.

"It's hard to find decent ones that size, and the way she's growing, it could be too small for her by then."

"Uh huh."

The disapproval was obvious in her voice, but nothing like it would have been if she knew the full truth. He'd spent months scouring the planet for the parts he'd installed on the bike and the frame was a custom build. All in, he had put about thirty hours and eight grand into it.

Claudia wrapped an arm around his waist as Anna disappeared behind the house. "Irene says she doesn't have anything for you on the horizon and the guys don't have another contract starting until fall. Does that mean you're home for a while?"

He retrieved the duffel that Anna had forgotten about and slung it over his shoulder. "For a while. Yeah."